surprises. I also loved the contemporary London setting and how the book showed the coming of age of the heroine, and the city itself' **Amy Heydenrych, author of *Shame on You***

'One of the most atmospheric and original thrillers I've ever read' **Charlotte Duckworth, author of *The Rival***

'*The July Girls* is a page-turning, atmospheric thriller about a serial killer, but at the same time a sensitively written coming of age story with a wonderful central character'
Jenny Quintana, author of *The Missing Girl*

'Thrilling, poignant and unpredictable, Phoebe Locke takes this serial killer chiller to a whole new level. I loved *The Tall Man*, *The July Girls* is even better'
Chris Whitaker, author of *All The Wicked Girls*

Praise for *The Tall Man*

'This summer's scariest thriller. If you liked Emma Cline's cult hit *The Girls*, you'll love *The Tall Man* – an addictive blend of psychological suspense and spine-tingling chills' ***Stylist***

'So chilling I had to put it aside for the few days I was home alone . . . Genuinely scary, *The Tall Man* carefully walks the line between psychosis and the paranormal, never quite letting the reader know its truth' **Alison Flood, *Observer***

'Genuinely scary contemporary novels are rare but Phoebe Locke's debut – a taut, complex but brilliantly constructed supernatural thriller – is not one to be read alone at bedtime . . . The writing is deft, the twists unpredictable, the tension unrelenting' ***Metro***

'If you read just one psychological suspense novel this year, make it Phoebe Locke's *The Tall Man*' ***Culturefly***

'Set to become a must-read summer chiller' ***Daily Express***

'Chilling' ***Bella***

'A gripping blend of dark psychological suspense and spine-tingling chills' *iNews*

'Spine-tingling' **Susan Swarbrick, *The Herald***

'I could not put this book down! A deliciously dark, twisty, absorbing plot . . . this will stay with you long after you've read the final page' **Lucy Foley, author of *The Invitation***

'So creepy and chilling' **Laura Marshall, author of *Friend Request***

'A compelling story that is original, cleverly plotted and brilliantly told. I was totally hooked'
Rachel Abbott, author of *And So It Begins*

'Outstanding. A chilling, relentless and needle-sharp thriller that will stay with you long after you reach the final page'
Cara Hunter, author of *Close to Home*

'An unsettling, original page-turner you'll still be thinking about long after you reach the end'
Amy Engel, author of *The Roanoke Girls*

'I absolutely smashed through this book. Terrifying and incredibly well written. If you're in the mood for something truly unnerving, you HAVE to read this!'
Darren O'Sullivan, author of *Our Little Secret*

'A must-read this summer!'
Emily Gunnis, author of *The Girl in the Letter*

'Loved this book. Utterly creepy and atmospheric'
Colette McBeth, author of *The Life I Left Behind*

'Do not use this book as a cure for insomnia. It turns shadows into threats. A brilliantly creepy, twisty story'
Julia Crouch, author of *Her Husband's Lover*

'Mesmerizing and terrifying – *The Tall Man* more than lives up to the hype' **Chris Whitaker, author of *Tall Oaks***

'A really superior, creepy, insidious thriller. I loved it'
Hannah Beckerman, author of *If Only I Could Tell You*

Phoebe Locke is the pseudonym of full-time writer Nicci Cloke. She previously worked at the Faber Academy, and hosted London literary salon Speakeasy. She lives and writes in Cambridgeshire.

Phoebe Locke is the author of two psychological thrillers, *The Tall Man* and *The July Girls*.

THE JULY GIRLS

PHOEBE LOCKE

WILDFIRE

First published in 2019 by WILDFIRE
an imprint of HEADLINE PUBLISHING GROUP

First published in paperback in 2020 by WILDFIRE
an imprint of HEADLINE PUBLISHING GROUP

3

Cataloguing in Publication Data is available from the British Library

ISBN 978 1 4722 4929 6

Typeset in Sabon LT Pro by EM&EN
Printed and bound in Great Britain by Clays Ltd, Elcograf S.p.A.

Headline's policy is to use papers that are natural, renewable and recyclable
products and made from wood grown in well-managed forests and other
controlled sources. The logging and manufacturing processes are expected
to conform to the environmental regulations of the country of origin.

HEADLINE PUBLISHING GROUP
An Hachette UK Company
Carmelite House
50 Victoria Embankment
London EC4Y 0DZ

www.headline.co.uk
www.hachette.co.uk

For my family

There is a moment with each of them. A look in their eyes when they know that it's over. He likes to watch that realisation finally dawn, see them accept that there is no escape. The feeling of it is electric. Each time, he holds them close to him. He cradles them, a calm taking over.

It's the calm, he thinks sometimes, that he truly craves. That second's peace, the fury he feels suddenly silenced. It doesn't last; it never lasts. And when the fury surges back, the hatred crackling through him, he will long for that moment. He will try to remember the way it felt as he killed them. Try to survive on it. But soon – too soon – he starts counting down, waiting through the cold months, the Christmas lights, the bleak early weeks and then the slow awakening of spring.

Soon he begins to look forward to the day when he can take the next.

2005

Before

1

The summer I turned ten, everything started to change. We still lived in the same flat we'd always lived in, second floor of a block on Brixton Road, where I could sit out on the concrete balcony and watch the top decks of buses sail by. But that year it started to feel less like home. The stack of bills with their red letters, left in a pile on the scarred kitchen table. The fridge sad and empty, humps of ice sliding down its back wall. Dad out at work when I went to school and when I came back and all night too, waiting outside hospitals, bars, airports. Anywhere he thought someone might be just desperate enough not to care about the cracked wing mirror, the croaky engine. The Magic Tree hanging from the rearview mirror where his licence should have been.

Jessie had started working more too. The wig shop was in one of the railway arches, trains thudding overhead, and Jessie had been helping out there since she was fifteen. She used to take me sometimes, if Laine was in a good mood, and they'd let me sit out the back, running my fingers through the boxes of acrylic hair until they crackled with static. It was Jessie's job to unpack them from their plastic, to brush them out ready for Laine to display; white polystyrene heads lined up in the window and on the walls for the full wigs, glass cabinets and racks for the weaves. Laine had a soft spot for me. She saved old magazines for me and would sit and twist my hair into complicated styles, her long nails tickling my scalp. But she loved my sister more. It took me a long time to look back and realise that that shop was too small for two people to work in there as much as they did; that even before that summer, it was only ever us in there, never any customers. Laine didn't need Jessie there, probably couldn't afford to pay her most weeks, but she still kept handing her those little brown envelopes each Friday. She loved us, or she felt sorry for us – I've always found it hard to tell the difference.

Often, after they'd closed up the shop, Laine would produce drinks from the locked cupboard under the till, and she and Jessie would sit on the display cabinet, legs swinging, and tell me to try on wig after wig. I'd get braver after a while, parading back and forth in Laine's heels, while they doubled over laughing. Laine was the only person, apart from Jessie, who could bring that out in me. But even that couldn't stay the same.

Her brother showed up one Saturday with a cardboard box, damp down one side, which he dumped onto the counter. I was sitting on my little stool in the tiny back room, but with the door propped open, and Laine was out getting lunch. It was Jessie behind the till, and I watched the way her hands went immediately to her hair, the way she pressed against the counter, one foot cocked onto its toes.

His hair was darker than Laine's dyed caramel; tight black curls which were shorn short all over. He was wearing mirrored aviators, blue and yellow tinged, and he tilted his head forward so they slid down his chiselled face and he could look properly at my sister.

'Hey,' he said, his voice smooth and low. 'Laine in?'

Jessie shrugged, her expression cool. But from where I was sitting I could see her foot tapping anxiously behind her. Her hair was growing out; mousy at the roots, yellowish white along the length, but Laine had been playing with her new straighteners and so it was shiny and smooth, no mean feat.

'Gone out,' she said, and then, to the box, 'What's that?'

'Product,' he said, and he took his sunglasses off. 'You're Jess, yeah?'

'Jessie.' I was glad she said that; glad she corrected him. Dad called her Jess all the time, Jessica when he was teasing or drunk or annoyed, and she never corrected him. I didn't like that. It was Dad who had chosen Jessica for her; Mum who had made it Jessie.

'Right. Jessie. I'm Laine's baby brother.'

'Elliott. I know.'

He looked at her differently then, a little smile starting at the corners of his mouth. It often surprised people, the hardness of her shell. 'Nobody calls me that,' he said.

'Laine does.'

Laine came in then, before he could reply, an open can of Coke in one hand, a half-eaten sandwich in the other.

'Oh,' she said. 'You're early.' And Jessie moved swiftly away, like someone almost caught doing something wrong. She started straightening the heads behind the till, brushing the hair, and so it was only me who saw the way he kept looking past Laine as she talked, his eyes drifting to Jessie.

The first boyfriend I remember of hers had broken up with her a couple of months before. We'd been walking home after she'd picked me up from school, and she'd got the text. I can still remember the exact way she looked then; the cropped yellow T-shirt, the toned line of her belly. The purple Air Maxes, their laces fluorescent yellow. The knot of her hair, the darker roots and the fluff of the ends fanning out from underneath. Her nose ring was new and didn't last long after that, and the third tiny hoop in her left ear was red-rimmed and crusted. She cared for me religiously; for herself, little. I remember the way she shrugged, shoved her phone back in her pocket. The way, a couple of minutes later, she hissed *Twat* under her breath.

'Are you okay?' I asked, and she squeezed my hand once and let it go.

'The only person you can trust is me, okay?' she said. 'Me and you, that's it.'

Dellar – and he was right; the only person who ever called him by his first name *was* Laine – came back a couple of days later. We were outside, Laine locking up the shutters, a stray acrylic red thread still stuck in my hair, a blue one sliding down the front of my school shirt. Jessie was laughing, her hand clawed up in front of her face as she told us a story about some guy she'd turned down the night before. It was weird, this aspect of our relationship: she was my mother figure but she was still seventeen. She was seventeen and she went out at night after she said goodnight to me and woke up in a single bed three feet from my single bed, make-up smeared across her face and her clothes abandoned in a trail from the door to her pillow. She was seventeen but she still woke me up for school, cooked me breakfasts – 'A hot breakfast in your belly makes you always ready,' she'd say, drumming up an omelette from the stray egg, the last piece of ham, and it'd be a year or two before she started adding, 'That's what Mum used to say, anyway.'

As Laine clicked the final padlock shut, we heard footsteps behind us, their sound a slow, assertive beat against the distant chug of a train somewhere down the track above, the clatter of shutters from the butcher and the fishmonger across the street. We turned and watched him come towards us, the early summer sun sliding behind the arches, Atlantic Road its most attractive in subdued orange. His sunglasses were back on his face, the three of us framed small and blue-tinted in both lenses.

'Hey,' Jessie said, when he got close, and he just grinned at her.

Laine tutted at him, but then she took my hand. 'I'll take Addie home.'

As we walked, I snuck glances up at Laine. In profile, her face was softer, less intimidating. She was quieter, just the two of us, away from the shop.

'Does your brother like Jessie?' I asked, and she looked down at me.

'Honey,' she said. 'Elliott likes everybody.'

We crossed the road and cut into the estate. 'She likes him,' I said, testing, and when she didn't reply, my heart sank.

2

After that, Dellar was always with us; he'd be there with Jessie, waiting for me after school. He was there, hanging around the shop while I sat in the store room, too shy to come out. And he was there, late at night or early in the morning, the blue hours in between, when I stirred in my sleep and saw not one but two bodies in Jessie's single bed. His smell, sharp and clean and completely different to our father's, soaked into everything.

Surprisingly, Dad didn't seem to mind – or didn't notice – him being around. Those months in my memory barely feature Dad, though. He'd always worked nights and weird hours but these were longer, stranger shifts, where he'd work for two days straight, come home and sleep for a few hours while Jessie, Dellar and I watched *Eggheads* and *Come Dine with Me*, and then he'd be out of the door again. I knew then, in a vague sort of way filtered through Jessie and overheard conversations, that he'd had to return his black cab, that he'd gotten into some kind of trouble at work. I knew that he'd bought a car from a mate down the pub, a navy Ford Mondeo with soft grey seats and a thick smell of cigarettes which three and then four and then five Magic Trees couldn't shift. I know now that he was driving it as a minicab illegally. I knew then that all of those bills that sat unopened were lettered in red, and that he only came home for those two or three hours of sleep when he started dropping off at the wheel. But I also knew – had always known – that we weren't supposed to talk about money around Dad. It was better, really, if we didn't talk at all. Safer.

I should have been annoyed that I was suddenly having to share Jessie's attention. For so long, I'd been all she cared about. What I wore, what I ate, whether or not I was working hard at school. She was the person who warmed a towel on the one radiator in the flat which gave off a decent heat, while I sat in the bath she'd run for me. She was the person who tucked me in, who told me she loved me just as I was floating into sleep. And then there was Dellar. There between us on the sofa, there beside me at the dinner table – his eyes firmly fixed on Jessie as she stirred a pan on the hob. There, waiting patiently in the lounge while she said goodnight to me and turned off my light, before going out into the dark with him.

But he made it difficult to be jealous. He talked about the things I cared about, tipped off by Jessie: dinosaurs; space; mermaids; the various ways to eat a potato waffle. One night while Jessie was in our bedroom, drying the hair she'd just bleached for the first time in weeks, Dellar turned to me during an advert break. 'What you reading?'

I'd been lying in my dad's chair, legs hanging over the arm with the book propped in my lap. 'It's called *Charlotte's Web*,' I said, showing him the yellowed, illustrated cover. It was one of a stack Jessie had dug out of a cupboard for me a few years before, each of them with our mother's name pencilled in careful letters on the inside cover: *Elizabeth Addison*. It was the fourth or fifth time I'd read it and mostly I just liked having it around.

'Oh I know that one,' he said, surprising me. 'That was Laine's favourite when we were little kids. With the spider, right? And the pig?'

'Yes!' I sat up straighter and looked at him properly, the book hugged close to me. 'It's *so* good. But it's really sad at the end.'

'Yeah, I remember.' He laughed. 'Our mum used to cry when she had to read that bit to us.'

I was interested in this, in imagining him tucked up in bed with a younger Laine, the two of them cuddling into a mother whose face I couldn't see. It made me like him more but it didn't make me jealous. Because it had been Jessie who had read stories to me before I could read them for myself, the two of us hiding under a duvet with her torch. I couldn't imagine anyone doing it better.

'What else did you like reading?' I asked, and he smiled

and stretched, settling himself more comfortably on the worn sofa.

'That's quite a long list,' he said. 'You ready?'

A couple of Sundays after that, the three of us were sitting in our usual places on the sofa, the plates from our breakfast still on the floor though it was past noon. I was working up the courage to tell Dellar what I'd thought of one of the books from his list – *Matilda*, which I'd loved more than anything I'd ever read before – when we heard the click of Dad's door opening, his stumbling footsteps down the hallway. I glanced at Jessie but she was staring determinedly at the TV. I could see the corner of her mouth twitching. She hadn't expected him to get up yet.

We were all silent, listening to him mutter to himself as he clanked the oily frying pan into the sink, shoved a plate in after it. The fridge opened and then slammed shut and I clenched my hands into fists to stop myself from flinching.

'Jessica!' His footsteps thundering back down the hallway. 'Where is all the *fucking* food?'

Jessie looked at Dellar and then jumped up and went out into the hall, closing the door behind her.

'I'm sorry,' I heard her say, her voice small as if that might lure his down, too. 'I'll make you something. I'll tidy up.'

'Too fucking right you will!' There was the slam of a cupboard, a hollow rolling sound as something was knocked over. 'Don't think you get to sit around here all day—' His voice was muffled suddenly, Jessie closing the kitchen door. He wouldn't like that, I realised. Her tidying him away, embarrassed in front of her guest. There was another dull thump as he smacked the counter, his growled words impossible to make out, and I did flinch, then.

When I glanced at Dellar, he was watching me, his mouth set tight. 'Want to go for a walk?' he asked, and I nodded.

We left the flat just as a glass shattered, Dad's voice lower again now in a way that made the hairs on the back of my neck stand up. We were quiet as we walked down the high street, past a crowd trying to push their way into Brixton station, its gates shuttered halfway across, and crossed the road at the corner where McDonald's was.

'Want a McFlurry?' Dellar asked, hands thrust into his pockets. He was wearing jeans and a white T-shirt even though the wind was cool, and he looked like a model. I nodded again. 'Come on then,' he said, and he pushed through the double doors.

It was busy – it was always busy in there – and we stood in the queue, Dellar's hands by his side now. I kept my eyes on the menu boards and didn't say anything. I wondered what was happening in the flat, wondered if she had managed to defuse things the way she usually did. Dad rarely got mad at me. But it was different with Jessie, who seemed to always disappoint him in ways I couldn't understand. And though she was harder to scare than me, it didn't always stop him trying.

Dellar glanced down at his trainers. 'You and Jessie, you're good friends, huh?'

I nodded. 'We're best friends.'

'You know she loves you, right?'

I nodded again, but this time I looked away.

He put a hand on my back, his touch cool and soft. 'I just want you to know that I'm not gonna change that.'

I glanced back up at him, but I still didn't say anything.

'I just figured,' he said, 'if it's okay with you – maybe we could all be friends together?'

Just then the family in front of us moved away with their brown bags of food clutched in fists, and so we stepped forward before I had to answer him. But as we walked away from the McDonald's, my ice-cream cup dampening in my hand and the Smarties from it gritty in my teeth, I felt warmer.

It was little things, really, but Dellar and Laine had a seven-year-old half-brother, Lloyd, so they both knew that it was the little things that counted. How he turned up one night with the first three Harry Potter books, the pages soft and curling, full of the dusty library smell I loved. How he fixed our DVD player and sat and watched all three *Jurassic Parks* with me while Jessie tutted and fidgeted and was pleased. How he always remembered what I was doing at school, remembered to ask. And he could draw, that was the most important thing. His drawing was entirely effortless, like everything he did, but there was a precision to it, a change in the way he looked as he did it, that made it special. He loved it, though he thought it was useless, and if Jessie was getting ready to go out, hair straighteners smoking, he could be easily persuaded to pause a DVD and sketch me Spider-Man or Nemo – or the Terminator, on the evenings when Jessie wasn't paying enough attention to what we were watching. I kept those pictures in a pile under my bed, and as the stack grew, so did how much I liked Dellar, until, one day, on a rare occasion when it was Jessie and me at home for an entire evening, I realised I missed him.

The next day was the day they had their first fight.

I was sitting in the bath, the water lukewarm and the skin on my fingers wrinkled and white. I didn't want to step out into the cold yet, the radiator-warmed towel too far out of reach. I sank my head under the water, listening to the rumble of their voices, comforting like the faint music from the TV that also made it through to me, until I burst back through the surface to catch my breath and realised that Jessie was angry.

'I *can't* go there. I don't have any money till Friday, I told you already.'

'It's on me.' Dellar sounded confused. 'Seriously, I've got this. He's a mate of mine, they only opened last week. It'll be fun.'

'I don't want you to pay again.' I could hear that Jessie was trying to control her voice, make it kind. She was good at that, at stuffing feelings down. She did it for me all the time. 'Let's go at the weekend.'

'It's just a couple of drinks, it's not a big deal.'

I sighed and sank back under the water. I didn't want to hear him getting her so wrong.

But maybe he understood her better than I did; or maybe with him, things were just different. Because when I finally got out of the bath and put on my pyjamas, I could hear her moving around in our bedroom, getting ready to go out.

She let him take her out for those drinks that night and that was when I really started to understand that things were changing. That maybe Jessie was ready to let someone take care of her for once.

3

There was a night, right at the beginning of July, when I couldn't sleep after Jessie and Dellar had left for a party. I lay in bed, listening to the sound of the traffic outside and the boys in the courtyard below playing music and laughing at each other. It had already been a hot and unsettled summer but the weather had broken that week, a cooler front creeping in and then sneaking away so that I didn't know each night whether I wanted my covers or not. I flopped onto one side and pressed my eyes closed for a while longer before giving up and getting out of bed. I went and curled up in the lounge with *The Prisoner of Azkaban*, which I'd nearly finished already, safe in the knowledge that it would be hours before I was disturbed. I liked to do that sometimes, to wander around the flat and pretend I was grown up enough to decide when I went to sleep. I only had ten pages left when I heard a key in the door, Dad's low cough as he kicked off his shoes. I lay on the sofa without moving and then, as I heard him hesitate, I called out to him.

'Hi, Daddy.'

He changed track, appearing in the doorway. 'Hey, kiddo.'

'You're home early.'

'Uh-huh.' He glanced around the room, a vein in his neck pulsing. 'Where's your sister?'

'She popped out,' I said, fear clutching at my insides. She wasn't supposed to leave me alone at night. 'She'll be right back.'

'Okay.' He smiled at me, a tight, tense thing which looked rigid on his face. 'I'm gonna jump in the shower.'

I listened to the boiler click on, listened to his jeans and his T-shirt hit the floor. I tried to focus on the words on the page of *Harry Potter* in front of me, but they swam and danced and in the end I sat and looked at the wall and waited for the shower to click off again, the hot water pipes to stop groaning.

He stuck his head round the door five minutes later, rubbing roughly at his hair with a towel. He gave me a smile which seemed to come more easily, sneaking across his mouth. 'Hungry?'

I wasn't. It was past eleven and my mouth was dry but I nodded anyway, smiled gratefully.

'Omelette?' he asked, and I followed him into the kitchen. It wasn't all he could cook, but it was all he could cook well. I watched him as he cracked eggs into a bowl, his back bare, jeans too baggy around his skinny frame.

The tattoo on his forearm: a rose entwined in ribbon, where once a name had been visible. His thinning hair still slicked back from the shower. He poured the egg mixture into the pan and left it on the hob. He winked at me as he passed, heading for his room.

When he came back, he had an old grey T-shirt on and his phone pressed to his ear. When she didn't answer, he left a message. 'Jessica, it's Dad. Where are you? Addie's on her own and I need to go back to work.' Simple, to the point. His temper in check. If she knew he was angry, she wouldn't come home.

He did love her. He loved us both with a fierce, unpredictable love that surfaced at the strangest of times – when you were stretching up to get a mug from the back of the shelf, when you passed him the paper, when you were laughing about something funny on TV. His arms would close round us, short and gristly with tendons, and he would kiss us on our foreheads, his eyes shut. He didn't show us often, but it was there. He loved us.

He tipped the omelette onto a plate and put it on the table in front of me as he sat down. He watched me fork up a mouthful.

'Aren't you hungry?' I asked him, and he shook his head.

'I'll eat later.' He scratched at a patch of something on the back of one hand and then stretched, the muscles in his back cracking. I forced myself to eat more of the omelette. 'So,' he said. 'Birthday girl soon, eh? Only a couple more days until lucky number seven. And then you're ten.'

I smiled, pleased. 'Yep.'

He scratched at the hand again and then considered me, his green eyes so much like Jessie's. 'I guess me and your sister better start thinking about buying you some presents then. Better start thinking about something you'd like.'

I was careful not to nod too eagerly, not to seem greedy. He didn't like that; it was one of his favourite things to pull us up on. Jessie, turning down pages in a magazine to mark the things she liked. Me, sneaking a slice of ham from the fridge, trying to chip off a corner of cheese when no one was looking. We were greedy girls and he was always happy to tell us so. Jessie didn't like it when he did.

His eyes narrowed and I knew I had tried too hard. 'Don't pretend there's nothing you want,' he said irritably. 'I know what you're like, you two.'

My mind turned blank. 'Maybe some books,' I said, and he wrinkled his face, processing this.

'Always got your head in a book.' But then he shrugged and I let myself breathe. He leant back in his chair, the old spindles creaking, and his attention fell to my plate where half of the omelette still sat. 'Come on. Eat up.'

I carefully pressed the edge of my fork in, marking out the perfect bite, but I was too slow again and I could feel the atmosphere changing in the room, hear his foot tapping against the leg of his chair. 'Stop messing around with it,' he said, the irritation growing. 'Decent omelette, that. You know we don't waste food in this house.'

The mouthful was bigger than I'd meant it to be, the egg cold and claggy by now, and it stuck to the roof of my mouth. I tried to chew it, feeling his eyes hot on me, and gagged.

'Eat it,' he said in a low voice. '*Eat* the food I made for you.'

But I could feel my gorge rising and, panicked, I spat the mouthful back onto the plate.

For a second, we stared at each other. It scared me most when his face went still like that, just the smallest of muscles tensing along his jaw. Because that was the moment when he would swallow the anger back – or he wouldn't.

Before either of us could move, there was the sound of the front door, the jangle of Jessie's bracelets and earrings and handbag. She clattered in the evenings, moving in a cloud of perfume and sharp sounds. I saw the storm pass across my father's face, his mouth set in a grimace.

'Hi, I'm home,' she called, tottering down the hall to the kitchen, and I knew then that she was drunk. I knew that Dad knew it too, and he got up from the table with a jerk, dropping my plate and the pan into the sink. He pushed past her without a word as she came into the kitchen.

We were both still, listening to him shrug on a jacket, grab his keys from the side. When the door slammed behind him, I saw Jessie let out her breath. But when she caught me looking, she rearranged her face into a smile and sat down at the table beside me.

'What are you doing up, little one?'

She had brought with her the fresh load of post which had been splashed across the mat. Menu after menu after menu, those stiff windowed envelopes of bills slotted in between like landmines. She flicked through them with her ringed fingers. The gold ring she wore on her forefinger was my favourite – a thin band with a perfectly round stone in the middle; dark brown, almost like wood. It had been our mother's, Jessie said, and one day she would give it to me.

'I couldn't sleep.'

'Really? I usually find it so easy to sleep sitting in a chair and eating breakfast foods.'

I rolled my eyes, trying to hide the shakiness I still felt. 'I was reading. He offered. I don't think he realised how late it was.'

She pushed the post away and sighed.

'Didn't you have a good time?' I asked.

Jessie turned and looked at me, her hand reaching out to smooth back my hair. She did this often, especially when she'd had a drink, and she'd once told me that she liked to look at my face because it reminded her of Mum's. 'Not really,' she said, surprising me.

'Why not?' I asked, my voice coming out small as if I was worried I might scare her out of her honesty.

Her hand moved away from my face and she sank back in her chair, looking suddenly younger, fragile. 'Laine's giving up the shop. She can't afford the rent.'

'Oh.' A fresh pang of fear went through me. 'Will you get another job?'

'I hope so.' She gave me a sad smile and reached out to hold my hand. 'I'm going to get us out of here one day,

Addie,' she said. 'It just might take a bit longer than I was hoping, okay?'

The fear went away and instead a terrible wave of something softer, colder washed over me. 'Please don't be sad,' I said.

She seemed to realise what she'd said, then; she blinked and took in a sudden breath, her hand releasing mine. 'I'm all right,' she said, shrugging and getting up from the table. 'Come on. Time for bed.'

4

Jessie only took me to the shop one more time after that, one afternoon after school when she and Laine were boxing up the last things, sweeping the floors. Dellar was there, unscrewing the shelves Laine had put in herself on the back wall, and all of them were quiet. I sat on my stool in the corner, holding the stack of magazines that I'd kept in the cupboard in the store room. When they were done, the three of them stood in the small space – even smaller, somehow, without everything in it – and looked at each other.

'End of an era,' Dellar said, putting his arm round Laine. 'Onwards, though, yeah?'

'Right.' She gave a scoffing sort of laugh and moved away from him. She leant against the empty counter, staring out at the market.

'What are you going to do with the stock?' Jessie asked, looking at the sagging boxes they'd dragged beside the door. 'I could put it on eBay for you, if you want?'

'I've got a mate on the market,' Dellar said. 'She'll take the lot. Probably not the most cash we could get for it, but, you know . . .'

'The quickest,' Laine said, and then she sighed and reached out to put some music on. 'Is this our closing down party, or what?'

They were happier by the time we left. The three of them were sweaty and breathless from dancing, and Dellar was making all of us laugh with a story about a man his cousin had arrested for streaking down Clapham High Street. We stood outside the shop, watching as Laine locked the shutters for the last time. It was early evening, sunny again after the afternoon's rain, though the faintly metallic smell of it still hung in the air. The kebab shop across the road had started cooking for the evening, a fresh slab of meat rotating slowly as one of the servers shaved beige strips from it. My stomach rumbled and I saw Jessie watching him too.

'Pub?' Dellar asked. 'I'm buying. We can go to The Crown, Addie'll be allowed in there.'

'Yes.' Laine threw an arm round him this time, her bad mood pushed aside. 'Come on, ladies.'

Jessie shook her head. 'I better get Addie home, get her some dinner. Maybe I can come meet you guys later.'

I saw Dellar open his mouth, about to argue, but Laine slid her arm through his, a little nod at Jessie. 'Sure,' she said. 'Catch you in a bit, hon. Bye, Ads – thanks for helping us, babe.'

'That's okay.' I felt shy, all three of them watching me. 'Have a good night.'

'Oh wait.' Laine put up a finger, made a show of suddenly remembering. 'I have something for you. Don't open it until the morning though, right? No cheating.'

She handed me a small parcel wrapped in sparkly paper and my face got hotter. 'Thank you.' I couldn't remember the last time someone who wasn't Jessie had given me a present.

'Sleep tight, mate,' Dellar said. 'See you tomorrow for some serious celebrating.' I nodded, that warm feeling bubbling up inside me again, and we watched as the two of them headed off in the direction of the pub.

Or I watched them, at least. When I glanced at Jessie, she was looking at the kebab shop window again, a naked longing on her face which I hadn't seen before. 'Well, let's go,' she said, shaking it away. 'Sorry you had to sit there for so long, I know it's boring.'

It wasn't boring at all. I'd always loved it in there, loved being with them. It felt like a secret place, away from the rest of the world, somewhere that had just been ours. Where we didn't have to worry. But as I looked back at the shutters, I realised that had never been true – not for Laine and probably not for Jessie either. And now it was gone.

Back at the flat, Jessie made me beans on toast with the last of the bread, eating the leftovers out of the pan as she stood and watched me. I pretended to be tired and got into bed quicker than I normally would so she wouldn't feel like she had to hang around with me, so she could go out and meet them. But she lingered anyway, fussing with her hair as I turned on my lamp and opened my book.

'When you wake up, you'll be ten,' she said. 'How mad is that?'

I smiled. 'Pretty mad.'

She leant over and kissed my cheek. 'Sleep well. See you in the morning, okay?'

I'd expected to lie awake for a while after she left but I'd only read a couple of pages before my eyes started getting heavy, the book drifting closer to my face. I put it down and turned onto my side and fell asleep before the last summer light had even left the room.

I woke to the sound of people talking and rolled over sleepily to greet them. But the voices were deeper than Dellar's and Jessie's, were coming from the living room. I checked the cheap plastic alarm clock on Jessie's side of the room: 2 a.m. I sat up. There was a low laugh, unfamiliar, and I got up and pressed myself against the bedroom door, heart pounding. But then another voice: 'Keep it down. My kid's asleep.' Dad.

Curiosity got the better of me and I creaked the door open, tiptoeing out into the hall. Dad was in the lounge, standing with his back to me. He was rummaging through one of the drawers in the manky dresser that had been in the flat longer than we had. I moved closer to the door to get a better view of the room and saw the rat in Dad's chair.

Leonard was the only friend Dad ever brought back to

the flat. A year or so earlier he had suggested that I call him Uncle Leonard but, in private, Jessie and I referred to him as the rat. Dad often did so to his face.

I turned, ready to creep back to bed – I didn't want to see Leonard, especially not in my summer pyjamas, an old vest of Jessie's and a pair of too-small shorts – but a floorboard creaked and I heard Dad slide the dresser drawer shut.

'Addie?' he called. 'What you doing up?'

Reluctantly I went back and stood in the doorway. 'Sorry,' I said, as if it hadn't been them who had woken me.

'Not got a hug for your Uncle Leonard?' Leonard grinned at me from Dad's chair, a can of beer in his hand. He was dressed the same way he always was: black cargo pants, usually with another can in one of the pockets, and a too-big plain white T-shirt, the kind that came packaged in plastic in sets of three or five. His hair, already streaked with more grey than Dad's though I knew he was at least ten years younger, had grown and was tucked greasily behind his ears. He wasn't bad-looking, but his face was pinched and sneaky somehow, and sometimes I still thought I caught a faint tang of the sewer even though it was over a year since he'd lost his job.

'Leave her be, Len.' Dad stood looking at me, a hand still on the dresser drawer. 'Back to bed, birthday girl. And don't wake your sister.'

I nodded, heart thumping again. If he didn't check – if they left before Jessie came home – he wouldn't catch her. As I closed the bedroom door, I heard Leonard say, 'She's all grown up,' Dad muttering something in response. A drawer slid open again and then another and I wondered what had been important enough for Dad to come home from work so early. I pressed myself against the door and prayed for them to leave, or for Dad to go to bed. Jessie would see his car downstairs, would know to sneak in, and everything would be okay.

'Here.' Dad's voice was gruff.

'Thanks.' Leonard sounded amused; I wondered how many beers he'd had. 'We can swing by mine after this. You can check out the goods.'

'Let's go now,' Dad said. He was speaking quietly but it wasn't forceful, not the way I was used to hearing him sound when he lowered his voice. 'I want to get back on the road.'

'You're a dedicated man.' Leonard laughed and there was the crack of a ring pull, a glug of beer. But I heard the chair creak as he got up, the two of them leaving the flat. I crept back to bed and lay there, listening to the traffic outside, the night-time sounds of the estate. I hoped Jessie was out there in a bright, busy pub, hoped Dellar was making her laugh again. As I closed my eyes, I realised that it was past midnight and that I was ten.

5

Jessie woke me up early the next morning. She did it each year, the exact same way – she jumped on my bed, bouncing with a foot on either side of me, and sang until I sat up or she landed on me. That year, it was the second option. When we'd stopped laughing and I'd untangled myself from the duvet, she pulled me into the kitchen, where she'd laid out my presents on the table, along with the breakfast I looked forward to all year round: Chocolate Marshmallow Pop-Tarts. She'd put a rose in a water glass next to my plate, a new touch.

It's one of my favourite things to look back on, how excited she got about my birthday. She barely remembered her own most years.

'Open this one first!' she said, pushing one of the carefully wrapped presents towards me. My eyes were still sticky with sleep but I stuffed as much Pop-Tart as I possibly could into my mouth as I sat down.

'Morning, birthday girl.'

We both turned in surprise as Dad came in. He shut the front door behind him, twirling his keys around a finger as he walked down the hallway. In his other hand, he had a blue plastic bag. 'Sorry I haven't had time to wrap it,' he said, putting it in front of me and leaning down to kiss the top of my head.

'Thank you,' I said, mouth still full of marshmallow. Suddenly, having both of them standing there smiling at me felt like the best present I could imagine.

But I opened the bag anyway. At first it looked empty, but when I rummaged in the folds of the thin plastic, my fingers touched metal. It was cold as I pulled it out and I opened my hand and looked down at the little spiral of chain. A bracelet, pretty and silver, three charms spaced out along it.

'Wow,' Jessie said, wary as if it might spring up and bite.

'You like it?' Dad asked me, his hand on the back of my chair, in the way that we all knew wasn't really a question.

'Yes,' I said anyway, leaning closer to look at it. And I meant it. It was the most grown-up, fancy thing I'd ever had. I didn't know what to say. I reached out a finger and touched each of the charms in turn: there was a little book, a heart and a tiny girl, the edges of her skirt sharp. I looked up at him. 'Thank you,' I said.

He shrugged and turned away, poured himself some of the orange juice Jessie had left out. 'It's no big deal. Just thought you should have something nice, now you're getting older. Ten's a special age, right Jess?'

Jessie nodded, though her eyes were still on the bracelet in my hand. 'Yeah. It is.'

'Well, I better get a couple of hours of kip,' he said, heading for the kitchen door. 'I'm gonna have to go out again tonight. Got a mate who needs some help with some deliveries.' He turned back, came and kissed me again – this time on my forehead, a bit awkward and misjudged so that his lips hit my skin too hard. 'You have a good day.'

'Thanks Dad,' I said, turning red. It wasn't a surprise he'd be working that evening. It had just been me and Jessie on my birthday night for my last three birthdays – the fact that he'd made it home in time to see me that morning was enough to make my heart sing.

'Will you put this on for me?' I asked Jessie once his bedroom door had closed. But she turned away, making a fuss about putting an extra Pop-Tart in the toaster for me, and I didn't think she'd heard.

'Well, are you going to open the others?' she asked, coming to sit back down and taking a bite out of my Pop-Tart before putting it on my plate. She glanced at the hallway and the closed bedroom door again before sliding an envelope out from under the biggest of the three presents.

'Mum sent you a card,' she said.

Jessie let me walk to school by myself that day. 'I have to go help Laine with that stock,' she said. 'And I guess you're all grown up now, right?'

'Yep,' I said, flushing with pleasure.

'I want you to go straight there though, okay?' I could see the doubt creeping in, knew she was about five seconds away from changing her mind.

'I will,' I said quickly. 'I promise! I'll be fine.'

She relented. 'I know you will. And I'll be there to pick you up, okay? We're going for pizza and ice cream, don't forget.'

My mouth watered. I'd been excited about that plan for weeks.

I didn't go straight to school, even though I'd set out with the best of intentions. Delirious with the responsibility – even though it was something I knew some of the kids in my class had been doing for ages – I ended up dawdling; looking in shop windows, watching people at bus stops, feeling impossibly adult. And then I reached the school gates and saw the empty playground, and realised I was late.

I ran all the way to my classroom, my shoes squeaking against the corridor floor, and made it inside just as Mr Geary finished doing the register.

'Good morning, Addie,' he said, marking me in, and I sat down at my usual place at the table next to the window, next to Henry – who elbowed me in the side and asked, 'Did you bring cake?'

Henry Zhang was my best friend and I'm not just saying that because he was my only friend, although that was true too. To be fair, I was probably his. He was loudly, unashamedly weird, prone to asking annoying and complicated questions about almost anything Mr Geary said, and had once got the entire school closed for the day after setting his brother Michael's tarantula free into one of the heating vents. 'They live in burrows in hot places,' he'd told us all, completely confused by all the fuss. 'It was perfect.' The spider clearly didn't think so; it had made its escape directly onto the head teacher's desk.

I'd forgotten that it was one of Mr Geary's special rules that people could bring in cake for the class on their birthday, which meant that I'd forgotten to ask Jessie if I could. She *had* bought me a cake; it had been sitting there with the presents that morning, still in its box, a mini Me To You one – she loved the little grey bears and all the cards she bought were from the range – that was the perfect size for us to share that night. Definitely not the right size for the thirty-two other kids in my class.

I shook my head at Henry and shrugged. He elbowed me in the side again.

'You suck,' he whispered. 'Also, happy birthday.'

Mr Geary had finished taking the register but he'd stopped talking. He was looking down at something under his desk, his face white, and I thought again about Michael Zhang's tarantula, which some kids still insisted had never been caught and lived in the school. But it was a phone Mr Geary was looking at – something I'd *never* seen him do during school time. He frowned and started to type but then remembered where he was and dropped the phone into his desk drawer, a smile put back on his face as he looked at us.

'Right,' he said. 'Time to get back to the life cycle of insects. I know you all can't wait.'

But a little while later, there was a knock on the classroom door and Miss Lewzey popped her head in and asked Mr Geary if she could speak to him outside. It wasn't that unusual for her to be wandering around the school (unlike the previous head, Mrs Yates, who had stayed in her office and was a mystery to anyone who wasn't naughty enough to get sent to her) but something about the way she looked at him, the way she pulled the classroom door closed behind her, told us all that something serious was happening.

Henry was the first across the room. He stood with his ear pressed to the wood of the door and four or five other kids joined him too. I wouldn't normally have had the nerve but something – maybe all the Pop-Tarts – made me feel different that day, invincible. I went over there too.

It was difficult to hear much with everyone whispering and laughing on our side of the door. But I made out Miss Lewzey saying '. . . waiting for advice from the police' before Tia Clark elbowed me out of the way.

When Mr Geary came back in, we all ran for our seats but he barely seemed to notice we'd been out of them. He went back to his desk and opened the drawer again, looking at his phone. It was only when Henry asked him if he was okay that he seemed to remember we were there at all.

*

It was breaktime by the time we found out what had happened. Henry and I were sitting in our normal corner of the playground, tucked in behind a low wall. That corner had been a spaceship, a castle and a jeep in *Jurassic Park*, but now we were older, it was usually just a place where we hid and read books or talked about them – or played games on the old pay-as-you-go phone Michael had let Henry have when he'd gotten his new one. And that day, we were just about to open the surfing game which was Henry's favourite (and involved jumping over pixelly sharks, submarines and giant octopuses) when Michael sent him a message.

Henry read it, his eyes going wide behind his round glasses, and then he looked at me. 'Someone's blown up the Tube,' he said.

By the time school was finished, everyone was telling different stories about the bombs and I'd forgotten it was my birthday at all – until, at the end of the afternoon, Mr Geary had brought a Colin the Caterpillar cake out of the art cupboard and made everyone sing to me. I could still taste the chocolate as I walked out onto the playground, looking for Jessie. There were so many more parents there than normal, some of them standing alone looking at all of us with their lips pressed into tight lines and their hands in pockets or arms crossed across their bodies. Others were grouped together, muttering, shaking their heads. They were talking quietly and looking serious but there was still a kind of excited feeling in the air, the way there had been in our classroom all afternoon as the rumours grew and spread. Tia Clark had been taken out of school at break-time and a couple of others had left at lunch. Michael Zhang had told Henry that there had been four bombs and that there were no Tubes and no buses in the whole city. It had seemed like a game, a story, but now that all of the adults were there, faces shadowed as they watched anxiously for their kids, I felt my skin turn cold.

Jessie wasn't there.

Jessie was always there. Whether she'd been working at the shop or not, she always showed up to pick me up, even if it meant taking me back with her. And that day there was the pizza and ice-cream plan; my birthday afternoon, just the two of us, the way it always was.

But she wasn't there.

I stood uncertainly for a minute, checking all of those anxious faces again in case I'd missed her the first time. They all looked blankly back at me, or didn't look at me at all. None of them were her. My grip tightened on the straps of my backpack, a horrible, looping feeling in my tummy.

'Addie?' Mr Geary had come up behind me, his own backpack slung over one shoulder. 'You okay?'

I nodded. My mouth had gone dry, the last traces of chocolate turned to sand.

'No Jessie?' he asked, his voice gentle. 'Do you want to come back inside and wait for her in the office?'

Something in the way he asked made me shake my head, even though the swirling feeling in my stomach had gotten worse. 'It's fine,' I said, 'we're meeting on the high street.

We're going for pizza for my birthday.' Saying the words made me feel a little bit better.

'Right,' Mr Geary said, his eyes already moving away. I wondered who had sent him the message that morning, who he was rushing home to. 'Well, have fun. See you tomorrow.' Watching him walk away made me feel better too. I've never really been able to take other people's pity, even back then.

But by the time I reached the high street, I was panicking again. I'd expected to bump into Jessie; probably running, full of apologies. But there was no sign of her, and the street was full of people – some milling around and talking, the way the parents had outside the school; some marching ahead without looking at anyone, a whole stream of them on their way home or on their way out, with no way to get there but to just keep walking. Outside one of the corner shops, the owner was standing holding a tray of bottled water, offering them to the walkers as they passed. Outside the pubs, people were standing holding pints and bottles, their voices angry and slurred. In every window, a TV screen showed rolling news footage, pictures of Tube station entrances with people spilling out; a woman being led by a man in blue plastic gloves, a white mask covering her face. I stood and watched a screen through the window of a café, a man with blood and something black spattered across his face being stretchered out of a crowd, and then I turned and looked up the street, waiting for Jessie to appear. Shoulders and elbows bumped me, someone's bag hitting me in the cheek.

'You all right, kid?' someone asked me, and that started me walking again. I didn't look back at them.

By the time I made it to the estate, my breath felt hot and spiky in my throat. I climbed the concrete stairs slowly, giving Jessie one last chance to appear. But then I was outside our front door, and the flat was dark, no one there to answer when I knocked. Standing still made the panicky feeling start clawing its way up again so instead I went next door to Mrs Klusak's.

A cat flew past me as she opened her front door, the light in the hall flickering.

'Addie?' She pulled her cardigan tighter around herself and peered at me. 'Are you okay?'

From behind her, I heard the TV turned up full – Mrs Klusak's hearing, or lack of, meant that we could usually hear whatever she was watching through our wall. 'We don't even need a bloody TV licence,' Dad would say, though I don't think we ever actually *did* buy one. There was a newsreader speaking, the missing words to the pictures I'd seen all the way up the street. *The Met continue to urge people not to enter London and confirm that all major Network Rail stations in the city, along with all Underground lines, remain closed. The Prime Minister will shortly arrive back in London after leaving the G8 summit in Gleneagles. He will go immediately into a COBRA briefing and is expected to give a further statement later this evening.*

'Addie?' Mrs Klusak asked again, fanning herself with a rolled-up menu from the Chinese round the corner. 'Everything is okay? Where is Jessica?' She pronounced it *Yessica*.

I snapped back to attention, trying to ignore the newsreader's voice. 'They're out,' I said, making my voice bright and polite. 'But I forgot my key. Can I have the spare?'

She frowned. 'Bad things are happening out there, darling. Do you want to come in and sit with me? You can wait for them here. Keep me company, no?'

But I didn't want to go into Mrs Klusak's house. I wanted to get under my duvet and read *Harry Potter* and wait for Jessie to come home and explain things.

'It's okay, Mrs Klusak. My dad's on his way home right now. He's bringing fish and chips for me.'

She frowned. 'You spoke with him?'

'Uh-huh. I need to go in and put the hot water on so he can have a shower.'

'Oh.' Her doughy face relaxed. 'Okay. Here. Let me get the key.'

She pressed it into my hand and kept her fingers wrapped round mine. 'Stay safe,' she said. 'You go home and stay there, okay?'

Her door closed just as another cat jumped onto the living room windowsill. It stared out at me as I fumbled to get the key into my front door, the newsreader's words muffled but clear.

There is still no official confirmation of the total fatalities, though a government source earlier suggested that the number already exceeds twenty, with hundreds thought to be injured.

I slammed the door, shutting his voice out.

The flat smelled stale; the drip of the kitchen tap the only sound. The box of Pop-Tarts was still on the side, the discarded wrapping paper and my presents still on the table, along with the little cake in its box. I dropped my school bag on the kitchen table and walked in a slow circuit through the empty rooms. I ate cereal out of the box. I started and switched DVDs. I took out my home-work book and laid it on the chipped coffee table, then didn't look at it again. When I got hungry, I stood in front of the fridge, looking in, taking bites out of a block of cheese, the clingfilm peeled back.

It grew dark, me hunched in the weak glow from the TV, and eventually I got up to switch on the lights. The little red digits on the oven blinked at me through the open kitchen door. Eight thirty. I made toast. I burned toast. I listened as Mrs Klusak laughed at the TV. She'd given up watching the news about an hour before, and I tried to find the channel she was watching, tried to share the joke, but our TV only showed soaps and news, all sirens and raised voices.

I slept. I woke once, to a late-night quiz show on the TV with a pretty redheaded host who talked and talked and filled the silence. I turned over and looked around at the empty room, everything still wrong. I closed my eyes tight again and forced myself back into sleep, wishing it all away.

The sound of a key turning in the front door woke me the second time. I sat up, Jessie's favourite scarf, which I'd wrapped myself up in, slithering to the floor. It was pitch black, the TV off. The door closed quietly and a breath of night air and smoke floated in to me.

'Jessie?' I called, but there was no answer. I stood up and wobbled over to the doorway, eyes still sticky with sleep and the fear growing again in my belly.

But it was Dad standing in the hallway, one hand still on the door. We blinked at each other, neither of us moving.

'Hey, birthday girl,' he said eventually, his voice coming out low and croaky. 'Wotcha doin'?'

'I was sleeping,' I said, tears turning the words gluey and thick. 'I was scared.'

I was too tired and confused to think about whether I'd be getting Jessie in trouble; the realisation that she still hadn't come home dawning and drowning everything else out. 'Dad,' I said, starting to cry now, 'the bombs—'

But he was already pushing past me into his dark bedroom, the smoky night smell and a faint trace of something ranker going with him. He didn't turn the light on or turn round as I followed him.

'Dad, Jessie—' I tried, and that did get his attention. His face was pale in the dark as he turned to look at me.

'She's not here?' He was pushing his shoe off with the toes of the other, stooping to remove the second one. When I shook my head, he swore and fished his phone out of his pocket. She didn't answer; I watched him throw the phone down on his bed as he pulled off his T-shirt.

'I'm getting in the shower,' he said, his voice tight. 'You need to go to bed, okay? It's late.'

Before I could say anything, he'd moved past me and into the bathroom, the door closing in my face and just that same strange, coppery smell left behind.

I usually did whatever he told me but instead I curled up on his bed and listened to the water patter into the plastic tray, willing his phone to ring from the foot of the bed. She would be sorry, and he would be angry, but everything would be okay again. That clenching feeling in my chest would go away and everything would be okay. I could hear the furious frothing of him washing his hair in there and I pulled his T-shirt closer to me, wanting to breathe him in; the warm, muggy *Dad* smell I knew, and not that dark, meaty scent he'd brought in with him. I lay back against his pillow, his T-shirt against my cheek, and fiddled with the hem of it, the way I did with my baby blanket when I was little, until Jessie had told me it was time to put it away.

My fingers touched a dry patch along the bottom of the T-shirt, a place where the fabric was stiff.

I looked down. Three roundish marks, one large, two small.

Dark. Red dried to rust.

Blood.

The water stopped running. I heard the curtain swoosh back, the wet plastic slap against the wall. The toilet flushed. I looked at the three spots.

45

He came out of the bathroom with a towel round his waist and finally flicked the light on.

'Did you hurt yourself?' I asked, and he frowned. When he saw the top in my hands, the stained part held out to him, his face went taut. I saw a scratch on one of his cheeks, red and angry. 'Was it the bombs?' I asked, starting to cry properly this time. 'Dad, was it the bombs?'

'What?' He came and sat down on the bed beside me, took the T-shirt from me. 'Is that what you're worried about? I was nowhere near the bloody bombs. Jessie won't have been either.'

'Oh.' I tried to wipe my nose on the back of my hand, tried to swallow back my tears. He never liked it when we cried. But that night he just reached for his phone and checked it, then spun it round to show me a text: Jessica: Sorry. On way home now. There were scratches on his arm too, two raked lines near his wrist.

'Then what happened to you?'

'There was a fight,' he said. 'Two lads against another outside some club. I tried to break it up, they were really giving him a kicking.'

We looked at each other. My mouth had turned dry again. 'Okay,' I said.

'Get into bed, Addie. It's really late.' His watch was next to me on the bedside table. Its face read 3.01 a.m. There were drying red flecks on the glass.

He picked up his phone again and left the room. I heard him filling the kettle, heard the pops as he pierced the plastic on a microwave lasagne.

And in the bathroom, I found what I was looking for. Balled up behind the toilet, smelling of that strange metal smell and sodden in my hands. His black jeans. My hands coming away red.

6

In the morning when I woke, Jessie was in her bed. I knelt on the edge of mine, listening to her snore, and watched from the window as my father cleaned his car in the court-yard below. There was a big bucket of soapy water beside him and I could see ribbons of blue bleach through it. Beside him, a bin bag flapped in the breeze, and I watched him take out the mats from each footwell and stuff them inside. It was 5.55 a.m., and my head ached.

Cleaning the car wasn't unusual. The time could have been, I suppose, although he worked so many late shifts that his sleeping pattern was unpredictable. It took me a couple of minutes to work out what about the scene was making my tummy feel funny. He was halfway in the car, one bent knee resting on the driver's seat, one foot on the concrete. He was scrubbing the steering wheel, the dash-board.

He was wearing gloves.

The plastic kind, the ones the dentist wore to poke

around in the depths of my mouth. Looking out at my dad, the powdery taste of them spread across my tongue. I looked back at Jessie, asleep with her face pressed into the pillow. The bones of her back rising and falling firmly between the shoestring straps of her vest top; a hand thrown up over her head, its bangles escaping down her arm. I looked out at my dad, his prescription glasses turning brown in the steadily rising sun, his head balding in a way I'd never noticed before. He gathered the neck of the bin bag in one hand, picked up the bucket with the other. His head turned in the direction of my window and I slid out of sight and back beneath my sheets.

I decided I wasn't speaking to Jessie but it took her a long time to notice. Her face was pale and puffy, her eyes still smudged with make-up from the day before. While I ate my breakfast, she stood listening to the radio presenters talk about the bombings with her arms wrapped tightly round herself and then, finally, she glanced at me and seemed to finally realise I was upset.

'I'm so sorry about yesterday, hon,' she said. 'I'll make it up to you.'

I pushed my cereal away. 'Where *were* you?'

She came and sat down, pulling her knees up to her chest so that her feet clung onto the edge of the seat and didn't answer.

'I was so scared,' I said.

'I am so sorry.' She reached out a hand and stroked mine. 'It was such a mess. Dellar was supposed to be picking Lloyd up from school but he didn't show up. None of us could find him and then my stupid phone died when I was halfway across town looking for him.' She sighed. 'Laine was supposed to come get you but I guess our wires got crossed. It was such a crazy day – I still can't believe it happened.'

'Did you find him?' My mind had flooded with images of those people being helped away from the bombs, bleeding, burnt. With a lurch, I imagined Dellar with one of the masks clutched to his face, someone holding him up.

'We found him.' I thought I saw anger flash across her face but it was gone before I could be sure. 'He's fine, babe, don't worry.'

I let out a sigh of relief as she drifted away, her attention drawn back to the radio. They were all okay. Already the fear of the night before was beginning to seem like a bad dream.

In school, the terrorists were all anyone could talk about. Everyone had spent the night watching the news with their families instead of trying to figure things out on their own like me. They had sat and listened to Tony Blair tell them all that we would not be intimidated, we would not be changed, we would not be divided. That we would not be terrorised, even as the death toll rose. But we were ten and we *were* intimidated, we were confused. Everyone talked about people they knew who had seen the bombs, things that older brothers and sisters had told them about who had made them and how it could and probably would happen again. Tia Clark was kept off school by her mum; Cyrus Farzan told us how his parents had made them leave half an hour early so they could walk instead of catching the bus. Henry stood in the middle of all of it, loudly explaining how homemade explosives were created and what it meant to be a suicide bomber, until Mr Geary came back from taking a crying Miley Turner to the nurse and told him to stop.

It was catching, the fever of it all. We understood hardly anything; we listened to the kids who thought they understood it all. We whispered about it and ignored our worksheets. For once, no one cared that Henry was being smug and annoying about all of the things he knew. For once, everyone wanted to listen. In the end, Mr Geary gave up on the comprehension exercise he'd planned and let us make cards for the injured. Mine had two people holding hands, cut out of black paper and glued on, but when I sat and looked at it, I thought again about Dad's black jeans, balled up and wet. Dark. I pushed the card away without writing in it.

That night, Dellar came round and put his feet up and the TV on, while Jessie wrestled with the contents of our shared washbasket in the kitchen. It felt normal, just for a minute, and I started to relax. But the channel Dellar had turned to was showing one of the early evening magazine shows; the presenters with serious faces instead of their usual smiles. They were showing photos and videos that viewers had sent in: the smoking wreckage of the bus, its top split open like a tin. More of the people being led out of the Tube tunnel, their faces smudged and smeared with blood. They were still counting the casualties, the silver-haired presenter said. There were still people unaccounted for.

'Fucking hell,' Dellar said, as they showed a photo of a blown-apart Tube carriage. 'Fucking bastards.'

Jessie came into the room, a tangle of wet jeans under her arm. 'Turn it off,' she said. 'Addie shouldn't be watching this.'

He started then, looked at me as if he'd forgotten I was there. 'I'm not a baby,' I said, annoyed. 'I know what happened.'

Jessie tutted. 'Just because you know about something doesn't mean you have to see it right there in your face. Turn it over, Dellar.'

But he didn't. His hand hovered over the remote and his eyes lingered on me, and he didn't do anything. 'She's fine,' he said. 'Look at her, she's fine. You can't protect her from everything, Jess.'

She turned on her heel and left without another word, slamming the flimsy door behind her. It wasn't like her to give up so easily; it certainly wasn't like her to take any advice on what was best for me. I glanced at Dellar and the muscles in his jaw were tight. On the TV, the presenters were interviewing a woman with a bandage covering one eye and ear.

'I'm not a baby,' I said, again, and felt like a traitor.

*

They fought after that, a hissed, fierce row in the kitchen with the door closed so that only the angriest of words made it out to me. *You don't get it* and *Don't tell me what to do* and – him, his voice rising – *Why can't you just chill out?* I knew he'd lost, then. Nobody told her to chill out and got away with it.

Later, when we were alone, I watched her taking T-shirts from the crooked clothes horse. The words bubbled up and out before I could stop them.

'Did you get Dad's jeans clean?'

'What?' She glanced up, huffing a strand of hair off her face.

'Dad's jeans that he was wearing last night? They were all dirty. From the fight.'

She straightened up. 'What fight?'

Something cold closed around my heart then. It was that same feeling of stepping close to the edge of something tall, knowing that everything was going to shift under me. Outside the city wasn't safe any more but inside, I didn't understand things either. And as soon as I said the words out loud, things were going to change again. Something I couldn't explain was wrong and as soon as I put it in front of Jessie, I knew I wouldn't be able to hide from it any longer.

'I thought it was the bombs,' I said, my voice turning quiet under the weight of her full attention. 'But he said it was a fight. There was blood – on his jeans and on the edge of his top and he . . . he was cleaning his car and—'

I started to cry, then, and she sat on the sofa beside me

and pulled me close, a hand holding my head against her chest. But she was still listening.

And so I told her. I told her about how he'd moved through the dark, stripping off his red-soaked clothes. How he'd put on the gloves to clean the car before anyone else in the world was awake to see him. I said all of the things that were facts and, as I said them, I realised that they didn't add up to the fear that I hadn't been able to get rid of all day.

But then I looked at Jessie's face, and she looked pale and afraid, too. She smiled when she realised, but it was a fake smile, an empty one, and it made my insides feel like they were cartwheeling.

'Don't worry, sweetpea,' she said. 'It was late and you were upset. It's nothing to be worried about, I promise.'

I let her pull me into another hug. I wanted, very badly, to believe her.

7

I fell asleep easily that night, full of cheese on toast and *Harry Potter*, the book flopped face down on the pillow beside me. But I dreamt of a dark tunnel, a train on fire. I was watching the train and then I was in it. There was smoke around me, and when I looked down at my hands, they were slick with blood.

I woke up sweating and for a minute I couldn't move. And then I rolled over and saw that Jessie wasn't in her bed.

I climbed out of mine and padded silently across the room. The door was pulled to but not closed and I creaked it open and stood in the hall, listening. Dad wasn't home; his shoes were still missing from the doormat. The TV was on in the living room, its blue flickering light reaching across the carpet, but its sound was muted. A breeze drifted in under the front door.

There was a scrabbling sound coming from Dad's room. The door was ajar and I pushed it carefully open a little wider. The bare bulb was swinging, as if someone had just swatted it, and in its light, Jessie was kneeling on the floor. The wardrobe was open and Dad's clothes were hanging out of it, a knot of them in her lap. She was going through everything, tossing jumpers and jogging bottoms aside, holding up T-shirts and pairs of jeans close to her face to examine them. Reaching the last one, she let out a grunt of frustration and stood up. I glanced at the corner of the room where his washbasket was already lying on its side, empty. My insides were cartwheeling again. She went over to the bedside table and started pulling out the drawers, most half-empty, crumpled old receipts and change swishing about inside. She heaved up the mattress; the sheets flapping, the lightbulb's swinging turning violent.

And then she pulled the bed away from the wall. She stood very still, looking into the gap she had made. The light slowed and then stopped altogether, the shadows regathering themselves in the corners of the room. The bed was blocking my view; I couldn't see what Jessie was looking at, but I could see the way the colour had drained from her face and it made me push the door all the way open and go into the room.

'Fuck,' Jessie said.

I made it round the bed just as she finally moved forwards toward whatever it was that she'd found. She didn't notice me there, and I bunched my hands up inside my sleeves and shivered as I saw what she had seen: a hole in the plaster behind the bed, a cubby in the wall. I wrapped my arms around myself as Jessie reached in and pulled out things – a roll of money tied with a rubber band, a gold chain. And then a dark, rectangular object which caught the light as she turned it over to look at it. A woman's purse.

'Jessie,' I said, and she whipped round, the purse clutched to her chest. 'Jessie, he did something bad, didn't he?'

From *Magpie* by L. K. Cooper, published by Whirlwind Press, 2011

Jennifer Howell turned twenty-three on July 7th, 2002. Despite the big day falling on a Sunday, she threw herself, and her twin sister Emily, a party at a bar in Bloomsbury, near to the publishing house where she worked as an editorial assistant. In attendance were several of her colleagues and around twenty of the girls' friends. Other patrons of the bar that night report seeing Jennifer at the centre of things, wearing a sash and a large badge that someone had bought her, as well as, later, a fluffy tiara presented to her by Emily (there was a running joke in the family that Jennifer was 'the princess' of the two). A bartender recalls them as 'a nice group, no trouble' and says that it was clear they were all having a good time. It was a warm evening, with the party spilling out into the bar's garden area. The only incident anyone can remember came when Emily, having had a couple of cocktails more than she usually would, tripped over a chair and landed – to much amusement from the group – in one of the bar's giant decorative plant pots.

Shortly after the plant pot incident, Jennifer took Emily to a nearby taxi rank. She helped her sister into the back of a black cab, before climbing in herself and giving the address of the flat in Clapham which she and Emily shared. The driver, Garth

Butcher, remembers Emily trying to persuade Jennifer to get out and go back to the party. But Jennifer insisted, he says. 'She kept saying, "Don't be silly, it's fine. I'm not going to leave you."' Emily was drunk, he admits, and he worried that she might vomit in his cab. But instead she fell asleep, her head on her sister's shoulder.

'I got chatting to her, Jennifer, after that,' he tells me when I meet with him in a café in East London. 'I noticed their sashes and so I asked if it was their birthday, if they'd had a good night, that kind of thing. She was a nice girl. Friendly. I told her it was early to have called it a night but she said she never liked her friends getting cabs alone after they'd been out. I weren't offended or anything. It's sad but true, isn't it? This is the type of thing young girls have to worry about these days. I've got a daughter of me own, I'm always telling her she has to stay safe.'

By the time they arrived at their destination, Jennifer and Garth were singing along to songs on the radio – Jennifer educating Garth on some of her favourites, including Ashanti and Alicia Keys, whilst Garth admitted having Avril Lavigne's album stashed in his glove compartment. He offered to help Jennifer get Emily up the stairs to the first floor-flat but Emily, when Jennifer woke her, seemed revived by the nap. The girls paid Garth and climbed out of the cab.

At that point, he insists, Jennifer made no mention of returning to the party. He went on his way, glad to see the sisters home. Safe.

Emily's memory of the evening is patchy. She remembers waking up in the cab; remembers Jennifer helping her remove her strappy sandals inside the flat. She remembers that her sister put the kettle on and made tea for them both. It could have been at that point, she thinks, that her sister received a text. Emily can't be sure.

We do know for certain, though, that Jennifer received a message at some point between 11 p.m., when Garth Butcher dropped them off, and 11.31, when Jennifer sent a reply. That message was from Jack Ward, a fellow editorial assistant at Attic Books. She and Jack had started work there within a month of each other and had grown close. The party had moved on, Jack told her. A group of them were coming south of the river, and it was only fair that Jennifer join them. It was her birthday, after all.

Emily can't remember if Jennifer considered resisting this request. Her reply, when she sent it, was simple: Oh go on then x

Jennifer said goodnight to her sister. And then she headed back out into the dark.

Emily woke the next morning at 6 a.m., feeling a strange, uncomfortable sort of anxiety. At first, she blamed it on a hangover – found herself searching through her memories of the previous evening for anything embarrassing that she might have done. Not finding anything, she tried to go back to sleep, but the sense of panic continued to grow. Getting up to get a glass of water, she discovered that Jennifer's door was open, her room empty. Her sister wasn't home yet.

Emily went back to her phone, checking for any text she might have read and forgotten during the night. It was highly out of character for either twin not to let the other know when they wouldn't be home. But it was still early – or late – and Emily tried to reason that the party might still be going strong; perhaps Jennifer had gone back to Jack's with some of her other work friends and had crashed out on the couch. She sent a text to Jennifer and, when she didn't receive a reply, gave in to her fears and tried to call instead. The call diverted immediately to Jennifer's voicemail. That was okay, Emily told herself. Her sister was always complaining about the pitiful battery life of her old Nokia. It had probably died hours earlier, and Jennifer's charger was plugged in and waiting for her beside her bed.

Emily got back into her own bed and lay, awake and alert, for two hours, praying for the sound of her twin's key in the front door. When it didn't come, she called Jack. Woken after only four hours of sleep, and still fairly drunk, it took him a moment to understand what she was asking. When he did, he was confused.

Because Jennifer had never returned to the party, he told a frightened Emily. When no one had been able to get hold of her, they'd assumed that she'd thought better of heading back out or had fallen asleep.

Emily hung up. And then she called the police and reported her twin as missing.

The hunt for Jennifer lasted for three weeks. With little to go on – Jennifer did not appear on CCTV at her nearest Tube station and the last train had departed shortly after she'd left the house in any case; nor did any of the cameras at bus stops or on Clapham High Street pick her up – the police appealed to the public for information. Jennifer's image was well publicised during the first two weeks though the media's attention peaked and then waned as growing concerns that Tony Blair would agree to an Anglo-American invasion of Iraq, along with coverage of the *Big Brother* final, began taking over the front pages. Despite this, Emily worked tirelessly, appearing on local and national radio, and continuing a door-to-door campaign with the twins' friends. No one seemed to have seen Jennifer; it was, as one police source carelessly remarked to a journalist, as if she had vanished into thin air. The quote appeared on the front page of a local paper the following day: *VANISHED*, a photo of Jennifer, beaming at the beginning of the party, beneath it.

But Jennifer had not vanished. And on August 3rd, 2002, Emily's worst fears were realised. Her sister's body washed up on the bank of the Thames Estuary.

A post-mortem revealed that Jennifer had been strangled. Attempts had been made to weight her body down but a particularly and unseasonably stormy couple of days had seen water levels rise and Jennifer's grave disturbed.

It was a mistake that her murderer would not make again.

2005

After

With Jennifer, he got it wrong. He knows that. Wrong place, wrong method. He got carried away, lost control. Didn't think about tides, weather, decomposition. He watched her twin cry on TV, he read every article. He waited, stricken, for the knock at the door. He was afraid he wasn't as smart as he'd thought before.

But the knock never came. And then it was July again. And again. And the girls he took those times were not found. He saved their pictures; snipped them neatly from the newspapers. Proof. A trophy. He likes to look at them sometimes, when the thing at the back of his mind starts its whispering. He has lived with it for a long time and it feels like a miracle that he has finally found a way to keep it quiet, if only for a little while.

Seven was his lucky number when he was a child, even when his life always felt so low on luck. But then she betrayed him and that day, the seventh day of the seventh month, will be a reminder of that betrayal every year that passes. But then there was Jennifer, and then the others; a way to make it lucky again.

And now the rest of the world will remember this seventh day as being one of death and destruction, a city in fear. He watches the news, listens to the radio, anger blazing through him. It feels ruined, defiled. His day. It makes him want to run out, find girl after girl, all of them finally getting what they deserve.

What she deserved.

The thing at the back of his head grows louder; he has to press his hands over his ears, close his eyes in an attempt to block it out.

He must stay in control. He isn't like them.

He turns off the news, closes the curtains against a city still in shock. Next year he will make this day his again.

1

Lex Emerson (born Alexander Andrew Emerson on the 25th of May, 1972, though I wouldn't know that until I read through his police statements, years later) graduated magna cum laude from Yale and walked straight into a job at Buxton & Wise; a shiny corner office on the ninety-fourth floor of the North Tower of the World Trade Center. He spent his days advising customers on their assets and where to move them, talking about portfolios and relationship managers, and he knew that he was good at it and that being good at it meant nothing to him.

On September 11th, 2001, American Airlines Flight 11 flew directly into the floors of the North Tower occupied by Buxton & Wise. One hundred and thirty-two employees were killed. Lex Emerson was not one of them. Lex Emerson was in bed with his colleague's wife at a hotel seven blocks away, just as he often was on a Tuesday morning.

It was a time when everyone around him became

watchful of money, fearful of what was to come. For Lex, it started to slide through his fingers in a way it never had before. He no longer slept with his colleagues' wives, who were now his colleagues' widows, but he liked to take one of them, a short, black-haired woman with bright blue eyes and a dimple in her chin, to bars some evenings. They would drink martinis and then beers and then whatever occurred to them, and they would take it in turns to rack up pillowy lines of coke on the backs of toilets, on the backs of their hands, on windowsills in alleyways and CD cases in other people's apartments. They talked and talked and said nothing.

And then he met the girl. He threw up in a cab one night – cocaine never made him sick but booze often did, especially when mixed with Valium – and he was standing on the pavement, letting the taxi driver, who had discovered he had no money left (in his wallet or elsewhere, in fact), punch him, once, twice and then three times, the man finding his rhythm and Lex finding himself loose and floating, the thuds on his jaw so very far away. And then a woman had come running up, her heels clattering furiously in the silent street, and swung her handbag so hard that when it collided with the taxi driver's head, it knocked him sideways. Lex had felt bad about that part; he had spoiled the man's backseat, after all.

But then he had looked into the woman's brown eyes beneath their smooth creamy lids. He had heard her voice, soft and concerned, those words in that clipped British accent: 'Are you *okay?*' And still, he had been floating away.

Almost four years later, his daughter was born: Cara Rebecca Emerson, dark-haired, dark-eyed. Quiet and intense, watching them constantly. She scared him sometimes, even as the love rushed through him, even as he held her tiny weight against his chest.

Three months after that, a secondary crash: my sister and I walked into his life.

Of course, the crash really began when his wife – Olivia, but Liv to everyone she knew and cared about – didn't come home on the night of July 7th. Lex was left holding the baby while Liv's purse wound up in a cubbyhole behind my father's bed. Her driver's licence in Jessie's hand while she looked up the address. My hand took its place in Jessie's as we stood outside the house a day later, staring up at its bright white walls, its huge, immoveable mass.

Pimlico was only three stops up the Victoria line but it wasn't somewhere I'd ever had any reason to go – by which I mean it wasn't anywhere Jessie had ever had any reason to take me. It was clearly unfamiliar territory to her, too, and she'd gotten us lost twice before finding this street with its beautiful three-storey houses and their shuttered bay windows, sleek cars parked outside.

'Bigger than I expected,' Jessie said, stroking my hand with her thumb before she let go. She took a folded sheet of paper out of her pocket and opened it up, smoothing out the creases. 'Ready?'

I nodded, and we climbed the stone stairs to the double front door, glossy black with twin gold handles. Jessie rang the bell – a shrill sound that echoed inside – and as we waited, I looked up at her. She hadn't straightened her hair or piled it into a knot – instead it was in a full, fluffy pony-tail tied near the nape of her neck. With no make-up, and wearing a floral-print T-shirt, cut-off jeans and ballet pumps, she looked more like she was thirteen.

After what seemed like forever, we heard footsteps coming towards the door. I shifted uncomfortably in my own pair of ballet flats, which Jessie had made me wear with a skirt and a cotton, sleeveless shirt which tied at the bottom and belonged to her. I wished she was still holding my hand, and then I felt like a baby for thinking it.

There was the sound of a lock turning, and then another, a chain sliding back. The man who opened the door was tall and broad with a face full of stubble. His hair was sticking up on one side and he was holding a sleeping baby, her head lolling like a doll's against his shoulder.

'Yeah?' he said, the way Dad sometimes answered the phone when he was tired.

'Hi,' Jessie said. 'We're raising money for charity. We're supposed to do something for you, like the hoovering or the washing up?' She held out her piece of paper for him to see, and he took it, his other hand holding the baby in place. I had watched Jessie draw up the document on a computer in the internet café that morning, googling a charity I'd never heard of and inserting their logo at the top of the page.

'What do they do?' I'd asked, and she'd glanced up at me, hovering beside her chair whilst the juddery old printer across the room whirred into life.

'Look after poor kids,' she'd said, and then, 'Dellar's mum works for them.'

This had surprised me – I'd never really thought about what Dellar and Laine's mum might do. I wondered what it must be like to have a mum who did charity work, a cousin in the police. Normal things. Good things. I wondered if Jessie felt the same rush of jealousy when he talked about it.

The man looked down at the sheet of paper and then up at Jessie again. He looked tired – his eyes were swollen and shadowed, and his T-shirt had a milky stain down the front.

'Oh,' he said. 'I—'

'We wouldn't get in the way,' Jessie said quickly. 'We'd really like to help.' I thought it was a strange thing to say. But he seemed to immediately sag, just a little, and he stared at her for a second longer before stepping back from the door.

'I guess I could find something for you guys to do,' he said, and his accent was like something from a TV show, not like anything I'd heard in real life before. I'd had an American teacher once, Ms Coogan, but she'd been from the south, her words soft and drawling, nothing like the sharp, glossy sounds of his. 'Come on in.'

The hallway was dark and cool. There was an oval mirror on the wall, a skinny white table beneath it with a black marble vase, a single white orchid. I looked up at the white wooden stairs which wound their way up two floors, a narrow runner of thick cream carpet down their centre. It looked like a home from a magazine but it smelled stale and slightly sickly.

'Umm, I guess come through here,' the man said, leading us into a living room, the baby sliding precariously across his shoulder. 'I guess I could find some ironing or . . . something.' He looked helplessly at us.

'Ironing is good,' Jessie said. 'Or dusting, maybe,' she added, looking down at the sleek black coffee table beside her, its faint coating of grime.

The baby stirred and immediately began to cry; a thin, mewling wail like Mrs Klusak's cats. 'Hey,' he said to her, pushing his hand through his hair again as he went back out into the hallway. 'Shh,' we heard him saying, over and over. 'Shh, shh.'

I saw Jessie's eyes travelling over the room; the expensive, modern furniture – a red suede chair, a white leather sofa. The walls were painted a bright turquoisey blue and lined at random with white shelves. She took a step closer to look at them; more big stone vases, some framed photos – of the baby, and of the man, with the woman from the driving licence. She was tall and thin – impossibly thin, thinner than anyone I'd seen before, the bones of her chest sharp and exposed – with long, shiny brown hair and freckles. Jessie stopped under the biggest photo of her and was still.

'Jessie,' I whispered, and she ignored me. After a second or two, she turned on her heel and went out into the hallway.

'Here,' she said. 'Let me try.'

'Oh—' I heard the man say, but when I turned to look through the doorway at them, Jessie was taking the baby out of his arms, flopping her onto her own shoulder with a practised look I didn't understand. The wailing got louder, but then, as Jessie began to rub her back, and walk slowly away from her father, the baby snuffled and was quiet. Her eyes, which had been scrunched up, opened, and she looked at me over my sister's shoulder. I stared back.

'Hello,' Jessie was saying, nuzzling right in close to her ear. 'Hello, little bear.'

The man and I looked at each other; him at the end of the hall, me in the doorway. He looked shocked, powerless.

'She hasn't stopped crying for days,' he said.

I took a step forward and held out my hand. 'I'm Addie,' I said.

We sat at the shiny stone bar in their kitchen on red leather stools like the kind they had in the American diner Jessie sometimes took me to when she'd been paid. I drank a glass of orange juice that tasted fizzy at the edges of my mouth and the man – Lex – drank a beer. Jessie was still pacing the kitchen but with the baby cradled in her arms now, goggling up at my sister in a contented kind of silence.

'Where are you from?' I asked Lex, trying to avoid looking at Jessie and the baby, whose name I now knew was Cara, though the way he said it was thin and alien: *Care-ruh*.

He glanced at me and then away again. 'Boston. New York. LA. Take your pick.'

I took a big sip of my orange juice and slopped some onto my chin, onto my borrowed shirt. Jessie had lifted Cara up high, her thumbs tucked gently in her tiny armpits, jiggling her until the baby's face creased in a wide, wet smile.

'You're good with her,' Lex said, his voice strained and raw.

'Yeah, well.' Jessie let Cara slump back to her default position across her shoulder. 'I looked after this one a lot, back in the day.' The nod in my direction felt painful and pointed; I shifted out of its reach.

Lex put his beer down too hard, the bottle skidding an inch or two away. His head tipped forward, his hands came up to meet it. We looked at him; Jessie, Cara and me, already a three, and we were quiet.

'I—' he said, from the hollow of his hands, but the doorbell interrupted him.

'Shall I get it?' Jessie asked, though Lex was already up, already smoothing out the creases of his face. She came to stand beside me, back against the bar and Cara between us, as he went out to answer it.

'Mr Emerson,' a man said. 'It's good to see you again. Can we come in?'

Jessie looked at me, and Cara looked at Jessie. Jessie's eyes were narrowed in panic, and the only person I could hear breathing was the baby, the sound snuffling and gently escalating, her mouth half-smooshed against Jessie's arm as she held her tighter.

'Yeah. Yeah, come in.' Lex's voice wavered and I looked at my fingertips, pressed into the surface of the bar until they turned white. My heart was bumping against my chest and I felt, suddenly, like reaching out and covering Cara's face with my hand. Squashing it.

There was the sound of shoes shuffling against the doormat and then the door closed softly with a click. Cara let out a coughing sort of cry and Jessie immediately shifted her to her other shoulder.

'I'm afraid I still don't have any news for you,' the man said. 'How are you doing, Mr Emerson? How's Cara?'

'She's—' Lex stopped suddenly, like he was about to throw up, and then he let his breath out, long and slow. 'We're okay. We need to know. What's going on up there?'

'Well, Mr Emerson – can we go through? Is that okay? There are still people to be identified, it's very . . .' Their voices faded away as they disappeared into the lounge and closed the door.

'I want to go home.' I hadn't meant to say it out loud, but that was so often the case with me and Jessie. She pulled truths out of my mouth like a magnet.

Cara started to cry properly and Jessie glared at me. 'We're here to help,' she hissed, and she flopped the baby back into a cradle position and stuck her pinky into her mouth. The baby started sucking immediately, eyes wide and focused, and Jessie turned away from me, rocking her as she moved over to the glass doors overlooking the garden, the sun-stretched shadows of the trees creeping over the grass.

'There's a pool,' she said, more to herself than to me, and I didn't go to look. I was frozen, listening to those muffled voices coming from down the hall, wondering if Jessie had brought the purse with her. I wondered if she would ever say to me what she thought had happened to the woman it belonged to. The same woman the baby Jessie was currently cradling belonged to, too.

When the lounge door opened, we all started, even Cara. Jessie moved away from the glass doors and came close to me again.

'We do understand it's an extremely difficult time, Mr Emerson,' a woman was saying. 'And there are many other families going through the same thing. Please do consider giving the support line a call.'

'No.' Lex's voice was flat. 'No, thank you. Just— I need . . .' He trailed off, didn't seem able to express what it was that he needed.

'We'll be in touch as soon as an inquest can be opened,' the man said, his voice gentle. 'We're doing everything we can.'

'Thank you,' Lex said again, although he didn't sound grateful. The front door closed behind them with a heavy thud.

When he came back into the kitchen and saw us, he jumped. 'I forgot— Sorry.' He went across the room to take the baby from Jessie. 'Oh. She's asleep.'

Jessie nodded.

'Oh,' Lex said again, and he sank onto one of the bar stools, a hand raked through his hair and propping his head up. I pressed my back into the doorframe and tried to get Jessie's attention; tried to will her to let us leave.

'Do you need a nanny?' she asked instead. 'Someone to help out for a while?'

He twisted his head to the side and stared at her. 'No,' he said. 'No, I don't think so.'

Jessie looked at me and then she looked at him. 'Okay,' she said, 'it's just that I'm looking for work and I've done a course. And she's such a lovely baby. I didn't mean anything by it.'

Lex had already returned his attention to the stone surface of the bar. The hand which wasn't holding his head up formed a fist and released, over and over again. 'I don't know what I'm going to do,' he said, though he didn't really seem like he was speaking to either of us.

'Shall I leave you my number?' Jessie asked, offering Cara back to him. 'Just for future use, you know?' As Jessie passed her over, Cara half-woke, letting out a croaky cry as her eyes flickered. Jessie stroked her cheek as Lex took her and Cara quieted, nestling into him.

'Okay.' He looked up at her with bloodshot eyes. 'Yeah. Thanks.'

He pushed a pen towards her, Cara balanced awkwardly in one arm, and Jessie strode over to the memo pad on the huge fridge and printed her name and number there in neat, careful strokes. 'We'll get out of your way,' she said, softly, and he nodded. He seemed to have forgotten why we were even there in the first place, which was good, because it seemed like Jessie had too.

In the hallway, I turned back to say goodbye, but Lex had moved away from us. He was standing looking out into the garden, perfectly still.

2

He called her, of course. It was the next morning, as I was getting ready for school, and when I stood close to her, I could hear Cara's frantic cries through the fuzz of the line.

'Yeah sure,' Jessie said. 'No, I'd love to.'

Her phone had rung all of the previous evening, desperately vibrating itself up to the edge of her crowded bedside table. Dellar, wondering why she wasn't responding to his texts, returning his calls. But she didn't pick up for Dellar. She picked up for Lex.

'You're gonna go there?' I put down my schoolbag and stared at her.

'Yes.' She picked the bag up and looped it over my shoulder. 'You're going to be late. I'll see you later.'

'Jessie, you can't go there!' My face turned hot and my chest started to squeeze in on itself, my bag slipping off and dropping to the ground again. 'We need to *do* something. Tell someone about the purse . . .'

Jessie tutted at me, pulled her ponytail tighter. 'Don't be stupid,' she said, looking at herself in the mirror. Then, glancing back at me, her face darkened. 'Don't you get it? They think she got blown to bits on one of the Tubes.'

'But she *didn't*,' I said, not able to stop my voice pitching up into the whinge I knew she hated.

Her answer was unexpectedly gentle in response. 'We don't know that. We don't know what happened. And until we do, this is the best thing for everyone. I promise.'

And because her promises meant everything, I picked my bag up. I let her walk me to school.

That morning, Mr Geary was trying to teach us about fractions but I couldn't concentrate. I kept picturing Jessie in that fancy kitchen, Olivia Emerson's baby daughter cradled in her arms.

'You're getting them all wrong,' Henry said, scribbling on the corner of my worksheet. 'These are *so* easy, what's wrong with you?'

'Nothing,' I said, pulling the sheet away from him sharply so that his pen drew on the table. What was Jessie doing? Feeding the baby? Doing their washing? Or sitting at the edge of that pool, her feet dangling in as she held the baby up and smiled at her?

'Oooooh.' Henry leant on the table, putting his face close to mine. 'Why are you so grumpy? Have you got your *period*?'

Michael had recently explained to him what periods were and he'd taken great pleasure in talking about them to anyone who'd listen.

'Right,' Mr Geary said, clapping his hands. No one else was really paying attention either, the classroom hot and stuffy and everyone flicking things at each other or staring into space. 'Does anyone want to tell us the answers they got? Or shall I just give up now, send you all off into life without ever knowing how to turn a fraction into a percentage?'

I'm not sure I ever really did find out how to. The rest of the morning passed in a blur. At break I was so quiet that Henry stopped teasing me. 'Are you, like, actually ill or something?' he asked. 'Do you want to go to the nurse?'

It was a tempting idea, because it was Jessie's number the office had on file. If I was sent home, she'd be called to collect me. But I remembered the way she'd snapped at me that morning: *Don't be stupid. Don't you get it?* I wasn't sure I could face making her angry by pretending to be ill, something I'd never been good at.

'I'm fine. I just . . .' Blood on a watch face. Lex opening the front door, his handsome face lined and shadowed and sad. I felt like something was gnawing away inside me, as if, if I wasn't careful, it might burst out. A part of me wanted so desperately to tell Henry what I'd seen the night of the bombings but deep down I knew I'd never say those words out loud again, not unless Jessie told me to. *This is the best thing for everyone. I promise.*

'You're being so weird,' Henry said, backing away. 'I'm going to go and hang out somewhere else today.'

Jessie had already told me that she wouldn't be able to pick me up from school but when I let myself in the front door that afternoon expecting an empty flat, I got a shock – Dad's shoes were on the mat, the radio on in the kitchen. I hesitated in the hallway but really there was no choice but to carry on into the room, to walk in as if everything was normal. He'd obviously only just got up. His face was still puffy from sleep and he was sitting at the table eating a bowl of soup, his phone in front of him.

'Hey kiddo,' he said, looking up.

'Hi.' I went to the fridge and looked into it so that I wasn't looking at him.

'How was school?'

'It was okay.' I took out a carton of apple juice and then put it back. He had bought food – I couldn't remember the last time that had happened. The shopping was Jessie's job.

'Where's your sister?' I could feel his eyes on the back of my neck; two points of heat.

I told the truth and surprised myself with its artfulness. 'At work.'

His phone started ringing; the old-fashioned *ring ring* he always had it set to. He got up to answer it, his bedroom door closing behind him, and I let out a breath and took out the apple juice again. I tried to listen to his half of the conversation over the humming of the fridge, the words muffled through the wall. 'I told you not to call,' I thought he said, then: 'We need to wait . . .' before the words tailed back off into a mumble that I couldn't make out. He didn't sound angry, the way he usually did on the phone. He didn't sound tired, either, the way he always was when he'd just woken up from the few hours of sleep he allowed himself. 'I know the place,' he said, louder now, his bedroom door opening. 'Yep, okay.'

He came back into the kitchen and smiled at me, sliding his phone into his jeans pocket. 'I'm going back out,' he said. 'You okay on your own?'

'Yeah,' I said, surprised. I watched him as he pulled on a jacket, as he drained the last of his tea. The scratch on his face had faded to pale pink; he'd cut himself shaving on the other cheek. And I loved him. When he came over and put one of his awkward kisses on my forehead, he was the same Dad he'd always been. He was the dad who had taught me to ride my bike in the courtyard outside, the dad who had sat and helped me write a letter to the future when Mr Geary made it our homework, who'd helped me seal it in a plastic sandwich bag and bury it in the park, keeping watch for anyone who might tell us to stop. The same dad who had run down the hill with me afterwards, laughing, and had bought us chips to share as we walked home.

'You sure you're okay?' he said, leaning down so that his eyes were level with mine, flicking back and forth as he searched my face. 'You look worried, kiddo.' And then, without warning, he folded me into a hug. I buried my face in his T-shirt and breathed him in, felt him place a kiss on the top of my head. 'You're wearing the bracelet,' he said into my hair. 'I'm glad.'

He was the same Dad and the London I knew was already putting itself back together outside our front door. Suddenly I hoped that everything inside might start to become familiar again, if only I wished for it hard enough.

But when Jessie got home, she smelled of the musky baby smell of Cara and something stronger, furniture polish and disinfectant, and I knew that none of it could be wished away. She turned on the oven and opened the freezer drawer and I sat at the table with my book and watched her.

'What you reading?' she asked, pulling out a bag of frozen mince.

I flipped it round to show her and didn't say anything.

'Addie.' She put down the mince and came and pulled out the chair beside me. 'Don't be mad with me, 'kay? I'm trying to do the right thing.'

I put the book down and tried to stop my lip wobbling. There it was again; that muddy, confusing concept that wouldn't leave me alone.

'The *right* thing would be to tell someone, wouldn't it? If you think he . . . did something. To her. Lex's wife.'

She sighed and twisted her hair up and away from her face, silent as she fumbled a band around the knot. 'Do you have any idea what would happen to you if Dad got in trouble, Addie? Do you know where they'd take you?'

'No.' I had a vague, cobbled-together idea that looked something like Harry Potter's cupboard under the stairs and an old film version of *Oliver!* we'd watched one Christmas, but I ignored it.

'They wouldn't let me keep you, babe. They'd put you in care.'

'They wouldn't!' I felt an itching spread through me; an anger. 'They wouldn't.' Who was 'they'? I didn't know. I didn't know about any of it, but that just made me madder.

She put a hand on both of my shoulders. 'Addie, we don't know the whole story. We don't know what happened. We just need to be smart about this, okay? It's you and me, just like always, and we'll figure this out together.' Her fingers were gripping me tighter but it didn't hurt; it felt good, secure. 'I need you to keep this quiet, right? Don't talk to anyone but me? I need you to trust me.'

I nodded. That was always true; that was a given.

She smiled at me, a hand slipping down to squeeze mine before she let me go. 'Good.'

'Are you going back there?' I asked, as she got up and poured the mince into a smoking frying pan.

'Yes. I'm going to work there for a while. I need money now the shop's gone and she's a cute baby. It'll be good for us, okay?'

'What are you going to tell Dad?'

She turned around and gave me a small, sly smile which I didn't like at all. 'I'll tell him I'm working for a friend of a friend.'

That night, when Dellar called, she didn't pick up either.

3

It was a while before I saw Lex or Cara again, though each night when Jessie came home I felt as if they had left their traces on her. A white crust of milk on the sleeve of her T-shirt, an unfamiliar CD tossed onto her bedside table. She worked later and later, would sometimes come home with chips or a carton of noodles from the Chinese for me to eat. I didn't ask her about her days even though questions about what she did there chewed at me endlessly. I waited to hear what her plan was and although I never lost faith that she *had* one (she was Jessie after all, and Jessie always had a plan), I eventually began to accept that she had no intention of sharing it with me.

Instead of shouting or whining or demanding, I turned all my fear and suspicion in on myself, keeping it knotted up tight inside me, the secret of what I had seen safely locked up there. I dreamt about my dad going to jail; I dreamt about him plunging a knife into Jessie; of blood circling around in the washing machine. Mr Geary had to tell me off most days for not listening in class, or not doing the work, or, once, pushing Henry after he'd teased me about something one time too many. I stopped myself doing it again after that but I didn't stop wanting to. All day long I wanted to push people out of my way, shout at them for getting things wrong. All day long I wanted to be left alone. I wanted to be with Jessie.

My routines, my rituals, started to form soon after she began working for Lex. I was alone in the flat and the sun was just dropping behind the building opposite. Our light was mostly blocked even on the brightest of days and that week had been hazy, the sky sullen shades of grey. So it was already getting dark and, as I passed through the hallway and into the lounge, I stopped to flick on the light.

It felt like something switched in me, then, although maybe that's all in the remembering. The gnawing fear which had never really gone from my belly suddenly became a wave which swelled up and crashed over me – a sudden, specific knowledge that *something bad was going to happen*. And with it, a needling voice told me that I had, in some way, not turned on the light correctly. These two things were, it seemed, inextricably and obviously linked. And so I reached up and turned the light off and then on again. Dad and Jessie were both born on a 5th (February and October, respectively) and it had always been my lucky number – it felt only natural, after the second flip of the light-switch to do it a third, fourth, fifth time. Somehow, it quieted my rising panic. When Jessie arrived home ten minutes later, I felt proud – I felt as though I had saved her.

Over the next month or so – and then in the years that followed – other rituals slowly began to emerge. Lying awake one night, an image of Jessie and my dad in the crumpled wreckage of his car surfaced in my mind and I couldn't force it away. I saw it all, on and on, the two of them slumped there, the windscreen smashed and bloody. I turned onto my back, tried – as I always did, my failsafe method – to think about the members of Dumbledore's Army and the animal produced by each of their Patronus charms (*Harry: Stag, Hermione: Otter, Luna: Hare*; my version of counting sheep). But nothing could shift that picture, the rising terror that accompanied it. Nothing – until I flopped onto my other side, a Biro taken from the windowsill, and etched their names into the wall behind my bed. Jessie. Dad. Somehow, writing them there made them solid. It made them safe.

As the weeks went on, a second set of attempted bombings hit the city, a fresh wave of panic. Jean Charles de Menezes was mistakenly shot and killed by police when running for a train one station up the Victoria line from us. And though the real suspects were arrested, the Piccadilly line going back into service and things slowly returning to normal, the fear was always there. There was always the voice telling me how I could protect us, and those letters became gouged into the plaster of my wall, the plastic casing of the pen starting to crack.

When school finished for the summer, I was on my own most of the time. I was supposed to sit in with Mrs Klusak but she seemed to have forgotten the arrangement that year and Dad had apparently forgotten to check. Mostly I sat out on the cold grey balcony and read, Capri-Suns sucked dry and curled up beside me. Sometimes I went to Henry's – he lived further up the hill in a terraced house where his bedroom looked out over the little flat roof of the kitchen and sometimes, if we didn't think we'd get caught, we'd climb out onto it and play games on his phone while we pretended we were at the top of a skyscraper or on a flying carpet or an island. Henry liked to play pretend just as much as me, as long as we weren't in earshot of anyone else, especially Michael. I remember us lying there one day when it was particularly sunny; Henry, who had a thing for old eighties action movies, had rolled up the sleeves of his T-shirt and pushed his thick dark hair into some kind of central fin with a strong combination of gel and sweat. He was lying on his front, flicking through a motorbike magazine (an interest he was trying out after Michael had claimed it as his) and eating Monster Munch when he glanced at me and said, 'My dad says your dad is bad news.'

I looked up from the ancient *National Geographic* I'd borrowed from the stack in his room – all of which Henry had pretty much memorised from cover to cover and often treated as some kind of catalogue for the settings of our games. 'Let's pretend we're on the Galapagos Islands,' he'd say, and so it was important for me to keep up. Sweat was trickling down my back. 'Shut up,' I said. The sun had burnt a strip across my nose and my face felt tight and sore.

'*He* says,' Henry continued, flicking the page over lazily even though he didn't care about the pictures on the paper any more. He had something much more interesting to investigate. 'That your dad is *dodgy*. He *says* that your dad is barred from all the pubs.'

'That's not *true*,' I said, sitting up.

'He said he didn't really want you hanging around here,' Henry said, pushing his glasses up his nose and staring absently out over the neighbours' narrow gardens. 'But me and my mum told him you were cool.'

I had only met Mr Zhang once before, when he had come to pick Henry up from school one afternoon when we were in Year 3. He had been dressed in a fleece and jeans, leather loafers that looked like slippers, and he'd stood with his arms folded across his chest, bouncing back and forth on the balls of his feet while he waited. At the time, I'd thought he looked boring. Now, my mouth turned sour with jealousy.

'You shut up,' I said, my voice coming out in a rough, hot way I hadn't heard before.

Henry rolled onto his side to look at me and laughed. 'Chill *out*,' he said, and I stared at him. I thought about how good it would be to shove him or kick him so hard that he rolled right off the roof and down to the concrete patio below. I could almost hear the thud. My fingers itched to do it.

Instead I got up and scrambled back through the window, thumping onto Henry's bed with a squeal of springs and running down the stairs and out onto the pavement.

I didn't see Henry again that summer.

I don't know how long it took me to realise that Jessie was not going to talk to me about Lex or Olivia or our dad; that she was hoping I would let the chain of events that had led her to that house go, let it float away like the string of a balloon. It stings, even now, that she thought I was that stupid, that trusting. It stings more to realise that she was *almost* right.

Because I almost did let it go. It was so easy to sink into those days, that stack of mildewed library books and the worlds they offered, a world away from my own. To go back to letting Jessie and Dad orbit me as the sun rose and fell, offering me meals and affection before disappearing back into their own realms. To pretend that I was cared for and safe and that things were carrying on as they always had. I *wanted* to. I wanted to forget, I wanted to sweep away the things that I had seen, to pretend that Lex's wife's purse had ended up in our dad's taxi simply by coincidence; dropped out of a handbag or picked up from the street by another punter. That he had been cleaning his car because he couldn't sleep; that the blood on his jeans really was from breaking up a fight. I wanted these things to be true so badly that the pen marks behind my bed began to bleed into each other, the names becoming unclear so that I had to begin again, a fresh Jessie and a fresh Dad beside them. A fresh start.

And perhaps I would have done it, would have managed to put it away and let my memory slowly fog it into nothingness, if it hadn't been for the Tuesday that August when Jessie had to take me back to Lex's.

It happened at 4 a.m., the glass shattering, two and then three sets of footsteps thudding into the house. I sat up in bed, the familiar panic already threading its way through me, electric and violent. But Jessie was there, she was there, and – my heart pounding suddenly to a stop – so was Dellar. For the first time in days, weeks, he had slept over. He had slept over and he was jerking awake as another thud came from next door, another splash of glass as something was tipped over. He turned his head and looked at me.

'Don't go out there,' I said, the fear resurging.

'Don't go out where?' Jessie, oblivious to the rest of the sound, woken up by me. In tune with me, always. She sat up, pushing her hair out of her face. 'What's happening next door?'

There was the sound of something else breaking; something heavy this time. I thought of the big brown lamp beside Mrs Klusak's TV. Then laughter.

'Someone's hitting up next door,' Dellar said. 'Stay here.'

My eyes met Jessie's in the orange half-light from outside. Her hand locked round his arm. 'No. Elliott, don't go out there.'

I started to cry.

'Where is she?' Dellar asked. 'Where's Mrs K? Is she in there?'

I shook my head but I couldn't make the words come out, and it took Jessie a minute to remember. 'She went to visit her son,' she said, dropping the duvet from around her and standing up on the bed to try and look out of the window behind me. 'Bournemouth.'

'Okay.' Dellar got up too, started pacing the floor. 'I should go in there. They're taking her fucking stuff.'

'No!' I threw myself in front of the door, stumbling as I did. 'Don't go out there, please.'

'She's right,' Jessie said, stepping down off the bed and putting a hand on Dellar's chest, her phone already at her ear. 'I'm calling the police.'

I sank down against the door, my body needled with fear and the breath trapped in my chest. The police, there, where we lived. Where our dad had hidden a purse and bleached a car. I couldn't get the words out and suddenly I couldn't get the air in, my lungs tight and the sound of me gasping echoing in my ears.

'Addie . . .' Jessie was crouched in front of me, her phone thrust at Dellar, who backed away, murmuring to the operator. I couldn't hear what he was saying, all I could concentrate on was Jessie. She took hold of both of my hands; tight, too tight. 'Breathe, babe. Breathe.'

And yet, for the first time, I couldn't do as she asked.

'Addie. Breathe. *Breathe.*'

For the first time, I could see panic in her eyes. She couldn't help me.

'Move, Jessie,' Dellar said, and she did. The panic meant she did. He handed her the phone and he sat down in front of me and the hollow whooping sound I was making kept on getting louder.

'Ads,' he said, gently gripping me by the shoulders. 'Addie, listen to me. I want you to look at me, okay?'

I managed to nod, stars dancing at the corners of my vision.

'Let's try and breathe together, okay?' I tried to focus on him, his eyes calm and kind. 'Take it easy,' he said. 'We're just going to breathe in through our noses, yeah . . .' He did it slow and loud, gave me a nod when I tried to do the same. '. . . and out through our mouths.' He blew out a long, gusty breath, mine sounding pathetic in response. 'You're doing great,' he said. 'Let's try it again – in . . . and out . . .'

And I did what he asked – slowly and painfully, my chest creaking open and the sounds shaky. The breaths came feebly at first and then stronger and I kept following his, listening to the air whoosh out each time until eventually I realised that it was no longer painful.

'You're okay,' Dellar said gently and, for that moment, I believed him.

And then Jessie was there again, bundling me up. 'It's okay, babe, it's okay. The police will take them away, don't worry. Keep breathing.' Pressed to her chest I couldn't see what she was mouthing at Dellar but from behind her hunched shoulder I could just read his lips: *No problem*. But I could see from the look on his face that she'd already turned away from him.

And so, the next day, when Dellar had gone, she took me with her. I hadn't slept again, disturbed by the flashing blue outside and the constant thump of footsteps next door, the faint buzz of a radio. I was clingy and terrified, my eyes flicking constantly to the door. I don't know, now, whether I was scared of them coming back or the police; whose boot I was imagining splintering our front door. I pushed the toast she made me around the plate and when she tried to pass me the jam, my hand wobbled or didn't grip, the jar sliding through it and smashing against the floor, clots of blackcurrant exploding across the vinyl.

She didn't shout. She took me with her.

And there it was again, that big black double door, with its glossy paint and its finger-smeared handles. Me on the front step, my palms sweating.

Lex opened the door, shoes already on and a leather jacket over his polo shirt. He handed Cara to Jessie, barely glancing at me. 'I've gotta go,' he said, sliding sunglasses on. 'I've got a – well, look, I've gotta be somewhere. Help yourself to whatever.'

'Sure.' Jessie looked up from making cute faces at Cara long enough to smile at him. 'Take your time. We'll see you later.'

She stepped into the cool of the hallway, leaving me to trail after her. I heard Lex thump down the front steps behind me and I couldn't help noticing the difference between this man and the one who had slumped over the breakfast bar only a couple of weeks before. I wondered what my sister had done to him. I wondered what my father had.

Jessie headed into the kitchen, Cara staring at me over her shoulder. She'd kicked her shoes off and I saw the way she moved through that room just the same way she did one of our own – cupboard opened and glass removed even as she walked, a quick glance in the fridge as she passed on her way to the sink. She murmured to Cara as she filled the glass with water, took a deep gulp as she stood and stared out at the garden.

She turned and saw me in the doorway. 'Well, come in then! Take your shoes off first though. Want a drink?'

I shook my head. It smelled cleaner in there than it had the first time I had visited but there was still something in the air that stuck in my throat, made me feel like I was suffocating. I watched as Jessie flicked through the post that had been left on the breakfast bar, noticed for the first time the way she'd dried her hair straight and shiny, had dressed in an old blue sundress which clung to her curves, straps thin against her freckled shoulders.

'What do you want, juice?' Jessie had ignored the shake of my head, too busy slotting a dummy into Cara's puckered mouth.

'No.' I moved back towards the living room but from

there I could see the pictures of Liv smiling at me from their shelves. 'I don't want anything,' I said, turning back to Jessie with a pout.

'Suit yourself.' She turned the key in the glass door. 'Cara and I are going outside to enjoy the sun. You coming?'

I looked out at the perfect green lawn, the bright blue pool and the sky blue above it too. I didn't want to stay in that dark cavern of hallway, watched by the many eyes of Cara's missing mother. I tiptoed across the sun-warmed tiles of the kitchen and followed Jessie out into the garden.

Up close, the grass was fake but the plants which lined it – exotic-looking trees in big stone pots and rose bushes in beds – were real. They were all beginning to droop and brown, petals dropping. There were dead insects and curling leaves bobbing on the surface of the pool, the first speckles of green mould growing on the blue-tiled sides where the water ended.

Jessie was busy spreading a blanket on one corner of the lawn. She looked up at me and gestured to a corner of the patio. 'Grab that, will you?'

A pastel yellow sun umbrella, ducks dangling from each of its spokes. I picked it up and knocked a spider from its handle, the last stray threads of web trailing away as I walked back towards Jessie. I was never scared of spiders or bugs or rats or snakes. Jessie was, though she pretended not to be, and somehow that had always been my little secret strength. The thing which I could take care of and she couldn't.

'Thanks, babe.' Jessie clicked the parasol open and flicked its stand down, propping it over Cara, who lay flat on her back and looked up at the ducks, hands clenching and uncurling. I sat down next to Jessie and faced the pool.

'I'm glad you're here,' she said. 'I know it was really scary last night.'

I chewed my lip and tried not to think about how I'd felt, hearing the glass shattering. I focused on the pool and reminded myself that I could breathe again. 'Is this what you do all day?'

'Some days.'

'He pays you to sit in the garden?'

'He pays me to look after the baby, Addie. He's having a really hard time.'

I turned to look at her then, but she was busy fiddling with one of Cara's socks, her hand creeping up and jiggling her fat little baby tummy.

'Where's her mum?' I asked, not realising my voice was shaking until all three words were out.

She looked at me then, her gaze cool even though it was one of the warmest days we'd had. 'I don't know, Addie.'

'Where do you think she is?'

'I don't *know*.'

I looked down and realised I was picking at a scab on my knee, the first dark bead of blood bubbling out. 'Where does Lex think she is?'

She sighed and looked away. 'They still think it's possible she was on one of the trains. Or that she's run away.' She glanced back as if realising that she was talking to me, not Dellar or Laine. 'She probably has, babe. Dad probably gave her a lift to the airport or the station or something.'

I looked down at Cara, her legs kicking against the blanket now. 'What, and just left her baby here?'

Jessie shrugged. 'Mum left you, didn't she?'

Lex came back just after lunch, sweat darkening patches of his T-shirt, his leather jacket slung over one shoulder. By then we'd retreated from the sun, Cara in her bouncer on the counter and me sat on one of the stools while Jessie loaded the dishwasher with the plates and mugs Lex had left by the sink. He was on the phone as he walked into the kitchen, Cara's eyes swivelling at the sound of his voice, and he carried on his conversation without looking at us as he dropped his keys onto the counter and opened the fridge.

'I'm going private,' he said, pulling out a beer and letting the door swing shut. 'The cops here don't know their ass from their elbow.'

Jessie rinsed the last mug and slotted it into place in the dishwasher, sliding the shelf in.

'I'll find her,' Lex said, uncapping the bottle with the opener stuck to the fridge door. 'I want answers.' He took a deep swig. 'No—' he said, but the person on the other end of the phone kept talking and he listened.

Jessie came and stood beside me, her hands assembling a bottle of formula without missing a beat while her eyes never left Lex.

'Sure,' Lex said, taking another long gulp of beer. 'I get it. Yeah, call me then.' And he hung up without saying goodbye. He dropped the phone on the counter and stared at it for a second. And then he glanced up and noticed me for the first time.

'Hi,' I said, when he didn't look away.

'We had a break-in at the flat next to ours last night,' Jessie said, the bottle angled into Cara's mouth. 'Addie was a bit scared to stay at home by herself today. I hope that's okay – I was going to ask you earlier but you were in a rush . . .'

Lex shrugged and finally his eyes left my face. 'Sure. I guess.' He drank the rest of his beer in three long pulls.

'Did it go . . . well? Whatever you had to do?' Jessie kept her eyes on Cara as she spoke and I couldn't stop my heart from hammering in my chest. I felt like she was walking a tightrope, dragging me along behind her.

Lex made a dismissive noise, pushing the empty beer bottle away from him. 'Another pointless meeting with that idiot detective. I'd get more help finding Liv from a fucking park ranger.' His eyes found me again. 'Sorry.'

Jessie smiled at him. 'You want to finish feeding her?' There was only an inch of formula left, Cara sucking hungrily at the bottle with her eyes locked on my sister.

'That's okay,' Lex said, pushing his stool back with a shriek. 'You're doing a great job. I have to go make some more calls.' And he stalked out of the room without looking at the baby.

4

I'd hoped that the night of the break-in had meant Dellar was back properly but, in the following days, a lot of his calls still went ignored. Some of them *did* get answered, though, and I wondered if secretly Jessie had been as shaken as I'd been by that night, if she'd been glad that he was there. Because one afternoon she came home from Lex's and started tidying the flat. 'Elliott's coming over,' she said, when she saw me watching, and although I didn't like the coolness of his first name on her tongue, I took it as a step in the right direction.

It got even better when he arrived, bringing me a DVD of the first Harry Potter film. He brought Jessie a present, too – a top I'd seen her looking at in a magazine a week or two earlier. She hugged him and I could see that she was pleased. When the three of us sat down to watch the film, I saw her move closer to him, her body tucked into his the way it used to be. I couldn't believe I'd ever felt jealous of that.

When I was alone in the house that week I played the film on repeat, watching all of the extra features until I felt as if I was actually on the set, part of the family. I laughed along with their jokes and I nodded wisely as the director explained certain details, certain character traits. When Dellar came round I made him watch them too, thrilled that he was as interested in the camera tricks of broom-stick-flying as I was.

Dellar was around a lot more after that, something which made me feel light-headed with relief although there was still less laughing between them than there had been before. He would show up around six, usually with food, and he and I would sit and eat it as the clock hands inched their way later each night. Sometimes when Jessie showed up her lips would be marked purple with wine; other times she arrived with food too and was annoyed that we had already eaten. Dellar never mentioned anything in front of me but sometimes when I was in bed and they were in the kitchen or the lounge, I'd hear him ask about Lex. *Who is this guy anyway?*

Sometimes, when it was just the two of us, I had to pinch my lips together hard to stop the answer to that question from bursting out.

And then, finally, Jessie did the thing I suppose I'd been afraid of all along. She didn't come home.

It was Friday night, boxes of chicken and chips half-demolished on the sofa between Dellar and me. It was her favourite – Dellar and I always picked Chinese if it was our choice, or a pizza – and it was cold. I knew he'd had plans to take her out somewhere; he was wearing a shirt and smelled of aftershave. But it was nearly eleven o'clock, *The Graham Norton Show* halfway through, and there was no sign of her. Dellar checked his phone again but it had stayed silent all night. I picked up a cold chip and chewed it even though it tasted like fat in my mouth.

'I guess you should be in bed,' he said, the phone still clutched in his hand. I stared back at him, icy fingers clenching my insides. I had tucked up my feet beside me and now my hand went to the one which, underneath the sock, had a *J* inked on it. I'd taken to doing this, drawing a spidery *J* and *D*, one on each foot each day. It was stronger than the names on the wall behind my bed; I'd decided it worked better, had more power. I pressed down hard on the *J* with my thumb and turned away from him. *By the end of the show*, I told myself. *She'll be home by the end of the show.*

But the performance from some singer I didn't know came and went, and then the red chair stories – Jessie's favourite bit – and then the credits were rolling and Dellar was leaving the room, phone pressed to his ear. He closed the lounge door behind him but still I heard his hissed voice as he left her a message: 'Yo. Where are you? We're worried.'

When he came back in, he gave me an awkward smile. 'Guess she got held up,' he said. 'He works her hard then, this new boss?'

I pressed the sole of my foot harder. 'I don't know,' I

said, stalling for time. 'She likes it there,' I added. I wondered if that gave him the same pang of fear it did me.

He fiddled with a tear in the arm of the sofa. 'I guess that's good,' he said, though he didn't sound sure.

The sound of a key in the door made us both jump, and I saw relief spreading across his face. But then we heard the muttered swearing of Dad as he dropped his keys, a shuffling sound as he kicked off his shoes, one of them thumping away from him down the hall. I froze. He was drunk. He never got drunk.

Dellar glanced at me. 'You should go,' I whispered, and he opened his mouth to argue but then seemed to change his mind. He got up and reached for his coat.

'See you later, Addie,' he said, reaching out to fist-bump me, but his face was still shadowy and scared, and I heard my father grunt at him as they passed each other, the front door slamming behind Dellar.

Dad appeared in the living room doorway, a hand put up to brace himself. His eyes narrowed as he looked at me. 'You should be in bed,' he said. 'Always up and around when you shouldn't be, kiddo.' He smiled but it was a hard, humourless thing; a sneer. 'It'll get you into trouble, some day.'

I bit my lip, wondered if I could duck past him, make it to the bedroom in time to close the door. But he walked carefully to his chair, sat down in it and let out a sigh. 'You're *all* trouble,' he said sadly. 'All of you.'

I kept my gaze on the ground.

'Where's your sister?' Dad asked, his voice low now.

There was a smell of smoke coming from him – the pub, I supposed, although it had a colder tang, something far more like November than August.

'She had to work late,' I said quickly. 'She asked Dellar to stay with me.'

'Lucky him.' He tipped his head on one side as he watched me. 'Who wouldn't want to hang out with Lucky Number Seven, eh?'

I tried to smile. Drink changed his face, made it looser, his features less predictable. What began as a grin or a laugh could so easily slip into something so different. I saw the beginning of a frown, his eyes narrowing, and my heart started to pound.

'When you were born,' he said, 'I called you my good luck charm. And then . . . well.' He leant forward and I instinctively tensed, waiting to see if he would spring up.

But instead he gave a hollow little laugh. 'Go to bed,' he said. 'Before trouble finds you, kiddo.'

I got up and moved slowly towards the door, still on uncertain ground. 'Goodnight, Dad.'

He didn't reply. I saw the way his hands gripped the arms of his chair, his eyes closed. The last traces of a smile twitched at the corners of his mouth. I turned away and went to my room, closing the door behind me.

I lay awake that night until the dark leached away again, my fingers pressed so tightly to the etched *J-E-S-S-I-E* on the wall that my arm went numb.

At 7 a.m., Jessie came home. She smelled of smoke and aftershave, too.

5

The next day, when my father had left again, Dellar came back to the house. I was sitting out on the balcony, a library copy of *Percy Jackson and the Lightning Thief* open against my knees, and he smiled at me as he went inside but he didn't stop to talk. The front door was ajar and I closed the book and listened as he said what he had to say. He wasn't angry but his words were strong enough to carry while most of my sister's – whispered, panicked – fizzled out before they could reach me.

'It's not right,' I remember he said. I remember that best of all.

'You don't get a say.' Her voice louder now, firm. And I knew it was over then. He had failed to understand the most basic of facts about Jessie. He had tried to tell her what to do.

When he came back out onto the balcony, he hugged me. 'Be good, Addie,' he said. 'I'll see you, 'kay?'

I nodded, even though we both knew he wouldn't. I listened to him thump down the steps to the courtyard, a tightness in my chest. I felt a sudden, urgent need to get up, flick a light-switch or write a new set of letters behind my bed. Instead I went inside to find Jessie.

She was sitting in the living room, her phone in hand. She looked up when I came in and I saw that her eyes were dry, her mouth set hard.

'Please don't break up with him,' I said.

She shook her head and looked away. 'It's complicated, Addie. You wouldn't understand.'

'Please. He loves you.' *He'll keep us safe*, an insistent voice said at the back of my head and it felt like the truth. I wanted to cry.

'We don't need him,' Jessie said, as if I'd spoken the words aloud. She got up and walked past me, headed for the kitchen. 'Come on, I'll make you something to eat.'

I swallowed back my tears, anger rising in their place, but she paused in the doorway and looked back at me with something closer to sympathy. 'We'll be okay, Ads. It's me and you now, just like it's always been.'

But I knew I wasn't her number one any more.

On Sunday morning, she ran me a bath and, while I was in it, laid out clothes on my bed. Smart things: my best jeans, a top of hers which she knew I liked. She sat me down cross-legged on the floor in front of her on the bed, and she dried my hair properly, with a brush, the way people did in the hairdressers.

'Lex is taking us for lunch,' she said, and my scalp started to burn.

'Why?' I asked, but it came out in the whingy, baby voice she didn't like and the brush tugged a little harder on my head.

'Because he's nice,' she said. 'And he needs me.'

She finished my hair without saying anything else but those last three words echoed in my ears. *He needs me.*

I hated that I couldn't stop my tongue from twitching with the weight of three of my own: *So do I.*

Lex – or Jessie – had chosen a pub near the house in Pimlico, the walls outside painted a dazzling white, neat baskets of flowers hanging between the huge windows. The picnic tables outside were full of people, all glossy and laughing with their cocktails and their huge glasses of wine. I felt small and stupid in my borrowed top, but Jessie took me firmly by the hand and led me inside. It was loud in there, people leaning on the bar and crowded round tables, glasses clinking and all of them talking, talking, laughing so loud it felt like a roaring wave which parted to let us through.

Lex was sitting at a table in one of the back rooms, where people were eating roast dinners, their conversations quieter. He had his back to us, Cara slumped against one arm while he talked on his phone, a half-drunk pint of lager on the table in front of him.

'Hi,' Jessie said, sliding into the bench seat opposite him, just as he ended his call.

'Hey.' His face shaven today, mouth creasing into a smile. He looked genuinely pleased to see her – both of us. 'Hey, Addie.'

'Hi,' I said, and I looked at Cara instead. She was dressed in a jumper that looked too hot for the weather, and leggings with an orange stain on one leg. Her fine strands of dark hair had crumbs of something caught in them and she only had eyes for my sister.

'You guys want a drink?' Lex was already rising out of his chair, Cara handed over the table to Jessie.

When he was gone, Jessie bounced Cara on her knee and brushed the crumbs from her hair. 'Hasn't she grown?' she asked me, though Cara looked as small and breakable as she had the last time I'd seen her. I picked at the hem of my borrowed top until Jessie slapped at my hand and told me to stop.

Lex came back with a glass of wine and a Coke. I'd never seen Jessie voluntarily choose wine before – sometimes she had vodka and orange juice or beer if Dellar had bought a six-pack. And I could tell from the way she was careful as she picked up the glass, the concentration on her face as she took a sip, that wine was still something she wasn't sure about.

I drank some of my Coke and then I fished out the slice of lemon and ate it, watching Lex but scared to look at him for too long. His T-shirt was creased and had a matching orange stain near the bottom. He looked at his phone again and then up at Jessie and the baby.

'She had a bad night,' he said. 'I don't get it.'

'She's probably having a growth spurt,' Jessie said, flashing him a sympathetic smile. 'Don't worry about it.'

Lex glanced at me. 'Your sister knows a lot about babies.'

I nodded. Apparently she did.

Jessie pushed a menu towards me. 'What d'you fancy, Addie? Roast?'

My mouth was so dry I couldn't imagine swallowing food but when I didn't answer, Jessie nudged me under the table. 'Okay,' I said, and when she shot a look at me I added, 'Please.'

Lex reached out and swung the menu round to face him and I looked at his big hand with its neat, clean nails and the thin gold band around the ring finger. His watch was big too, several sets of hands arranged around the huge face. He saw me looking at it and smiled.

'Nice, huh? It was a wedding present from my wife.'

I looked at Jessie but she kept her gaze on Cara. I was embarrassed when I risked a glance at Lex and saw tears welling in his eyes. But he blinked them away and took several large gulps of his beer.

When Jessie finally turned to me, I saw something I liked even less in her expression. 'Lex's wife is missing,' she said to me, her eyes daring me to react. 'It's a very hard time for them.'

Lex swallowed and looked away and I stared at my sister. But she was already rising from her seat, Cara slotted neatly on her hip. 'I'll go to the bar and order food,' she said. 'Lex, you want to come with?'

He shook his head, unfolding notes from his wallet and handing them to her. 'I'll keep Addie company.'

Jessie hesitated for just a second before smiling. 'Okay, great. And a roast for you, too? Chicken?'

I wasn't surprised that she could already guess what he'd choose but it still sent a spike of something cold through me.

'Yeah, thanks.' Lex watched her as she weaved her way through the tables and then turned back to me. 'Your sister has been an angel,' he said, looking down at his hands. 'I don't know what I would've done these last few weeks if you guys hadn't shown up at my house that day.'

Guilt churned in my stomach and I pushed my Coke away from me. The sweetness of it had evaporated in my mouth, the taste turning coppery.

'I guess you're kind of young to understand about Liv disappearing,' he said. 'It's been a complete f— A nightmare. I keep thinking I'm going to wake up.' He rubbed a hand over his face. 'And then I don't, and she's still not home, and I'm sitting here ordering a roast dinner and drinking a beer like any of this is normal.'

I glanced at the bar, where Jessie was laughing with the server, tossing her hair over her shoulder and hugging Cara closer.

'We thought she'd been on the train.' Lex was still looking at his hands. 'That was her route, you know. Victoria line to King's Cross, Piccadilly to Russell Square. And that front carriage, that's where she always stood, cos that's where the stairs and the lifts are, right? She hated getting stuck at the back of the queue for the lifts, she was bad at small spaces. So that's where she would've been, right there next to the fucking asshole—' He caught himself too late that time, carried on anyway. 'But they still can't tell me for sure. Only the coroner can record the verdict, and the inquest . . .' Finally, he looked up and seemed to remember properly who he was speaking to. 'Sorry,' he said. 'I don't have many people to talk to. Sometimes, it . . .' He waved a hand about helplessly. 'Sometimes I can't stop it.'

'It's okay,' I said. I looked down at my own hands and remembered them red.

'I guess what I'm saying is, the worst thing I could've imagined has happened. And your sister is somehow making me able to carry on. That's why I wanted to take you guys out for lunch. To say thanks.' His voice had grown tight over the last few words and he coughed, like he was trying to ease the pressure somewhere in his throat.

I stared at him, my hands clammy in my lap. 'I—'

'All sorted.' Jessie slid back into her seat, plunking Lex's change down on the table in front of him, along with a bucket of cutlery and napkins. 'They're out of beef though, unlucky for me.' She took a sip of her wine and glanced at both of us. 'What have you two been talking about?'

I looked away, face turning hot. Neither of them seemed to notice.

'I was just telling Addie how grateful I am for all your help,' Lex said, taking a napkin and knife and fork from the bucket and setting them carefully at his place. 'This is the worst—' He stopped suddenly, as if he'd choked on the next word. He closed his eyes, tapped a fist once and then twice on the table as if that might dislodge it. The heat in my cheeks deepened, my nails digging smiles into my palms. I looked at Jessie but her face was calm. She reached out a hand and laid it over his clenched one, Cara still balanced in her other arm.

'Don't,' she said, softly. 'It's okay. You don't have to do this. You don't have to pretend with us.'

He looked up at her with bloodshot eyes and nodded once, his hand still held in hers.

When the food arrived, I couldn't swallow a single mouthful.

When we got back to the house, I could tell Jessie was cross with me. 'You'll have to make toast if you're hungry,' she said, as if wasting my dinner was the thing I had done wrong, instead of sitting silently for the whole uncomfortable meal. Uncomfortable for me, anyway; Jessie and Lex seemed to find it easy enough to fill the quiet with comments about the food, Cara, the area. With each sentence, I'd heard how Jessie's voice had changed in small, subtle ways; the words crisper and more careful, everything calm and controlled and kind. She laughed differently too, when she was around him. It was a giggle, musical and polite, nothing like the belly laugh she did when something was really funny.

'I'm not hungry,' I said, and went to our bedroom. Falling out with Jessie – even in such a quiet, uneventful way – only made my stomach swirl more. I listened to her clanking plates around in the sink, my fingers tracing her name behind my bed. It was starting to feel like it wasn't hers any more. At lunch, Lex had called her Jess and she hadn't corrected him.

I flopped onto my side, my back to the Biro names on the wall. My own baby face looked back at me from the framed photo I kept on the bedside table. I was about five months old and I compared the image to Cara – I was a fatter baby, with round pink cheeks and a goofy, dribbly grin. But I had dark hair like Cara's, soft flyaway strands of it, and dark eyes like hers. We weren't so different. It wasn't a pleasant thought and I pushed it away.

I looked at the person holding baby me instead. She had dark hair too, and her nose was narrow and delicate like Jessie's. She was smiling at the camera, her hands spread wide on either side of my belly, holding me up proud and happy. It was Christmas, and she had on a sweatshirt with a snowflake pattern and a long strand of beads round her neck.

I had lots of complicated feelings about my mum, and so I'd got used to putting all of them away, like there was a box in the back of my head where I could keep things I wasn't ready to look at properly. But thinking about Cara, and the way Jessie had cooed at her and cuddled her, made me think about Mum too. She hadn't called on my birthday but I'd spoken to her three days later, a quick call like every year, with people laughing and shouting in the background. When Jessie had come back from work she'd asked about the conversation but there wasn't very much to tell. There never was.

It wasn't that I didn't want to talk to her. I looked forward to those calls each year – birthdays or Christmas or sometimes out of the blue on otherwise ordinary afternoons. I kept each card she sent me, hidden in the back of one of my old picture books where I knew Dad wouldn't find them. But then she was on the other end of the line and she was a stranger. Neither of us really knew what to say to each other and there was always someone there, telling her to hurry up in a language I didn't understand. Sometimes they sounded friendly, more often they were angry. It scared me, even though Jessie had tried to explain how there were only two phones for everyone to use and so people got impatient. It felt like they were shouting at me.

Jessie had tried to explain a lot, the older I got. How Mum had met someone she loved and moved abroad with him. How she had gotten into trouble over there and ended up in prison. How Dad didn't like to talk about it. She'd explained it all.

Though she never would tell me what Mum had done.

It was half a story but they all were, back then – it's only looking back now that I see the missing pieces. Then, it was all I'd ever known, and all I'd ever needed. I was happy, me, Jessie and Dad. I looked forward to those calls and cards but, when they were in front of me, I felt scared. Because someone else was there, on the edges, threatening to change things.

But now that there was Lex, a different person who was

changing things, I found myself thinking about Mum. I looked at the baby version of me in the photo and my stomach started churning again. Because we weren't that different, Cara and me. But at least I knew where my mum was.

There was a soft tap at the door and Jessie came in. I ignored her.

'Hey,' she said, sitting down on the bed beside me. 'I'm sorry for being cross. I know you're just worried. But I need to tell you something that Lex mentioned to me today.' I held my breath, determined not to look at her. 'He told me that Liv lost her purse. So you don't need to worry about that any more.'

'Really?' I rolled onto my back and stared at her.

'Ages ago. Someone stole it out of her bag.' She reached out and stroked my hair. 'See? It didn't mean anything. She wouldn't even have had it with her that day, when she got on that train.'

'Are you sure?' Relief rushed through me, my smile matching hers. 'Did you tell him that you found it?'

She shook her head. 'I thought it might sound a bit weird. Don't you?'

I frowned. 'Couldn't you say that we went there because we wanted to give it back?' Honesty was something she had bred into me; being guided away from it, even by her, unnerved me.

She sighed. 'Don't you think it's kind of special? That we showed up at his house, just when he was most desperate? And we've helped him. We've helped both of them.'

I looked at the photo of me and Mum again, thought of the way Cara beamed whenever Jessie was near her. 'I guess so,' I said uncertainly.

'The important thing is that we're making things better for them,' she said, tucking my hair behind my ear, her hand resting for a second beside my cheek. 'It doesn't matter how we ended up there in the first place, right?'

I think that, even then, I could hear the thing she was really asking of me. *Don't ruin this for me.* She loved him; she loved them. And because I loved her, I nodded. I let it be.

From *Magpie* by L. K. Cooper, published by Whirlwind Press, 2011

Katherine West was London born and bred, growing up in a small semi-detached house in East Dulwich. She was a happy, outgoing child – a favourite in the local community centre's Drama Club. She harboured a desperate ambition to be a *Blue Peter* presenter aged five, though by the time she came to choose a career path, she opted instead to train as a veterinarian. By twenty-three, she was working as an assistant at the South London Animal Hospital, and by twenty-nine, the age at which she would die, she was one of the more senior vets there. She lived in a flat fifteen minutes from the house she grew up in, and was, by all accounts, a bit of a homebody. She turned up at her parents' every Sunday for a roast, and she met her father for a pint after work each Friday.

On the night of July 7th, 2003, Katherine had arranged to meet a friend, Julia, for drinks at a bar in Brixton. But Julia was delayed – she'd dropped home after work in the hope of changing into comfier shoes, only to discover that her flat had been broken into. By the time she got hold of Katherine to explain that she had the police there, Katherine had already arrived at the bar. Katherine being Katherine, she immediately offered to go round and help but Julia told her not to. It wasn't going to take much longer, she explained, and then she would need a drink. Would Katherine mind waiting?

Katherine did not mind. She took a seat at the bar and ordered a cocktail, then sat and read a copy of *Metro* which someone had left behind.

By 9 p.m., Katherine had struck up a conversation with Dean, one of the bartenders working that night. He remembers her as happy, too – 'Most people would be annoyed if their friend left them hanging like that, but she seemed like she was having a nice enough time on her own. One of those people who make the best of a situation, you know?' They'd got talking about Dean's new puppy, a French bulldog he'd named Louie. He showed Katherine some photos and she talked him through some basic training techniques he could use. At 9.30, Dean had a break and he ended up spending it with Katherine, the two of them chatting about music now. It was completely innocent, he's quick to clarify – he had a girlfriend and Katherine a boyfriend and they spoke about both of them. It was just an interesting chat between strangers, which Dean, who'd moved to London from Manchester in 2001, had noticed wasn't all that common in the capital. 'She was so friendly,' he says, 'and not automatically suspicious or on her guard, like a lot of people. I guess at the time I thought what a nice quality that was to have.'

When Dean's break was up, he says Katherine checked her phone. Julia had texted again, upset at having discovered that a necklace her grandmother had given her had been taken in the break-in. Katherine decided that she would go round there and surprise her, perhaps picking up a bottle of wine or some choco-late on the way. Again, Dean remembers thinking what a nice person she was; he hoped that they would become friends. He made a mental note to register Louie at the vets where Katherine worked.

Katherine's next steps are easy to trace. CCTV belonging to the bar shows her leaving; the cameras belonging to several other venues and shops in Brixton capture her journey along the high street. Footage from Brixton station shows her hesitate, noticing the gates that had been pulled across the entrance, the station closed due to a fatality further up the line. But Katherine was not easily deterred; Julia's flat wasn't far away, a short bus ride or a brisk walk. It was a warm evening. She carried on. The last image we have of her was captured by a camera mounted on the wall of a pub on Stockwell Road. Shortly afterwards, she turned onto a residential street and was lost from sight.

Katherine was reported missing on the morning of July 8th, when she failed to show up for work and the surgery called her emergency contact – her father – after being unable to reach her. After failing to get a response from either her mobile phone or her landline, David West went round to her flat with the spare key Katherine had given him. There was nothing there to immediately alarm him. Things looked much as they ever did; the flat was tidy but full of *stuff*, the way Katherine liked it – rows of framed photographs on shelves and windowsills, stacks of magazines and books, jewellery hung over the edges of mirrors and little pots and boxes of things lined up on the desk in her bedroom.

But as he made his way around the flat, a sense of unease

began to grow. Katherine's work uniform was still hanging on a clothes horse in the kitchen. The bowl and spoon she had used to eat her soup before going out the night before had been tossed carelessly into the sink, but there was no sign of breakfast things. The bed was made. Katherine's coat was missing from its place beside the front door, along with a pair of heeled boots, but the black rubber-soled shoes she wore for work, and her favourite trainers, were still in theirs.

David West knew in his heart that his daughter had not returned home the previous evening. He phoned Julia. And then he phoned the police.

DS Leyton Jones was pleased to be assigned to Katherine's case. It was a nod from his superiors, who'd noted some keen work he had done on another misper – a fifteen-year-old girl who had eventually been found. Jones wanted to prove himself again; he wanted Katherine to be found as quickly as possible. He wanted a happy ending for the distraught father he found waiting for him at Katherine's flat, and he resolved to do everything he could to bring her home.

And he did everything right. With the help of David West, he made lists of Katherine's friends and contacts, and he and his colleagues interviewed all of them. He went to the bar and spoke to the manager and then to a shaken Dean, who was shocked to hear of Katherine's disappearance. (He may also have been relieved, had he learnt he was initially a person of interest, that he was quickly eliminated as a suspect by DS Jones.)

But no one knew anything. No one had heard from or seen Katherine, and no one had any reason to believe she might have disappeared voluntarily. A feeling of unease grew in Leyton Jones's gut. The potential for a happy ending seemed suddenly to be getting far smaller.

Something else was playing on Jones's mind, too. It was a case a friend and fellow officer, DS Keeley McCarrow, had worked on the previous year: the murder of Jennifer Howell. There were some obvious parallels in the cases – Jennifer and Katherine were of a similar age and had disappeared within two miles of each other in South London. Jones also knew that Jennifer had gone missing in July – a fact he remembered because his own birthday was at the end of June. It was only when he paid Keeley a visit and the two of them revisited the file that he realised the two women had disappeared on exactly the same day, a year apart. Still, it seemed like an odd coincidence, and though Jones tried, he couldn't make the two cases link up in any other way – Jennifer and Katherine had no friends in common, didn't seem to socialise in the same places, had never made contact. Jennifer had been found dead whilst Katherine was still missing, and there was no CCTV evidence to support a third party's involvement in her disappearance.

Desperate as DS Jones was to bring Katherine West home, months ticked by without a lead. The West family continued to search for their daughter throughout the winter, but when the summer of 2004 rolled around, Katherine remained missing.

Anita Khan hadn't particularly wanted to attend her colleague's leaving party. She'd been working in the advertising department at Hartwood Mills since January 2004, and had only had a handful of conversations with the sales director who was leaving.

But she knew that it was important to the senior team that everyone showed their faces at social events; she knew it was an opportunity to impress. She knew she had to take those whenever they arose.

Anita had moved to London in 1999 to attend Kingston University. Having grown up in Sheffield (where her parents and brother still lived), she wasn't exactly a country bumpkin, but still, she revelled in life in the capital. Weekends saw her dragging coursemates to galleries and museums, though she had a particular love for theatre. She was fiercely clever but not especially keen on studying – her aversion to the library meant several exams saw her 'winging it' and her final year was a bit of a game of catch-up. She pulled it off, though, graduating in the summer of 2002 with a 2:1, and, more importantly, a place on the graduate scheme at Hartwood Mills.

There, she showed a keen sense of initiative and a willingness to pitch in which got her noticed by management. She arrived early and worked late, and she was polite but confident, just as happy to recommend an exhibition to a senior partner as one of her fellow interns. She was one of only three to reach the end of their placement and receive an offer of a permanent job. Her life as a young professional in London was officially beginning.

The party was held at the home of one of the directors of Hartwood Mills, a beautifully converted seven-bedroom Victorian property in East Dulwich. A violinist played in the living room, where a cocktail bar had been set up, whilst through the vast glass doors at the back of the house, a DJ booth had been set up beside the swimming pool. It was July 7th, one year after Katherine West, whose family home was just a short five-minute walk from the party, had disappeared, and the weather had been unseasonably cool and wet. Guests shunned the garden and gathered in the kitchen and living room whilst waiters circled with canapés.

It was not the usual kind of social gathering Anita had experienced during her time at Hartwood Mills. Those tended to be raucous and wild, the team she was part of often propping up bars in Soho before drunkenly staggering to late-night karaoke places. Almost the entire company seemed to have shown up at this party, and Anita knew that this was an opportunity to get her face known, to ingratiate herself with some of the senior team. She threw herself into it with her usual brand of determination and humour and impressed both her line managers and the director whose home it was.

'She was easy to get along with,' a fellow guest remembers. 'The kind of person you want in one of those awkward small-talk chats at a party. She knew how to carry a conversation, she always had something to say.' Another Hartwood Mills employee agrees: 'She got the balance right between confident and cocky – not all of the younger ones hit that mark but she really got it.'

Something else Anita had perfected early in her career was knowing when to leave a party. Whilst everyone else was making their way through the free bar, inhibitions abandoned accordingly, Anita gathered her things and prepared to make a discreet early exit – a move she'd become well known for among her friends. She didn't quite manage it undetected on this occasion, however: Jasper, a fellow intern who'd also secured a coveted permanent role at Hartwood Mills and whom Anita had become close to, saw her in the hallway. He offered to walk her to the station but Anita declined and Jasper said goodbye to her there and headed back into the party.

It was Jasper who, two days later, reported Anita missing to police after she failed to turn up for work for the second day in a row. Jasper had been alarmed to discover that her housemates also hadn't seen her since the morning of the party and began to fear the worst.

It was several days before the connection was made and DS Leyton Jones was informed of Anita's disappearance. During this time, little progress had been made. Anita's frantic family hadn't heard from her and, though footage from various CCTV cameras in the area was checked, no sightings of Anita were found. Though Jones and his supervising officer, DCI Mina Barton, tried to find ways to link the cases, they were at a loss. They were all women, they had all disappeared in South London, with exactly one year separating each of them. But there was no body in either Katherine or Anita's case. No evidence that suggested they had been harmed, or by whom.

Somewhere in the city, a man was performing the ultimate magic trick: making girls disappear into thin air.

But is it satisfying, pulling off a trick with no one there to watch you? That man, who would come to be known as Magpie, had decided that it was not.

*

On the morning of 21st September, 2004, a letter was delivered to Scotland Yard, addressed to David West. A plain white envelope, the address label typed.

Inside it was a single earring. A silver stud in the shape of a paw print.

When David West saw it, he began to weep. The earring had been part of a set given to Katherine on her fourteenth birthday, and though she had long ago lost its pair, she always wore the remaining one among the three studs in her left ear. And now here it was, returned to him by an anonymous sender.

One week later, another letter arrived, this time addressed to Emily Howell. Inside was a necklace belonging to Jennifer: a silver pendant with the initial 'J'. It was particularly hurtful, as, in the intervening two years, Emily had become increasingly upset that the necklace was not recovered with Jennifer's body – she had wanted to add the 'J' to her own matching 'E' necklace. Her wish had been granted in the cruellest possible way.

By now, DS Jones and DCI Barton had the attention of the department. It seemed that the man who had murdered Jennifer Howell was claiming credit for Katherine West's disappearance – was, perhaps, openly bragging about it. DCI Barton, whose own daughters were fourteen and seventeen, was furious. She threw every possible resource at the investigation, analysing the envelopes tirelessly; no trace of DNA, the make of envelope and address label generic and widely available. They had been sorted by different postal offices within the city, suggesting the sender had taken care to select postboxes at different locations. And then, a week before Christmas 2004, a third envelope arrived, this time addressed to the family of Anita Khan. Inside was a silver ring; a thick band with an inset stone of deep red. It had been given to Anita by her grandmother in India and she wore it religiously. To DS Jones, it felt as if the sender was laughing at them, taunting him. It became personal.

The team assembled to investigate what was now, within the walls of the Met, being considered three murders, often referred to the killer as Magpie, thanks to his habit of taking trinkets from his victims. For Mina Barton, the playground rhyme echoed in her head: *One for sorrow*. And DS Jones, too, refused to use the moniker. It was too chipper a name, too much like a joke, for the spectre who haunted Jones's every thought. The killer who seemed able to move through the capital like a ghost, taking a single victim with him each year.

And every day, the calendar above Jones's desk counted down the months to July 7th, 2005, when the lives of countless Londoners, including my own, would be changed forever.

2008

Three years pass after the bombs, three Julys and another three girls gone. The dreams which have haunted him since childhood are more vivid now; he has given them faces. When he was a boy, they were a blur of hair and skin and blood, the screams his sleeping brain conjured like those he heard often at night from the pigs in the slaughterhouse across the fields. But now he knows exactly what each of these women sounded like as she died. Now he remembers them, over and over.

He thought it would help but it doesn't.

Instead the urge grows stronger. He finds himself in the middle of May, following women as they make their way through the city. He tells himself it is just for fun, just for honing his skills. He spends whole days finding the perfect places, the little nooks of London where there are no cameras, no places to be seen. He notes them down, thinks often of the possible problems, the women he has seen walking there. But the days grow long and the thing in the back of his mind is impatient, screeching. He follows women and they all become her and it's all he can do not to break into a run, clamp his hand around their mouths. Drag them from the road and crush the breath from them.

There have to be limits. He has always known that. He has to be better than them, has to play by the rules. One girl, one night. He will keep doing it until it feels as though the scales have been balanced. Until the anger is gone.

The anger doesn't go.

Instead he feels it flaring up unexpectedly – at people serving him in shops, at drivers who pull up beside him at traffic lights. He imagines his hands closing around their necks, his knife shoved deep inside their chests. The desire is so strong that often he blacks out, thinks he is doing it. He is surprised when he blinks and sees them alive, staring back at him.

He has to stay in control. And so he thinks of them, each of the girls. He thinks about the way they looked, the way they sounded. The life he took from them.

The life he will take next.

1

Arlo was born on a Sunday in September. I sat for hours in that cubicle, playing songs for Jessie on the phone she had bought me, holding her hand, letting her snap at me. Trying not to listen to the woman in the next room groaning and insulting the nurses. Hours of nothing, hours of waiting, hours of Jessie swearing and screwing her face up tight, then babbling giggled sentences like she was drunk after another puff of gas and air. I ate sweets from the vending machine and then wished I hadn't when Jessie threw up in a kidney-shaped cardboard tray.

When Dad arrived, she was in the middle of a contraction, bending over the bed with the sheet bunched in her hands and her feet bare and blueish against the hospital floor. He stood there, watching her, a bunch of flowers hanging by his side. When she let out a moan, he took a step towards her and then seemed to think better of it, moving round the bed to sit in a plastic chair beside it. 'Easy does it,' he said quietly. 'You're doing great.'

He hadn't mentioned her pregnancy since she'd told him, ignoring her bump as it grew, ignoring the clothes and blankets that she'd started saving up for in the later months. But then, a week earlier, he'd arrived home with a brand-new cot and sat in our room assembling it, a beer on the floor beside him as he tried to make sense of the diagrams. And now he was there, sitting calmly as she paced.

'Keep it together,' he said in a low voice, watching her. She stopped and looked at him and I saw a flash of challenge there, though it quickly disappeared. 'You can do this,' he muttered, his final word on the subject, and then he turned his attention to the paper he'd brought with him.

Jessie was quiet after that, gripping the edge of the bed when her contractions came, watching Dad as he flicked his way through the paper and then went out to buy another. But his words had seemed to get through to her; she seemed calmer, surer. She took the gas and air in long, controlled breaths, her eyes closed. A sort of peace settled over the three of us.

But when she was examined and the midwife told her it was time, the panic came back. She grabbed my hand again, her face turned away from Dad. 'I want Addie here, I just want Addie with me.'

His expression didn't change. He simply nodded at the midwife, closed the magazine he'd moved on to, and stood. I listened to his footsteps echo down the corridor. And then it was just me.

Me, who had to watch as she turned red and then purple with each push, her voice dark and strained and nothing like the one I knew. Who had to watch as she started to cry and told the midwife, with an empty certainty, 'I can't do it.' Who had to try to join in as the midwife told her she could, my words coming out weak and worried and no help at all to anybody. I sat at the head of the bed as she knelt on all fours and in between contractions she rested against me, her hair damp and animal-smelling. When the midwife asked if I wanted to see him crowning, we both stared at her until she shrugged and carried on with what she was doing.

And then he was here, and everything had changed again.

I don't remember much about what came after. The people who moved around us – things tidied away, things checked and measured and mopped up – all passed by me in a blur. And then, just as quickly, we were alone again; Jessie propped up against her pillow, Arlo an angry pink and bundled up tight in her arms.

She let Dad in then; she and Arlo milk-drunk and the air around us warm and sleepy. He appeared in the doorway, his expression unreadable, his shoulders hunched. But Jessie's face stayed soft, her eyes barely leaving her son's. 'It's okay, Dad. You can come in. Come and meet him.'

And I watched as she handed Arlo over to him, the blankets trailing between them. For the first time ever, I saw an uncertainty in Dad's face; a sadness. He cradled Arlo to his chest awkwardly, ran a finger over his tiny cheek. I looked at my sister and saw something which also felt strange and new.

She looked at peace. She looked at home.

She wouldn't tell us who the father was.

2

Jessie and Arlo came home later that evening and all of us settled into a new kind of life. Jessie sat and fed him and rocked him and Dad and I crept around them, the two of us a sort of team now. He did the shopping and together we attempted to cook, burning toast, boiling pasta to mush. It frustrated him each time, I could tell, but he held his temper. When Arlo cried in the night, his bedroom door stayed shut, and when I peeked in there one morning after he'd left for work I saw a pair of ear plugs on the pillow. There was a quiet in the house and, for the first time since the day of the bombs, I didn't feel the constant hum of building panic.

On the third day, flowers arrived; huge and waxy under their cellophane. A big blue ribbon tied round them. The card, when she tore it free, was cream and thick, the message typed. *Well done. We can't wait to meet him. Love, L and C xxx*

Lex and Cara. It had only been a few short days without

their presence in our lives but this sudden reintroduction made me cold with anger. They had had Jessie for three years and now she needed us again, now we were a family like before. When Jessie wasn't looking, I tore the card into pieces and shoved it to the bottom of the kitchen bin.

I should have known she wouldn't let them go just like that, though.

When Arlo was ten days old, she dressed him in the tiny onesie Laine had sent, the little hat knitted by Mrs Klusak. She strapped him to her chest the way the health visitor had shown her and she stood in the hall, studying herself in the smudgy mirror. She looked beautiful, her hair down and shining, her cheeks and lips pink. She'd started dressing differently a couple of years before, once she'd decided she would stay as Cara's nanny; floral dresses and grown-up boots, smart dark jeans and shirts under jumpers, the collars bright and white and turned out. The clothes had appeared gradually, though she never shopped, until I didn't recognise anything in her wardrobe. But now, since Arlo, she had changed again. The top she wore was loose and flowing and she wore it over those same smart dark jeans but with ballet shoes on her feet. I tried to remember where I had seen that outfit before and it wasn't until she was opening the front door that I thought of the large picture of Olivia Emerson that Lex had hung in the hallway of that Pimlico house the July of the year before. I looked at the top, immaculate folds of cream, and felt certain it was the exact same one.

I was thirteen and chubby and I hated to stand beside her in front of that mirror. I wore a faded old Hufflepuff T-shirt and refused to brush my hair – but when she asked again, I let her do it because I was afraid she'd leave me behind.

When Lex opened the door, Cara came thundering down the hall behind him, colliding with his legs in her hurry to get to my sister. It had been a couple of months since I'd last seen her – a trip to the park when Jessie, her bump huge, had dragged me along with them – and she'd grown again, her legs spindly in their stripy tights. Her face had lost some of its baby roundness and, for the first time, she really looked like the picture of the woman which hung in the hall behind them, watching us all with cool, cautious eyes.

'Lemme see him, lemme see him,' she said, tugging at Lex's shirt until he scooped her up. He reached out with the other arm and ushered Jessie in, his hand coming to rest on her shoulder as the three of them leaned in to gaze at sleeping Arlo. I was left on the step, forgotten.

'He's beautiful,' Lex was saying quietly as I stepped in and closed the front door behind me. 'Isn't he, Carey?'

'He really really is.' Cara leant her head against Jessie's shoulder as she reached out to touch the few strands of fair hair on Arlo's soft head. Her own hair had been put into an untidy ponytail, bumpy where it had been scraped back and lopsided on her head. The tights she was wearing had holes in both feet. It was obvious that even a couple of days without my sister was too much for them both to deal with.

But then Lex surprised me. Letting Cara slide to the floor, her hand already seeking Jessie's, he turned to me, arms open.

'Congrats, Auntie Addie,' he said, and before I realised it, he was hugging me. His chest warm through his shirt, his smell soap and lemons and something darker, more expensive. He pulled back from me, those white teeth bared in a grin. 'Didn't she do great? Come on in, I got cake and stuff.'

In the kitchen, he had set out a cake bigger than I'd ever seen, two tiers covered with smooth white icing and decorated with blue stars, Arlo's name spelled out on top. There was a bottle of champagne and three crystal glasses, though he filled mine with cream soda, a new favourite that I was surprised he'd remembered. He filled a glass with champagne for Jessie and held it as she sat down at the table and unstrapped Arlo from her chest.

'He's sooooo cute,' Cara said, leaning on Jessie's knee as Jessie cradled the baby in the crook of her arm and took the glass from Lex. Ten days and it was like she'd been doing it forever.

'I hear you were at the birth, Addie,' Lex said, leaning against the counter to look at me. 'That's pretty brave.'

I nodded. I was still feeling strange and unbalanced from the hug and the remembered cream soda. 'It was pretty gross,' I said, and felt unexpectedly happy when he laughed.

'She was my rock,' Jessie said, taking a sip of her champagne. 'I couldn't have done it without her.'

Arlo woke then, his face creasing and his hands twitching dreamily.

'Him eyes are open,' Cara said. 'Oh, him crying!'

'He's hungry,' Jessie said, smiling at her. I noticed how, instead of putting the glass down on the table, she handed it to Lex before lifting the edge of her flowing top and unclipping her maternity bra (an ugly, thick-strapped thing which made me feel funny when I looked at it).

Over the past ten days, I had got used to seeing Jessie's blue-veined, swollen breasts but to see her take one out there, in that sunny kitchen with its fancy cake and another child clinging to her, I felt dizzy and embarrassed. Lex carried right on talking, still leaning against the kitchen counter.

'You know, I was there to see this little munchkin get born but my wife, she wanted me next to her, holding her hand. I didn't see the whole thing and I remember being glad, because I knew I was too chicken for all the gory bits.'

I took a sip of my cream soda and tried to find something to look at that wasn't my sister or him. Three years and I could count the number of times he'd spoken about Liv in front of me on one hand. In the house, the evidence that she had existed beyond the photo frames that hung everywhere had slowly been tidied away until only a few forgotten traces remained; an inhaler in the bathroom cabinet, an earring fallen between cushions on the couch. I tried not to watch as the echo of saying her name out loud rippled across his face, the muscles taut as he tried to keep it from showing. The water that built up in his eyes anyway, his mouth twisting.

'Are you going to cut the cake?' I asked, a comment that would usually earn me a telling-off from Jessie. But she was too busy watching Arlo, her fingers stroking his cheek as he fed.

Lex laughed again, blinking the tears away. He cleared his throat as if something had risen and gotten stuck there, but when he spoke, his voice was normal. 'Yeah, sure. We've got plenty to get through.'

He picked up a knife and slid it through the icing. The piece he handed me had the O from Arlo's name, gaping red like a mouth. I stared at it as I ate around it, shoving cake in though the crumbs turned dry in my throat, suffocating me.

'And for you, madame,' Lex said to Cara, who had given up staring at Jessie feeding and was twirling around her father's legs, humming in the off-key way she did when she was bored. She squealed and snatched the plate from him with both hands.

The doorbell rang then, making me jump. Lex frowned, putting down the knife.

'Who's that, Daddy?' Cara asked.

'I don't know, sweetheart. Delivery maybe? Can't remember ordering anything though.'

He went into the hallway, leaving the kitchen door open, and the three of us watched, Arlo lulled to sleep again. Lex opened the right-hand side of the double door and the light was so bright that we couldn't really make out who stood there.

'Jessie, are *you* going to eat some cake?' Cara asked but still I could just make out Lex's voice – confused, polite.

'DCI Barton, I wasn't expecting—'

I turned to look at Jessie, and her face had lost that dreamy smile she'd had ever since they first put Arlo in her arms. She stared at Lex's back and when Cara opened her mouth to ask again, Jessie reached out a hand to silence her.

'Mr Emerson, I'm sorry to show up unannounced. You remember DS Jones?'

'Yes.' Lex's voice had turned watery and I saw how he reached out for the doorframe, like he couldn't hold himself up. DCI Barton must have seen it too, because she spoke quickly then, her tone suddenly soothing.

'I don't have news about Olivia, I'm afraid, Lex. DS Jones and I just wanted to update you about some developments in our investigation.'

'Oh.' Lex was still holding onto the doorframe, and her words didn't seem to have soothed him at all. There was a moment's silence and Cara tiptoed closer to the door.

'Can we come in, Lex?' DS Jones prompted. He sounded kind too but there was something harder-edged there, something that scared me.

Lex turned to look at us and then, relenting, he stood back and held the door open. 'It's not a great time,' he said, showing them into the living room. 'My nanny just had a baby, we were celebrating . . .'

He closed the door behind them and, just like three years earlier, we were shut out. Jessie stood up abruptly, handing me Arlo. His eyelids trembled, mouth sucking in his sleep. 'Take Cara in the garden,' she said, and I watched her move slowly and steadily towards the living room door.

'Garden, Addie,' Cara said, pulling at my jeans with cakey fingers. 'Shall I show you my playhouse?'

I hesitated. Jessie was leaning against the hall wall, her back to me.

'Aaaaaddie.' Cara's voice rose to a whinge and Arlo's eyelids fluttered again, his lips crinkling into a pout.

Jessie whipped round, her face furious. *Get – her – out*, she mouthed at me, hand waved at the garden with a vicious snap. And I was so stunned that I did.

Outside, Cara ran ahead but I lingered at the edge of the house, Arlo propped awkwardly in my arms. The police were there. The police had made *developments* in their investigation.

I knew then that Jessie had lied to me. The feeling was disorientating and I wanted to squirm away from it, but it wouldn't leave me. Because if Liv really had been on that train, why were the police here again? Why couldn't I stop picturing myself on that night three years ago, my dad's jeans balled up on the bathroom floor and my hands streaked with blood?

Cara came barrelling back towards me. 'Addie! Come in my playhouse!'

I forced myself to crouch down to her level, made myself smile. 'I've got an idea,' I said. 'Let's play hide and seek instead.'

It was a game Lex and Jessie had tried to dampen her enthusiasm for, because it was a game she was good at. They had lost her in a supermarket once, had found her an hour later, curled up on a shelf behind stacks of kitchen roll. It was the only time she could stay quiet and she took it seriously, would stay for hours in a chosen hiding place, ignoring their repeated calls.

Her face lit up. 'Okay! Can I hide?'

I nodded. 'Yep. I'll go round here to count so I can't see you, okay?'

She was already running off. 'No peeping!'

'No peeping,' I agreed, and I made my way carefully around the side of the house, hoping Jessie was too distracted to pay attention to what we were doing out there.

When I reached the living room window, I ducked down, Arlo twitching in his sleep against me. It was open, just a crack, and the air was warm and still, their voices drifting out.

'I'm afraid we can't return it, Mr Emerson. It's crucial evidence.' This was the woman, DCI Barton. Her voice was cool and clipped but I heard sympathy in it too.

'It's her wedding ring.' Lex was angry, angrier than I had ever heard him. 'The ring that *I* gave to her. And you guys have had it for almost three years. And now you're telling me that you're no closer to catching the, the, the *cunt* who did this—' The word seemed to wind him the way it had me, and he stopped, took a breath. When he spoke again, it came out in a growl. 'You're telling me that this has happened to yet *another* family—'

Arlo squirmed against me, his face puckering, and I rocked him desperately, trying to lull him back into sleep.

'I understand that this is deeply upsetting, Mr Emerson.' DS Jones's voice was gentle now; I believed him when he said he understood. 'But we're getting closer. We *will* catch him, I promise you that.'

Arlo let out an angry squawk and I scrambled away from the window.

When they'd gone, Lex packed up the rest of the cake for us, only leaving a chunk for the two of them when Jessie insisted. It was like he wasn't listening to or seeing any of us properly, like he was somewhere else. I watched him as he stood and stared at the kitchen counter. Smeary crumbs of cake and jam, the knife abandoned there. Jessie came back in, Arlo's dirty nappy tied in one of the little peach bags Dad had bought in bulk from some friend who worked at a cash and carry. She was trying to act normally, I could tell, but her voice was tight when she spoke.

'Come on, Addie, get your shoes on. Little man needs his bath.' When she passed Lex, she stopped. After a moment, she reached out and put a hand on his arm. 'Call me,' she said quietly. 'If you . . . If you need anything.'

He nodded and, with what looked like a huge effort, lifted his gaze from the knife. 'See ya, Addie.' A weak smile, white teeth kept away. 'Enjoy the cake.'

As we left, I heard Cara in the kitchen behind us. 'Daddy, is it time for pasta now? Daddy? Daddy!' Just before the door clicked closed, she started to cry.

3

That evening, while Jessie napped on top of her duvet, I lay on the bedroom floor with Arlo on his back beside me. His eyes were big and deep blue, not like either mine or Jessie's, although she told me that they would probably change. I thought about the way Cara had looked that first day we'd walked into their house, three years earlier. She had seemed so small to me back then, so fragile. And now here was Arlo, smaller, newer, looking back at all of us with such trust. I didn't think we deserved it.

I slid the laptop towards me. It was a chunky, clunky thing that Mrs Klusak had given me as if it was no big deal – 'Oh darling, I don't like this technology, you better have it' – and it was easily the most expensive and most exciting thing I had ever owned. Jessie was surprisingly uninterested in it too. She let me use it for writing stories and playing games and, since she'd been pregnant, she seemed to care less about checking up on what I was actually doing online. I flipped open the screen and waited for it to creak into life.

The background image I'd chosen was a photo of Jessie and me which Dad had taken a year before, just after my twelfth birthday. We were standing on the balcony outside the flat, the sky bright and sunny, Jessie's arm round my shoulders and mine looped shyly round her waist. I remembered him taking it – insistent on trying out the camera they had clubbed together to buy me, ushering us together. *My girls.* I remembered hating the way my belly pudged out compared to Jessie's, the way the little flabs of flesh which had started to appear on my chest stretched out the T-shirt which had been my favourite then: a Simpsons one which Dellar had bought me before they broke up and which I had started wearing again, even though it was way too small, to spite Jessie the longer she spent with Lex and Cara.

I felt a rush of shame, then, thinking of that – thinking of the way I had resented them even that afternoon. The way I had focused on that feeling, used it to push down the fear and the knowing that something was wrong, that something else had happened to Liv and that my dad was involved somehow. The way I had listened to Jessie's lie about the purse being lost because it was easier than confronting the possibilities that existed otherwise.

I knew I had to confront them now. I opened Google and typed in DCI Barton's name.

The first link in the results was an article that had been posted that day:

Magpie claims another victim, says Met

I drew in a breath and clicked on it.

> Police announced today that they believe Maria
> Lopez-Hardcastle, last seen leaving a restaurant in
> Chelsea on the evening of July 7th, was the victim
> of the killer who may also have taken the lives of
> six other women including Jennifer Howell. DCI
> Mina Barton, leading the investigation, said that
> all victims had been abducted on the 7th July,
> though six years separates Jennifer, the first
> known victim, and Maria, the latest. Though
> Maria is still missing, DCI Barton confirmed that
> the Met had received a bracelet belonging to her,
> a known calling card of a suspected serial killer
> known as Magpie.

The words blurred in front of me and I could feel my chest
getting tighter, my throat closing. July 7th was my birthday. July 7th was the day Liv had disappeared. I slammed
the laptop shut as if the words might jump out and bite me.
*Suspected serial killer. The first known victim. A known
calling card.*

The wedding ring. Lex had been asking for Liv's
wedding ring back because DCI Barton had it, along with
a bracelet belonging to this woman.

I pulled the laptop towards me again but Arlo began to
kick, his face wrinkling. He started making the first stutter-
ing cries that usually meant he was hungry and I picked

him up, tried rocking him to see if he might go back to sleep. But Jessie was already sitting up, only half-awake, already holding out her arms for him. I stood up and passed him over and she blinked, yawning, as she took him in one arm, the other already sliding the strap of her pyjama top down, unclipping her bra.

'You okay?' she asked, looking closer at me as she guided Arlo's head into place. I backed away.

'Yeah. I—' *Taken the lives of six other women.* 'Just thirsty. I'm going to go get a drink.'

When I left the room, she was whispering to Arlo, stroking each of his fingers with one of hers. I closed the door behind me, shutting them away.

Dad was sitting in his chair, the TV on with the volume down low. He glanced up as I came in.

'The baby okay?'

I nodded, not trusting myself to speak. The floor lurched in front of me as I stepped over a bag of shopping.

'I got more nappies. And wipes. You going to give dinner a try tonight?'

I nodded again and sat down on the edge of the couch. My chest was still too tight to breathe properly and I tried to focus on the room, tried to stop the panic spiralling out. The light of the TV flickered over Dad's face in the dark, yellow and then blue and then grey, his eyes hidden in black sockets.

'Dad,' I started, the word coming out in a croak. I couldn't get any others out, my fingers gripping the arm of the sofa. And the funny thing was, in my silence he seemed to understand. He looked at me and, for a long moment, neither of us said anything.

'I know it's hard,' he said softly. 'I know everything seems different now.'

My heart thumped painfully against my chest and I pressed a hand against it, trying to draw in deeper breaths through my nose the way Dellar had taught me.

He smiled. 'It's difficult to accept. Hard for you to understand. I get it.'

I stared at him. *Suspected serial killer.* 'You get it?' I whispered.

He sighed. 'Having a baby is a big change for anyone. And I know . . . Well, I know she's always been more like a mum to you. I know it's going to be tough to share her.'

Tears stung the backs of my eyes but I was suddenly, unexpectedly, angry too. It lurched up in me and all I could picture was that photo of Olivia Emerson staring down on her husband and her little kid and my sister, taking over and putting herself right in the middle of it all.

'I'm worried she's made a huge mistake,' I blurted out, and it felt good to say it, so good, so traitorous, that I felt dizzy.

But Dad just kept on looking at me, his face flashed with shadows. 'People make mistakes all the time. Sometimes they end up sorry for them and sometimes they don't. But the best thing that can happen to anyone – I *promise* you – is to have a child. You girls are the thing I will *never* be sorry for.'

'What are the things you're sorry for?' I asked, my voice small again.

His face split slowly into a grin. 'Nice try, kiddo.' He turned his attention back to the TV.

4

It took me a while to start to understand. To find out the things I needed to know. But that was okay – I had time. There was still ten months until July 7th came round, and I had nothing better to do at school.

It was weird that the first thing I wanted was to talk to Henry. I hadn't thought of him in months. When the rest of us had gone from Year 6 to the normal, nearest senior school like everyone always did, he'd moved away. His dad had sold his business and they were suddenly rich, Henry going off to some private boarding school in Surrey which I pictured as a castle like Hogwarts where he slept in a dorm room with nine other boys. He'd written me letters the first term but they'd soon stopped and I'd been too busy hating my own school to care very much.

Now that argument we'd had one summer's day three years ago came back to me. *My dad says your dad is dodgy.* I sat in the library, the same way I did most lunchtimes, and thought about messaging him. But I didn't know if our school accounts were monitored and the library computers wouldn't log on to MSN. And something else was stopping me from contacting him, a feeling deep down in my belly. Henry was good at projects and I knew he'd be able to help. I knew he'd have theories and evidence and list upon list before I'd even really got started. But this project, I decided, was just for me. I didn't want anyone else presenting me with facts or stories or theories. I wanted to think for myself. Right then, I was the only person I trusted.

I opened Google and a new notebook and began.

It took days. Me in the library, working through the few news sites we were allowed access to. Me curled up on the balcony with the laptop, my heart stopping every time I heard Jessie moving around in the flat behind me. But the pages of my notebook filled up. I wrote down details, I scratched things out.

It had been hard for the police to be sure, especially at first. Girls went missing all the time. Girls went missing and bad things happened to them and sometimes people cared and sometimes they didn't. Sometimes people could pinpoint the moment they had gone and sometimes they couldn't. Girls had friends and did jobs and were loved and then, when they were gone, they were missed and mourned and celebrated. Girls took drugs and sold their bodies and then, when they were gone, they went unnoticed, unreported. Who could really say whether a girl who disappeared on a day in July was any different from a girl who ran away on a day in January?

But then the jewellery would arrive and he would claim them as his. One on the same day every summer. The list getting longer with each year I got older.

Sitting in my room one night when Jessie had taken Arlo to see Lex, I started with DCI Barton again. I looked at the picture of her that came up, some link from years before when she'd been given an award. She was wearing a black dress, her dark hair swept back and her smile tight. She looked clever. She didn't look like someone you should mess with.

I went back to the most recent article, the woman who had gone missing only two months earlier. Maria Lopez-Hardcastle, aged thirty-five, a mother of one. I read DCI Barton's statement slowly, whispering to myself, trying to soak the words in.

> This person has terrorised our streets for six years now, taking advantage of women who find themselves alone and vulnerable. I will not rest until they are brought to justice.

'She will not rest,' I murmured, and felt sick. I went back to my results page and read on.

I read and read and read until the flat was dark and my head ached. I read about Jennifer Howell who had been killed the day I turned seven and she turned twenty-three. I read about her twin sister Emily who had started a campaign to let young women travel for free on public transport late at night.

I read about Katherine West, who loved animals as

much as I did, and I read about Anita Khan, whose family were so devastated by her disappearance that they had to sell their house because her father could no longer work. I read about Anna Rowe, who was a year younger than Jessie and had left her home on an estate just like ours after an argument with her mum, never to be seen again, and Mae Lin, an exchange student whose necklace had been posted to her family on July 11th, 2007.

I read until I couldn't breathe.

5

I lay awake that night, my stomach churning. My fingers itched to reach out for the familiar letters etched on the wall but somehow I couldn't bring myself to touch either of their names. Instead the names of the women I had read about repeated over and over in my mind. *Jennifer Howell. Katherine West. Anita Khan. Anna Rowe. Mae Lin. Maria Lopez-Hardcastle. Olivia Emerson.*

Olivia Emerson.

Olivia Emerson.

Just before dawn, I slipped out of bed and crept down the hall to my dad's room. The door had been left ajar and I pushed it open without a sound. The air in there was hot and fusty and he lay on his side, one hand pushed up under the pillow, the other in a fist by his face. He was still, so still, when he slept. He slept like the dead.

I moved closer and stood there, watching him. I took in the hard lines of his face, the rough stubble around his jaw, the raw edges of his fingernails, and I thought of girls climbing into the back of a car, girls burned and buried and drowned. In the dark I thought I saw his eyes flicker and I held my breath, blood thumping in my ears. But he was still, so still, and the silence went on.

I turned and went into the kitchen and to the drawer. I looked down at the knives. The long bread knife with its wooden handle and its jagged teeth, and the fat, sharp butcher's knife Jessie used for chopping chicken. My fingers traced their handles and I imagined picking one up, carrying it back down the dark hallway. I pictured myself taking it in both hands, plunging it down. Blood splashed on a T-shirt, soaking into jeans.

'What are you doing?'

I spun round. Jessie stood in the doorway, Arlo cradled to her chest.

'You weren't in bed,' she said, yawning. 'You okay? It's, like, four a.m.'

I blinked. I looked back at the drawer. The thumping in my chest would not go away. 'I don't know,' I said.

'Did you sleepwalk? You haven't done that since you were teeny.' She reached out her free arm and I stood and stared at her. She had told me that everything would be okay. She had told me that Olivia Emerson had probably been on the train from King's Cross to Russell Square, that she had lost her purse long before that day, that I should forget what I had seen. And then three other women had been taken while she made herself at home in that big house. I thought of the picture of Liv in the hallway and I thought of the picture of Maria Lopez-Hardcastle in the news article. I thought of Anna Rowe leaving her house and I thought of Mae Lin getting on a plane to London. I stared at my sister and I hated her and I wanted her to make everything okay again.

'Addie? You okay? Did you have a nightmare?' She was still holding her arm out to me and I walked numbly over and let her fold me into her.

She smelled of milk and sleep and Jessie, and I let her lead me back to bed.

When I woke it was late and the house was empty. I wandered through it, my stomach aching, and found a note from Jessie on the kitchen table.

You seemed like you needed sleep so I rang the school and said you were sick. Don't say I never do anything nice for you! And don't tell Dad. Arlo and me are taking Cara to playgroup and then a birthday party today, back in time for tea. Text if you need anything. Please do the washing up – you owe me! xxxx

I should have felt happy but the words turned me cold inside. 'Don't tell Dad,' I whispered to myself and then I studied the way she had written 'I said you were sick' instead of 'ill', the way Lex might say it, and I really did feel sick. I folded the letter until it was small enough to squeeze in the palm of my hand, and then I went to our room and got dressed.

Out on the street, I wanted to run and never stop. I started walking with my hands shoved into my hoody's pockets and suddenly, under my sleeve, the charm bracelet I'd worn every day since my tenth birthday felt white hot, like it might bite. I'd never asked Dad where he'd got it from.

When I got to the high street, I found myself turning onto Atlantic Road, passing the arches where the wig shop had been. There was a phone stall there now, rows of covers and cases lined up in the window. I kept walking.

The bar didn't look like anything special. When I stood on the pavement opposite it, nothing happened. It didn't feel like anything. It was the last place Katherine West had been seen alive five years earlier, but it didn't feel like anything. I fiddled with the bracelet round my wrist and then, when someone came out with a cloth and bucket and started cleaning the windows, I turned round and kept walking.

All night long I'd looked back at each of my birthdays and tried to find a memory where my dad was home with us. I'd tried to remember where he'd been when I was eight and Katherine West was sitting at the bar I'd just left behind. But all I could see was him sitting in the lounge with shadows flitting across his face; dark drops of blood across the glass on his watch while the hands ticked slowly round.

I walked. I walked through Clapham and up to Battersea and through the park until I was standing looking out at the river, imagining, somewhere far along it, Jennifer Howell's body being washed up wrapped in weeds, her feet and legs sucked pale and new by the water.

I was thirteen, don't forget. I didn't know then what happens to a body when it spends so long in the Thames.

Across the bridge was Chelsea, where Maria Lopez-Hardcastle had last been seen two months earlier. I wandered through the streets of neat houses with their shiny doors, their leafy gardens, sweat spreading down my back, under my arms and under the edges of the sports top I wore instead of the bras Jessie had bought me the summer before. Jessie. The thought of her made me numb. It seemed impossible that she hadn't, in the past three years, seen any of the stories about the missing women, about the man they called Magpie, and wondered. I knew for sure that if I'd googled DCI Barton, Jessie would have too. And maybe she hadn't even needed to – maybe Lex was confiding in her everything the police were telling him, maybe Jessie had known from day one that Liv was being considered a victim. Didn't she care? That also seemed impossible, but I was learning that my sister would never stop being able to surprise me. I felt raw inside, like someone had torn away a part of my body I hadn't known was detachable.

Underneath all of it, insistent, was the fear. What would happen to us now? I made it to the Natural History Museum and wandered round, thinking the whole time of being taken away, of being the girl with both parents in prison. I stood under the dinosaur skeleton and imagined Jessie moving in with Lex; Cara and Arlo growing up together. But that wouldn't happen, I realised, not when he found out who she was. The thought gave me a vicious stab of pleasure and that made me feel sick again. I didn't recognise any of us any more.

It was getting dark when I got back to Brixton and I knew that if Jessie was home, she'd be angry. I hesitated outside our block, looking up at the balcony. I didn't have to go in, I thought. I could just turn around and keep walking, be another one of those girls who slipped away and left everything behind. I could keep on walking until the fear was gone and I was alone.

But there was a light on in the living room and I imagined Jessie up there, Arlo sleeping in the Moses basket next to her. And it was home, and they were my home, and nothing I could do would ever be able to change that.

'Addison.' I turned and saw a man standing in the shadows at the bottom of the stairwell. For a second, I thought it was Dellar but he was shorter, and older too, dressed smartly in a suit with his handsome face clean-shaven. He had his hands in his pockets as he took a step closer and glanced in the direction of my father's empty parking space. 'Don't be scared,' he said.

I looked at the stairs and wondered if I would make it past him. Better to turn and run the way I'd come, out to the main road. But somehow I couldn't make my feet move and, while I stood and stared at him, I realised why I recognised him.

'Addison, my name is DS Jones. I want to help you.'

Another swell of feeling rose up and choked me. 'You can't,' I said.

'I can.' He took another step closer, but it was cautious this time – slow and measured, his eyes never leaving mine as if I was an animal he was worried he might frighten away. 'You know, don't you, Addison? You know what he did.'

The fear dropped away and all that was left in that moment was relief.

'Yes,' I said. He nodded gently and I followed him to his car.

From *Magpie* by L. K. Cooper, published by Whirlwind Press, 2011

Most people who were in London on the 7th July 2005 will tell you they remember clearly what they were doing that day. I am not one of them.

I had lost my job a month earlier, my bosses finally unable to ignore my erratic behaviour, my missed shifts. Most of the copy I turned in during that time was littered with typos and errors and I kept a bottle of vodka in my bag most days. At night, I mixed prescription drugs in various combinations, desperate to sleep, half hoping I wouldn't wake up.

On the morning of July 7th, I did wake up. I staggered out of bed and made myself a coffee; added the last slug of whiskey I'd left in the bottle the previous night. Somewhere in the fug inside my head, I had forgotten that I didn't have a job to go to and I drank the whiskey-laced coffee down, determined to do better that day.

I was living, at the time, in a bedsit in King's Cross. It was a dirty, miserable place but I was a dirty, miserable man then. It had felt fitting. I stumbled out of it into the flow of normal people going about their normal lives, the morning rush well underway. A glance at the huge clock above the station told me that it was 8.40 a.m. and that I was running late. I quickened my pace and headed for the entrance to the station to catch the Piccadilly line train I needed to get to the office.

I walked straight into rush-hour traffic.

I was lucky. The lights fifty feet beyond me had turned red, and the van which clipped me had already slowed right down. Its wing mirror caught me on the shoulder, knocking me back instead of under its wheels. I fell, hitting my head against the pavement, the wind knocked out of me. I was barely aware of the person I had brought down with me until she was on her knees beside me, telling me to stay still.

She was hurt too – a sprained wrist and a smashed phone, her takeaway coffee spilt over her clean white shirt. But she was kind. She told me I might have concussion. She stopped a man among the many people walking past us, ignoring us, and borrowed his phone to ring an ambulance. When she was told how long that might take, she changed her mind. She stood up and flagged down a passing taxi. She helped me inside and told the driver to take me to the nearest A&E.

Somewhere in the tunnels beneath us, on the train that we both might otherwise have been on, a man detonated a bomb.

I never even asked her name, but three years later, I would see that woman again, when I opened a newspaper and found her photo in a line-up of seven. I learnt that her name was Olivia Emerson and that on the same day I had saved her life, someone else had taken it.

One week after I opened that paper and saw Olivia's face there – the 25th September 2008 – DCI Barton and DS Jones were finally able to make the move they had been hoping for. After spending five years of their careers on it; countless sleepless nights, weekends spent trawling CCTV with only coffee and each other for company, they were ready to make an arrest.

It had been Jones's cousin, Elliott Dellar, who had first set them on the trail of Paul Knight. It had been a moment of chance, the two of them at a family barbecue for their grandmother Patsy's eightieth birthday. A few too many beers in, the cousins, who had been close growing up but saw little of each other as adults, found themselves discussing life and love at one end of the garden. When Jones began talking about the unsolved disappearances he was working on, something he said gave Elliott pause. It had long been a theory, Leyton explained, that some or all of the women could have been picked up by a taxi driver. On a whim, Elliott mentioned the father of an ex-girlfriend, a minicab driver he knew could be violent. Someone he'd always considered a bit . . . *creepy*.

It was a throwaway comment but Leyton Jones was getting desperate; had *been* desperate for the past five years. The next day he found himself doing a search for Paul Knight. He figured it couldn't hurt to run his number plate through an ANPR search.

A day later, Jones was becoming very interested in Paul Knight.

ANPR had logged Paul's car in the areas of both Katherine West and Anita Khan's disappearances, close to the times of their last sightings. It had also logged him close to the bar where Mae Lin worked on several occasions in the week leading up to her disappearance.

Jones dug deeper.

He found a complaint that had been made to TfL which had led to Paul's black cab licence being revoked. The female complainant, who had been taking a taxi home after a night out, had claimed that she'd fallen asleep in the back of the cab and had woken to find the car pulled over and the back door open, Paul climbing in beside her. She claimed he had his hand on her thigh and that her skirt was pulled up. While TfL ruled that this was clearly unacceptable behaviour and revoked Knight's licence, criminal charges had not been brought by the Met.

But there was a problem. Six women were still technically missing. Despite Barton and Jones's arguments, the supervising officer, Detective Superintendent James Kielty, decided it was too early to make an arrest. The evidence was circumstantial at best. DCI Barton was forced to order that surveillance be placed on Paul Knight instead, in the hope that he might lead them to the girls. There was little hope, at this point in the investigation, of finding them alive.

Leyton Jones was not satisfied with this decision. Days went by, Paul picking up and dropping off fares without incident, and the spur of energy that had momentarily gripped the team began to fade. But Jones was surer than ever that he had found Magpie. Despite warnings from DCI Barton, he began staking out the Knight family home alone. And one evening, seeing Paul Knight's younger daughter, Addison, arriving home by herself, he couldn't resist the urge to talk to her.

It was an urge that would swiftly be vindicated.

*

Less than twelve hours later, police raided Paul Knight's home. In a cubbyhole behind his bed, they found – as Addison Knight had told them they would – a leather purse belonging to Olivia Emerson. A forensic examination of his car would later find a trace of blood confirmed to be Olivia's on the inside of one of the doors.

What they didn't find was Paul Knight. Like the women he had abducted, Knight had disappeared without a trace.

2011

He is careful as he puts the necklace into the envelope. His hands in gloves, the tape on the envelope's seal peeled slowly off. He smooths the flap down, then turns the envelope over. Peels the address label from the sheet, still warm from the printer. Centres it precisely on the envelope, strokes the air bubbles out.

He looks at it there, thinking about the moment it will be opened, the jewellery discovered and examined. He has watched footage of the Met's press conferences, watched the way DCI Barton and DS Jones field questions with their eyes downcast, their teeth gritted. They both look so much older now than when he started.

He is smarter than them. But this is not a surprise. He knows they won't find him.

His mother always told him he was smart. Too smart for your own good, *he remembers her saying, a finger pointed at him whilst the rest of the hand remained wrapped around her glass. He can't remember now if that was a day which ended with hugs on the sofa or with him locked in the cupboard, backs of his legs still throbbing from her belt. He remembers another day; that glass, or one like it, thrown at his head. Remembers her forcing him to walk across its pieces in his bare feet because he had complained that his shoes were too tight. He thinks that that night, when he dreamt of death, it was her screams he heard. But he remembers how carefully she bandaged his feet, can almost taste the cake she baked him for breakfast the next day.*

He never knew with her whether he was good or bad; the rules constantly changing, her games unpredictable. But he was always smart.

He still is.

He pushes back his chair and picks up the envelope.

1

On the morning of my sixteenth birthday, I sat at the kitchen table and opened three cards, just the same as I had the year before. One from Jessie, one from Arlo – this year, a heart made from his footprints. Jessie had written it but she'd made him sign it too, an undecipherable squiggle that took up most of the page.

And one from DS Jones: the picture on the front a pug looking at a cupcake, the message inside written in small, neat letters: *To Addie. Happy birthday and best wishes. Leyton.*

There was a package too, a lone present in a padded envelope. The address label typed. I reached for it and carefully slid a finger under the flap.

There was no card, just as there hadn't been on the days I turned fourteen and then fifteen. Instead I tipped the envelope up and stared at the slash of silver as it tumbled onto the table. A necklace, the chain tarnished in places. I leant closer to study the charm: a crescent moon, a star at its tip. I picked it up, held it close to my face. The star caught the light as it turned slowly, slowly, and I wondered who it had belonged to before.

I opened the envelope carefully and dropped the necklace back inside. It would go to DS Jones, just like the others had. And that year I would not tell Jessie about it.

It had taken almost a year for me to start to feel safe in my new home. A bedroom alone for the first time in my life and every time I lay down in bed I felt exposed, vulnerable. I had dreams about people standing watching me sleep, pointing, screaming. Cameras flashing until I couldn't see anything, people jeering and calling my name.

They weren't really dreams, of course. They were made of memories.

We'd tried, at first, to carry on. We'd stayed indoors like the police told us, waiting for him to be caught, for all of it to be over. Waiting for the courtyard to empty, for people to get bored of staring up at the flat and whispering about the man who'd lived there and the daughters who still did. But they didn't. They kept coming, every day, journalists and our neighbours standing out there with their long lenses and their camera phones, waiting for us to come out. The tabloids weren't supposed to use pictures of me or Arlo but Jessie was fair game. I saw my face pixelated in print so many times that for a while, I'd started to forget what my features even looked like. The panic attacks I'd had in those weeks had made me feel as if I was dying.

Eventually, we had to be moved.

I think Jessie might have fought harder – that was her instinctive reaction to most things in those days. But when other people in the estate started complaining and my social worker started wondering if it was the best environment for me – or Arlo – Jessie started listening.

Perhaps she thought we'd end up somewhere better, just like she'd always hoped. But at the same time, her stubborn streak refused to let us leave Brixton, the place we'd both called home. She wouldn't be chased away, not by him. Even though every night I pictured him in the dark outside, waiting. Watching us. Even when, night after night, men stood guard at our door, helicopters circling above the city.

In the end we were moved to a flat that looked a lot like ours, further up the hill, and we acted like that would be enough for people to give up.

It was him they wanted, of course. Him they cared about. But he was gone, and the girls he had taken were still missing, and so all that was left was us.

And each year, he let me know he was thinking of me. With a bracelet and then a ring and then a necklace. They couldn't find him but he never had any trouble finding us.

That evening I sat in the kitchen again, listening to Arlo splashing around in his bath; the occasional gush of the tap as Jessie added more warm water. I ate the leftovers she'd brought home. Strawberry that day, the soft pink swirls studded with chunks of fruit and white chocolate. She knew it was one of my favourites and she always tried to get it when the last of a batch was going out of date and destined for the big industrial bins behind the restaurant. The blue bubblegum flavour made me feel sick so I put the styrofoam cup with its plastic lid into the freezer for her to eat later.

When bathtime was over, Jessie brought Arlo in to say goodnight to me. He was wrapped up in his towel, his blond curls slicked back, his little cheeks pink and warm as he reached out to kiss me. 'N'night, Addie,' he said.

'And what else?' Jessie prompted.

'And hap-pea birfday!'

I gave him an extra kiss on the cheek. 'Thanks, little bear. Sleep tight.'

He waggled his index finger at me, finished the sentence the way he always did. 'Don't let the bedbugs bite!'

'You got it,' I said. 'Night night.'

I listened to the click as Jessie shut their bedroom door behind her. The space nightlight he loved would be switched on, the ceiling scattered with stars. She would get into bed beside him and read until his head was heavy against her shoulder. I wished I could remember what it had been like when I was almost three and she had done the same for me.

I moved to the window and looked out at the still-light summer sky, the first purples of evening streaking between the buildings, and wondered where he was looking up at that same sunset. I wondered where he had found the girl from whom he had stolen the moon and star necklace; who he had chosen that year and what he would take from her.

I wondered if he would spend the rest of the summer watching us instead. Waiting for the moment to come home.

When Arlo was asleep, I watched as Jessie fried eggs, oven chips slowly browning in the oven. She went to the washing machine and took out her uniform; the black trousers and the hot-pink shirt which matched the leather of the booths in Sundae's. She studied the fabric and sighed. 'These are knackered already.'

'Well, you do wash them every day.'

She raised an eyebrow. 'You'd be surprised how sweaty you get standing in front of a row of giant freezers.'

The first job Jessie got after Dad ran was at a café on Coldharbour Lane. She lasted a week before word got round and kids started showing up to peer through the window at her, taking photos on their phones. A week after that, an old woman spat at her when Jessie put down her cup of tea and, a week after *that*, the manager told her it wasn't working out – because even though more people were going to the café than ever before, the pavements cluttered with them gawking, they weren't buying anything. It was the same in the second, and the third, and after that the call centre where someone in the booth beside hers started giving out her extension number to his friends so that people would call up and ask her about Dad or whether she thought she might turn out to be a murderer too. Finally she'd ended up at Sundae's, where the owner had taken pity on her and put her safely in the dim area behind the vast bar of ice creams, waiting for the order slips the waitresses brought her, scooping up portion after portion for them to deliver to their tables.

She wasn't good at it the way she had been at caring for Cara. But that wasn't an option any more.

She turned off the oven and the hob and plated up the food. 'How was the boy today?' she asked, putting mine down in front of me.

'He was funny.' I splurted ketchup over my plate and passed it to her without needing to ask. 'You know how he's started changing the words to songs on purpose?'

She smiled. 'And then he giggles to himself like it's the best joke ever?'

I laughed. 'Yep. He really does like his own company.'

Jessie sliced through an egg and speared a section of it along with half a chip, shovelling on some beans. She always ate like that, haphazardly grabbing whatever she could as if she was afraid someone might take it away if she took too long. It wasn't until I was much older that I realised that actually she'd just got used to being short on time, ever since I'd been alive.

'Did you go to the library?'

I nodded. 'He made me take out *Some Dogs Do* again.'

Going to the library was my favourite thing to do with Arlo when I picked him up from nursery and soon the summer holidays stretched ahead, full of the stacks of books I wedged under his buggy or shoved into my back-pack. The thought filled me with longing; at school I was a freakshow, someone to be avoided and whispered about, the kid who was allowed to spend her breaktimes in the staffroom in case yet another girl decided to corner me in the toilets, yet another boy decided to throw his lunch at me or trip me as I walked past.

'He knows what he likes.' She pushed back her chair and collected her phone. As she sat back down, I caught a glimpse of her inbox, rows and rows of unread emails. Before we'd moved – before Jessie had refused to get another landline – the phone had rung all day and most of the night sometimes, the offers flooding in. People wanting Jessie to tell her story, on their TV couches or in their glossy magazines. She turned them down, politely and quietly, but she didn't stop answering their calls. I knew that the money they were offering was life-changing. I wondered if she spent her shifts imagining what she could have bought with it. But she never would have done it to them.

I didn't know what Lex had said to her when, finally, the truth about who we were had come out. The truth about where we had come from. As the police had raided our house, our father was already running – but then it was Jessie's turn to run, too. She had left me there, had tried to get to Lex before them. Tried to explain.

When she came home, her face was swollen with crying. She didn't speak for hours, didn't even move from the spot on the sofa where she'd curled up. She was broken, and it was me who had done that to her.

We didn't go back to the Pimlico house again.

'I'm so tired,' Jessie said, pushing her plate aside. 'I

swear, if Arlo keeps waking up at four I'm going to die this summer.'

I flinched. She often made comments like this, her voice harsh and a challenge, daring me to stop her. She'd grown thinner, her hair straggly, everything about her bearing the threat of a snap.

'You go to bed,' I said. 'I'll tidy up.'

She rose out of her chair with a sigh. 'Thank you. See you in the morning.' In the doorway, she stopped. 'Happy birthday,' she said.

I dreamt that night, as I always did, of Liv.

2

The next day, I sat across the table and watched as DS Jones drank coffee from a plastic cup. The necklace had already been sealed in an evidence bag and taken away for testing. They still, even then, hoped that one day he would make a mistake. Give himself away. I knew better.

'How are you doing?' DS Jones asked me.

'Thanks for my card,' I said, which was easier than answering.

'You're welcome.' He took a last sip of coffee, crinkling the cup in one of his hands. 'You should know that we haven't had any reports of a missing girl yet.'

'That's good,' I said, although I didn't really believe it was. Somewhere, somehow, he had found another one. It was just that now he chose to send their things to me instead of to their families. Now he chose girls who were less easily missed, kept them for himself.

'But you should also know that the sighting we were

checking out from a couple of months ago turned out to be a dead end.' He rocked back on his chair, his hands dropped down by his sides. He looked drained. Empty.

'Okay,' I said. I wondered if the farmer who thought he had seen a man matching my father's description sleeping in one of his barns had unwittingly set the force of the Met on a homeless man, or if he'd imagined the whole thing entirely. He wouldn't have been the only person jumping at shadows. Every night, right before I went to sleep, I thought I saw him. Climbing out of my wardrobe, crawling out from under the bed. Come back for me, the daughter who had betrayed him.

'And the press? Has anyone else been bothering you?'

I shook my head. 'Not recently. I guess, with the date, you'd expect it but . . . no one's approached me.' I thought of the unread emails piling up in Jessie's inbox. Once again, she was shielding me from it all. But the thought filled me with anger now, that lie about the purse circling, as it always did, in my head. *I need to tell you something Lex mentioned to me today . . . Liv lost her purse.* I knew she had told it to remove the worry for me, to take it all on herself. But that had never been her right, and it still stung.

It didn't stop me from trying to protect her now, though. Last year the parcel which had arrived on my birthday had frightened her – doors and windows kept locked at all times, extra bolts added to them. I had woken in the night a couple of times and found her standing rigid, watching at the front window. I'd had a horrible feeling that she had been standing there for hours. She was just as afraid as I was of him coming back. It was just that in daylight she did a better job of hiding it.

And so, when the necklace had arrived this year, I had decided to keep it between me and the Met.

'Okay. That's good.' The last three years had been kinder to DS Jones than they had to Jessie, but I still noticed the creases that had formed by the sides of his mouth and across his forehead. 'But you should tell us, Addie, if you don't feel safe at home. We can do things about that. Your safety is my number one priority, it always has been.'

I nodded, because he was kind. Because I think, deep down, he believed that what he was saying was true. But I knew that what really drove him, what drove all of them, was catching my father. It had been almost ten years and, as far as I knew, Leyton Jones had not married or had children. He had dedicated himself to a man who slipped through his fingers at every turn. I knew that, eventually, it would ruin him.

'Thank you,' I said.

'And obviously, it goes without saying but . . . You have my direct line and my mobile number. Call me straight away if anything else arrives. Or if, you know . . .'

'I know.' But both of us knew that really there was no chance of my father showing up on the doorstep, giving me the opportunity to call DS Jones or DCI Barton, sending those helicopters into the sky to search the streets for him again.

He was far cleverer than that.

I hadn't told Jessie that I was skipping school, something I did as often as I thought I could get away with. The first year hadn't been so bad. They'd made allowances for me, sent work home. But when Dad wasn't found, when we were all still waiting six months and then twelve down the line, my social worker started to get a bit uncomfortable. A bit worried about me 'getting behind'. Jessie was in no position to home-school me. And so I was sent back. Sent back to taunts, to things thrown at me in class, in the hallways, in the canteen. Changing schools didn't help. If anything, it made it worse.

But that had been back in the days when I was still terrified that Jessie might slip back into one of her silent, still moods, and so I had just put my head down and hoped it would get better. I didn't want to add to the things she had to worry about. I didn't want to push her any further away.

And when I thought I could get away with it, I skipped school. Spent the time reading in parks or nursing a single milkshake in a café for hours on end. Or visiting the detective still trying to catch my father and find the women he had murdered.

I spent the rest of the afternoon wandering aimlessly round the Tate and then walked back to Brixton to pick Arlo up from nursery at the usual time. He came running out, clinging to a still-wet painting, holding it high above his head to stop it trailing on the floor. 'Addie, *look.*'

I did my best to admire the smeared mass of paint on the paper, his name carefully printed at the top by one of the staff. I did my best to smile at them as I signed him out, because they were nice, the people who worked there, and had never acted as if they knew anything about me even though they had to have regular briefings with police in case my dad took it upon himself to try and catch a glimpse of his grandson. I collected Arlo's scooter from the row of identical and more expensive scooters and started the long walk home. Arlo had walked early, at eleven months, and had refused to go in the buggy not long after. But he was easily distracted, interested in everything, and it made getting anywhere fast an impossible task. It wasn't easy for me to relax about this even two years on. I had learnt long ago that flicking switches or writing down letters on my body wouldn't keep us safe; *hadn't* kept us safe. I'd had to find new tactics, and so I'd gotten used to scuttling out of sight as quickly as possible whenever in a public space, trying to keep my head down and avoid anyone's gaze.

'Has you got my picture, Addie?' He glanced up from his earnest scooting, making himself wiggle clumsily across the path.

'Yes, I've got it,' I said. 'Eyes on the road, maniac.'

But we were passing the park now and he stopped, attention caught by something through the railings. I stopped and tried to guess what it was – recent journeys home had been held up by several dogs, a man's hat, a funny cloud, a scary tree, a lady's shoes and a sad pigeon. But then I saw a man making his way up the path, a little boy on his shoulders.

Arlo had been intrigued by men even as a baby – sometimes shy, sometimes straining to get to them. He'd taken a particular shine to Leyton Jones whenever he'd visited the house. I supposed he didn't have many male figures in his everyday life; their differences probably *were* interesting to him. He laughed at their deep voices, was endlessly fascinated by beards. But it was only that year that he'd started talking about other kids at nursery and their daddies. It was only that year that he had asked whether *he* had a daddy.

It was a harmless, innocent question, one which he'd first asked after he'd picked up a book at the library about a family of squirrels whose daddy got lost. It was another thing I had attempted to hide from Jessie, though I knew that Arlo must have asked her too. When things interested him – funny clouds or scary pigeons or what a daddy was and how they got lost – they stayed on his mind for days, were the things he talked about while halfway through his breakfast or almost asleep at night. I wondered what she had told him. It wasn't something we had ever talked about.

Suddenly, in the bright July sunshine, my own father's latest gift to me in a forensic lab somewhere, I felt furious about that.

3

I skipped school again the next day, an unusually daring move which risked Jessie getting a phone call that evening. I'd got good at faking her handwriting – and, on two or three occasions when the situation had required it, her voice – but there were only so many heavy periods, sickness bugs and summer colds one person could suffer from over the course of a term. If I ever stopped to think about it – which I tried not to – I hated how sneaky I had become, how good at deception. My father's daughter.

I waited for the Tube with the rest of the rush-hour crowd. We were the start of the line, each train that pulled into the platform emptying of passengers entirely, and yet the station still felt swamped, the carriages filling immediately. I had never been good with small spaces and now, with an intense fear of crowds, of being out in the open, I tried to avoid the Tube wherever possible. The temperature down on the platform was already soaring but the sweat which trickled down my back had nothing to do with heat.

I focused on a spot on the wall in front of me, listening to the strange roar of warm wind from the tunnels, a train coming closer. I focused on breathing in and then out, willing the tide of panic to recede.

My skin prickled. I couldn't shake the feeling that I was being watched. Carefully, trying not to meet anyone's eye, I looked behind me, checking for any obvious signs that someone had recognised me. But the crowd that had built up were all concentrating on their phones or the copies of *Metro* and *Stylist* they'd collected on their way into the station. I thought I saw a shadow move, a figure shifting out of my eyeline, but when I glanced over my other shoulder, I didn't see anything suspicious there, either.

The next train pulled into the platform, the people behind me pushing impatiently forward before the doors had even opened. I stood aside to let the couple of people left on the train off, a man with a briefcase and sweaty forehead shoving past me and them to claim a prime seat. Others followed and I let myself be carried on, wedging myself next to the emergency door between carriages. I never liked to sit down on the Tube, never liked to feel trapped in the centre of the carriage as more people got on. I liked to always be near the exit and I wasn't sure any more if that had started after 7/7 or if it had always been there. If it had only got worse when I realised I might actually need to escape at any time.

The sliding panel on the door had been opened to let air in and, as the train moved off, I turned my face towards it, trying to breathe deeply. It was only three stops, I told myself. I could make it three stops. I watched the damp dark walls of the tunnel pass and tried to ignore that same, hot feeling of someone's eyes on me. When I risked a glance at the carriage behind me, I saw nothing – pages of newspapers turning, a woman applying lipstick in a mirror. In the centre of the carriage, people were standing, holding onto the railing; a girl with a paperback held open in one hand, a man with a bike leant against the glass partition. Another man in a dark hoody, the hood pulled up, face angled away from me.

The carriage jolted as it moved onto a different section of track. The girl with the book turned a page. The boy with the bike thumbed his phone out of his back pocket, checked the time. The man with the hood was still, very still. I couldn't see his face. The longer I watched him, the more I felt like that was deliberate.

The doors opened at Stockwell and more passengers got on, filling the aisle between us. I found myself facing inwards now, caring less if anyone noticed me, leaning further to the side to try and get a glimpse of the face of the man with the hood. I watched as he moved to accommodate someone with a suitcase, his arm coming up to hold the bar and his face safely hidden behind it. I tried to ignore the ripple of fear that went through me.

I was so distracted that I almost missed my stop and had to push past people to get out of the doors before they closed. Out on the platform I spun round, half expecting the man with the hood to have gotten off too. But there was no sign of him and I watched as the train pulled slowly away, his figure still there in the carriage, his back to me.

Stop it, I told myself, and I made for the stairs, headed for street level.

The house looked better than I remembered; its white walls given a fresh coat of paint, the double gold door handles polished to a shine. But the shutters in every window were closed tight, the world kept out. I climbed the steps and rang the bell, my heart thumping. At the sound of footsteps on the other side, a chain being drawn back, I had to fight the urge to turn and run away.

And then the door was opening, her suspicious face looking back. I stared at her.

'Can I help you?' She frowned, opening the door a little wider to peer nervously round me, as if I might have a camera crew in tow.

I had absolutely no idea who she was. Tall and thin, white-blonde hair tied back in a low ponytail, she was dressed in a simple cotton T-shirt dress, a pretty shade of pale yellow.

'I—'

'Lilly, who is it?' Another face peered round the door at me and my heart started pounding again. Cara was tall for six, her hair lighter than I remembered it; a warm chestnut brown cut in a thick fringe which hung in her eyes. I couldn't believe how much she'd grown. How much she looked like her father. Like her mother. 'Who are you?' she asked.

'I . . .' I tried again, sweat soaking through the back of my T-shirt. 'Lex. Is he here?'

Lilly put a hand on Cara's shoulder and ushered her back. 'No,' she said. There was the faintest trace of an accent to her soft voice but I couldn't place it. 'Who are you? What do you want?'

My heart sank but somewhere deeper inside I was relieved. Seeing Cara had shaken me. She was a real person, a girl who was growing up and whose life had already been ruined irrevocably by my family. I didn't know why I had come. 'I'm no one,' I said. 'Forget it. Wrong house.' I backed away, turned to go down the steps.

'It's okay, Lilly.' His voice low and controlled, that New York twang lingering. 'I've got this.'

I turned to look at him, one foot on the first step. He was dressed in a suit, shirt collar unbuttoned, a tie in his hand. His face clean-shaven, hair longer than I remembered, brushed back in waves. Lilly disappeared into the shadows behind him.

'What are you doing here?' There was no anger in the way he said it. If anything, he sounded afraid.

'Can we talk?' It sounded ridiculous out loud. I couldn't believe I had come.

He bit his lip. The hand holding the tie had gone to the door handle; I watched him consider closing it on me.

'Please,' I said. 'It's about Arlo.'

He studied me for a second longer and then he stepped out. He glanced down at the tie in his hand as if he'd never seen one before and then tossed it back into the house, pulling the door shut behind him.

'Five minutes,' he said. He glanced around at the street, at the windows of the other houses. 'This way.'

He took me to a bar around the corner; a fancy place with dark wooden tables and velvet seats. It was empty at that time of the morning, the bartender barely looking up from the bottles he was uncapping, a tub of speed-pourers at his elbow.

'I didn't think I'd ever see you again,' Lex said. He could hardly look at me.

'I'm sorry.' I found myself suddenly dangerously close to tears. 'I know I shouldn't have come. I know you must hate us.'

He looked away. 'Why *did* you come?' he said eventually. 'You said it was about Arlo? Is he okay?'

And I saw it there, in that flicker of concern. I knew it was true. 'You're his dad,' I said.

He was silent for a second. 'Is he okay?' he asked again.

My tears were suddenly forgotten, some of that fury from the previous day surging back. 'He's almost three years old,' I said. 'He's been asking if he has a daddy like some of his friends do.'

I saw the muscles in his jaw tighten. 'I'd imagine his mother's more than enough for any kid to cope with.'

'He's innocent in all this,' I blurted. 'You can't just shut him out. He's your *son*. He needs you. Don't you care about that?'

He laughed, a harsh, bitter sound that set my teeth on edge. 'Tell me, Addie – how did having your dad around work out for you?'

I bit back my anger; ignored the sting. 'I know you must hate us,' I said again. 'But we weren't the ones—'

'No,' he interrupted. 'Don't try and excuse any of it. Please. You came into my home, both of you, and you *lied* to me. You made yourselves a little place in my life, you took my money, you touched my *daughter* . . .' He shook his head, could barely get the words out. 'You knew my wife was dead and you saw your opportunity.'

Not me, I wanted to say. *Not me not me not me*. But that was wrong. I couldn't put all the blame on Jessie, I saw that now. I had let myself be carried along with her plan but that was no excuse. I had been ten and scared but that was not the same as innocent.

'It wasn't like that,' I said instead. I could hear the plea in my voice but I wasn't sure if it was for him or myself. 'I didn't understand. I didn't *know*. I would never . . .' I trailed off. I didn't know what I would never do. Because I had. We had.

He shook his head again but the fight seemed to have gone out of him. 'You were a little kid, Addie. Fine. I get that. But you have to see how impossible this is. Your father killed my wife and your sister helped cover it up.'

That isn't true, I wanted to say, because hiding it from Lex was not the same as helping Dad. But it was semantics. And the shame that swept through me repulsed me.

'You slept with her,' I said instead, shocked at the spite

with which the words emerged. For a second I saw anger flash across his face but it was gone just as quickly, leaving him deflated.

'It was just once,' he said. 'I was drunk. I know that's no excuse.'

I shook my head. 'I don't believe you. There were so many nights when she came back late or didn't come home at all.'

His eyes widened. 'I was a mess, I don't deny that. I spent most nights that first year drinking. Crying. Not coping. And yeah, sometimes I liked company. She *made* herself the perfect companion. Always there to listen, always there to stroke my arm, refill my glass. I shouldn't have let her the way I did, I know that. But I would *never* have made it sexual with her. She was seventeen years old back then, for fuck's sake. She was my nanny.'

I raised an eyebrow. 'But you *did* have sex with her. I pick the proof up from nursery every bloody day, Lex.'

'Once.' His face flushed, his voice raised. 'I made one mistake, much later. It was the fucking third Christmas Liv had missed and I was struggling and Jessie was there. She was there for me. And I gave in one time and, and . . .'

'And now you have a son.'

He was silent again. 'We agreed,' he said eventually. 'It was too confusing for me, for Carey. I needed time to get my head around it, to figure out how to make things work. She was fine with it. For us to just carry on the way we'd been, keeping things normal. For all of us. For *you.*'

I was quiet too. What a nice plan that had been.

'And then the police show up at my door,' he said. 'Asking me if I know a Paul Knight. A Jessica Knight.'

'I get it,' I said. I didn't need to hear the rest, didn't need to remember that day. 'It's a fucked-up situation.'

He laughed again but this one was softer, hollow. 'That's one way of putting it.'

'But none of that is Arlo's fault,' I said.

He looked up at me, eyes watery. 'I know that. Of course I know that. But what choice do I have? I can't forgive her. I can't.'

I stared back at him. 'She never wanted to hurt you. I know it sounds crazy, but she really did think she was doing the right thing.' When he scoffed at this, pushing his chair back as if he was going to leave, I changed tack. 'This isn't about her. Or about you. It's about a little boy who hasn't done anything wrong.'

He bit his lip again and I thought for a minute that he would cry. But then he shook his head, pushed his chair the rest of the way back and stood.

'I can't,' he said. 'I'm sorry. I just can't.'

4

The weeks after my birthday were quiet again until, near the end of July, the papers got hold of a story about a young girl who'd gone missing from her home in Surrey the previous summer. The girl was a drug addict, estranged from her family. In the picture they plastered across the front page, she was thin and fragile-looking, her hair lank. Around her neck she wore a necklace: a silver crescent moon and a glinting star.

Someone had told them that that same necklace had been placed in an envelope and posted to London by Magpie.

I was oddly grateful that whoever had leaked this information from inside the Met had omitted the detail about the packages coming to me. It seemed that it wasn't only Leyton Jones who felt protective of Jessie and me – whoever had sold out to a tabloid had drawn the line at selling us out, too. But it didn't matter. The news that Magpie was still out there, still taking girls, brought people back to us anyway. The emails stacking up in Jessie's inbox, a reporter approaching me when I tried to collect Arlo from nursery. At school, people whispered wherever I went. Someone cut out the photo of the missing girl and Sellotaped it to my locker. A parent complained about me being allowed to attend, said it put the other pupils in danger. I didn't know if they meant from my father or from me.

In the last class of the last day of term, the boys in the row behind me took a tube of fake blood they'd bought at a joke shop and sprayed it across the back of my blazer, the collar of my shirt. It was warm against my neck, smelled faintly of rubber and strawberry. I'd planned to ignore it, let it turn gummy and dry, but when Mrs Lemar, our long-suffering French teacher, passed, she tutted and sent me off to the toilet to clean it up as if I had somehow inconvenienced her or done it myself.

The hallways were quiet, a rare peace, and I dawdled, in no rush to get back to the lesson. In the girls' toilets I went into one of the cubicles first, reading the graffiti as I peed. *Katie Lee loves Sam R. Mrs Lemar is le bitch. Amber B sucks dick.* I pulled a couple of sheets of toilet paper free from the dispenser. The door to the bathroom swung open, quick footsteps padding across the floor. I listened to the other cubicle door slamming shut, the lock sliding across. The shuffling of shoes, the creak of someone leaning against the cubicle wall. Then I saw it there, scratched painstakingly into the door, half-hidden by a smudge of hot-pink lipstick: *Addie Knight's dad eats girls alive.*

I stood, pulling my trousers up. I didn't care what they thought. In an hour's time, I would leave that place and never have to see any of them again.

In the cubicle next door, the person shifted, let out a little sigh. I unlocked mine and crossed to wash my hands, blotting my neck and collar with one of the paper towels from the dispenser. I shrugged off my blazer and stuck it under the tap, wondered if I should just stuff it into the bin. I'd never wear it again.

There was another sigh from the other cubicle, this time shakier, and then a shuddery sob. Someone was crying in there.

I stopped what I was doing and listened. I had locked myself in toilets in that place so many times over the past eighteen months, crying and willing the day away. Wanting them to leave me alone, wishing I was someone else. How many times had I hoped someone, just one person, would come and knock on the door, ask me if I was all right?

There was another sob, this time louder and then cut short as if the person was embarrassed to have let it out. I went over to the door and knocked softly. 'You okay in there?'

The sob came again, muffled now as if the person had clamped their hand over their mouth. 'Mmhmm,' they mumbled, a high-pitched, unnatural sound. They didn't tell me to go away.

'Do you want to talk about it?' I asked, leaning closer to the door.

There was silence for a moment and I could hear wet,

shaky breaths. And then the latch on the door slid back, the door creaking open. I put a hand on it, went to push it wider, took a step inside.

The door slammed back, hard, hitting me in the face.

My forehead and nose took the impact, the pain bright and white and shocking. I stumbled backwards and tripped on a broken tile, landing on my tailbone with a thump.

The cubicle door was opening now, slowly. Deliberately. A hand appearing at its edge, fingers bone white, dirty-nailed.

I pushed myself away but the door to the bathroom was creaking open too, someone reaching out and getting hold of a fistful of my hair. Yanking my head backwards.

'You're a freak.' A waft of bubblegum breath in my face. I saw a flash of blonde and blazer, the grip on my hair getting tighter so that I was staring up at the mouldy, crumbling ceiling tiles. 'Kick her,' the voice said, and there was a giggle from the cubicle, hurried footsteps coming towards me. Two, three, four kicks to my ribs, the wind knocked out of me, dots dancing across my vision. And then they were running away, leaving me crumpled on the floor, drawing in shrieking, wispy breaths, blood trickling onto my top lip.

I cleaned it off along with my blazer and returned to class.

And then I was free. Then it was day after blissful day of Arlo and me, books and walks and endless tubs of old ice cream stacking up in the freezer. I tried not to think about the latest missing girl or how close to London Surrey was; far closer than I knew DS Jones had imagined Dad might dare be.

And then one lunchtime, Arlo and I were eating sandwiches on the balcony when there was the scuff of someone's shoes on the steps; a heavy tread, someone moving fast. A man's awkward throat-clearing cough. Arlo and I looked at each other and he put his sandwich down on his little plastic plate.

Lex rounded the corner and stopped short when he saw us. We stared at each other, my heart thumping.

'Hi,' he said eventually.

'Hi,' I said.

'We're eating samwidges!' Arlo added.

'I can see that.' Lex came closer, his face wary. He wore Converse high-tops under his jeans and a plain white T-shirt, an expensive-looking leather messenger bag slung across his body. 'Nice day for a picnic.'

'Do *you* want one?' Arlo held out the plate with his three remaining squares of peanut butter sandwich, all of which had at least one bite taken out of them.

Lex looked at him, his smile wobbling. 'I'm good, little man,' he said, his voice suddenly thick. He glanced at me, cleared his throat. 'Is Jessie here?'

'She's at work,' I said. He nodded and I couldn't tell if he was relieved or not. 'She'll be back at six,' I said uncertainly. 'But I could text her. Ask her if she can come home?'

He took a sudden, deep breath, shook his head. 'You know what, it's not important.'

'Important enough for you to come here,' I said. Slowly, carefully, I moved over to make space for him on the old blanket. 'Want to sit down?'

This time, when Arlo offered him the plate, Lex took one of the nibbled sandwiches. He held it gingerly between finger and thumb but didn't eat it. 'I've been thinking a lot about what you said,' he said to me.

'That's good.'

'Not really.' He ran a hand through his hair. 'It's so tough, Addie. I have no idea how this could work.'

I fiddled with the edge of the blanket, hoping he wasn't expecting me to have the answer. 'I guess this is a good first step,' I said.

Arlo had finished the last sandwich and he put the plate down in front of him. 'Do you want to see my scooter?' he asked Lex.

Lex laughed. 'Um, sure. Why not?' Arlo grinned and I felt my heart swell hopefully. But then Lex turned to me. 'I actually came here for another reason. I need to show you something.'

I felt a sudden surge of dread. 'Okay,' I said, trying to keep my voice bright for Arlo. 'Why don't we go in then? Arlo, maybe you can pick an episode of *Peppa Pig* to watch.'

'Yesssss!' Arlo bounced up and ran into the flat, me hurrying to pick up the picnic things.

'Go through,' I said to Lex, who was standing awkwardly in the doorway. 'I'll just set him up and then . . . we can talk.'

When Arlo was happily wedged on the sofa, I went into the kitchen. Lex was hovering near the door, taking in the mess I'd made making the sandwiches, the papers stuck to the fridge with magnets – Jessie's shifts for the fortnight, Arlo's doctor's appointment, the handprint flowers I'd helped him paint for her on a piece of yellow construction paper. I'd carefully printed 'For Mummy' underneath and let him draw three shaky kisses. Lex stepped closer and ran a finger over one of the blue paint handprints. When I edged past him, he jumped.

'Want a cup of tea?'

'Sure.' He sat down at the kitchen table, his eyes still on that stupid painting, his legs folded awkwardly under the wobbly chair. I let the kettle boil and made the drinks, my back to him.

'How . . . how have you been?' I cringed at the sound of the words as I said them. They sounded stiff and wrong, me playing grown-up.

He blew out a breath, as if the question had flummoxed him. 'I've been . . . To tell you the truth, Addie, I've been pretty shitty.' I forced myself to turn and face him and, when I did, he gave me a sad smile. 'But then I guess you'd say the same,' he said.

I nodded. I walked over and put his tea down with a shaking hand.

'What was it you wanted to show me?' I asked.

He hesitated for a second before reaching for his bag. Opening it, he took out a book and slid it across the table to me. 'A journalist buddy of mine got hold of an early copy. I guess he thought I ought to see it.'

I studied the front of it. A dark street, a car pulled up beside the kerb, its headlights blasting twin streaks of white across the bottom left quarter of the cover. The letters of the title were large and glossy, stamped across it all: *Magpie*. At the bottom, in deep red, the author's name: L. K. Cooper.

'It's about him,' I said, flatly, not needing to turn it over to read the blurb. 'Dad.'

Lex couldn't meet my eye. 'Yeah.'

'Am I in it? And Jessie?'

'Yes.' He sighed and sat back in his chair. 'You guys. Me. Liv.' Her name, like it always did, seemed to cause him physical pain, his mouth twisting. 'Fucking guy makes out he saved her life. She helped him on 7/7, supposedly. He's a fucking piece of work.'

I drew the book closer, touching the edge of the cover but not quite ready to flip it open. 'Do you think people will read it?'

He sighed. 'Honestly? Yeah. I do. The whole world's obsessed with the story. With *him*.'

Him. Dad.

Lex looked down at the book again. 'Every time I think I might be able to start getting over this, someone's there raking it all up.'

'I'm sorry,' I blurted. 'I know you don't want to hear it but—'

'Addie, don't. I didn't come here for that.'

'I just . . . if I could go back and change things . . .' My voice, thick with tears I hadn't been expecting, trailed off.

Lex looked sadly back at me and then gave a small shake of his head. 'No good playing that game, believe me,' he said gruffly. 'I've spent so many nights lying awake, wondering if I could have changed things.' He sat looking into space for a second, while I tried to stop the tears from actually spilling out, ashamed. 'I never even wanted her to go to work that day,' he said after a minute. 'Cara was so tiny and Liv was making herself ill – not sleeping, asthma worse than I'd ever seen it, just from the stress of worrying about catching up, doing these keeping-in-touch days. I looked at her that morning and I thought, *Don't go. Stay here with us, life's too short for this.* But instead we ended up having a fight about the stupid bottle steriliser. That was the last fucking thing I said to my wife – that it was a waste of money buying a better one when the one we had worked just fine.'

'You didn't know,' I said.

He shook his head again. 'You can drive yourself crazy with this stuff,' he said. 'But nothing you could have done would have changed this, Addie. I do know that.'

The *Peppa Pig* music came from the other room, followed on cue by the sound of Arlo's footsteps. 'It finished, Addie! Can I have another one?' He came into the kitchen. 'What's that?' His little voice so loud and proud, finger pointing at the book.

'That, buddy, is a present for your mom,' Lex said, clearing his throat and getting up from the table. He looked at me, the pained expression back on his face. 'It was good to see you, Addie. Both of you. I mean that.'

'Don't you want to wait?' I asked. 'Jessie will—'

But he was already leaving.

5

When Jessie came in that evening, she brought a medium-sized tub of salted caramel swirl, a half-empty bag of chocolate cones and a foul mood.

'Some absolute *dick*,' she said, before she'd even shut the door behind her, 'didn't close up properly last night. You should have seen the state of the place this morning.' She handed me the bag of leftovers, kicked her shoes off. 'And *then* some *idiot* lets his kid eat two giant sundaes in a row and the kid threw up all over the booth. We had to close for an hour to clean it. Biohazard, apparently.' She shuddered. 'Urgh. I need a drink. Hey, buddy!' She crouched and gave Arlo a hug.

'A man came here!' His greetings were never subtle but this was a new low. I winced and Jessie glanced up at me, the beginnings of a smile starting.

'Did he now?'

'Jessie,' I cut her off. 'It was Lex.'

She straightened up immediately. 'Here?'

I nodded. 'He brought a book—' It was coming out all wrong. 'There's a book coming out. About . . .' I'd wanted to say *Dad* but I could feel Arlo watching me. 'About Magpie.'

'Magpies are birds,' Arlo said knowledgeably. I wondered who'd taught him that.

'They sure are, babe,' Jessie said, her words coming out stiff. 'Tell you what – shall we practise our shapes today? Why don't you go and get the cards out of the toy box?'

'Okay!' Arlo hurtled back into the lounge, where I could still hear the *Peppa Pig* music playing on a loop. I had used as much of the afternoon as I could to flick through *Magpie*. The glossy photo section in the centre had been particularly difficult to look at – and yet I hadn't been able to stop myself turning back to it.

'Show me,' Jessie said in a low voice, but before we'd even made it into the kitchen, she asked, 'He came here to warn us?'

'Not exactly,' I said. 'Yeah, I guess so. Sort of.'

She picked up the book from the counter. 'Fuckssake. This is actually going to be in shops?'

'Yep.'

She tossed it aside without opening it. 'And we're in it?'

'Yes. Bits. I haven't looked properly.' At random, I had opened a page in a chapter where it explained in detail how pivotal my initial statement had been in the investigation. I had flicked to another where Jessie was described as 'a product of her upbringing' and had slammed the book shut for several minutes, forcing myself to tune into the episode of *Peppa Pig* that had been playing instead.

'Well that's all we fucking need.' Jessie went to the fridge and pulled out a beer, uncapping it on the opener magnet she kept on the door. It always made me sad, seeing how it and the brand of beer were the same as the ones Lex had had at his. 'So.' She leant against the counter, took her first sip. 'What did he say? Was he okay?'

'Look, I need to tell you something.' I forced myself to meet her eye. We wouldn't keep secrets like this from each other, I'd promised myself that. 'He didn't show up just randomly. I . . . I went to see him a couple of weeks ago.'

'Did you?' She took another sip of beer, considering me. 'Why?'

I shifted, uncomfortable in the full beam of her attention, the first signs of a storm crackling. 'I went because of Arlo. It's not right, Jessie – he can't just pretend he doesn't have any responsibilities. That he doesn't owe Arlo anything.'

She was quiet for a long time. 'That wasn't your place,' she said eventually and I felt sick. She sighed. 'But thank you.'

I let out a breath. 'I don't think it did much good,' I said. I had seen how quickly Lex had left the flat, the mix of emotions that had crossed his face as he looked at Arlo. *I have no idea how this could work.*

'Mummy . . .' Arlo appeared in the doorway. 'I has got the cards out of the box. There's a square!'

212

She smiled. 'Good work, buddy. Shall we check what's on the next one?' She glanced at me. 'Coming?'

I shook my head. 'I think I'll go for a run.'

Running was something I was trying out, something which the internet promised would stop the crawling, constant anxiety that teemed through me and which I no longer had rituals to control. But it involved going out in the open, something which usually only made things far worse, and I was still trying to figure out how to get over that hurdle. I'd found that dusk, one of the busiest times of the day, was somehow the best – everyone on their way home or their way out, no one really caring who was passing them by.

I wasn't fast or fit, my lungs burning within a few minutes, my feet sore as they pounded against the pavement. But I wound my way through the streets around ours and it felt somehow like I was escaping. As I went through the gate to the park, the sun sank behind the skyline, the air cooling. I felt like I could breathe, even as sweat soaked through the waistband of the cheap yoga pants I'd bought in the sale at the sports shop on the high street.

I always made myself run round the park, even though every step there reminded me of Dad. I ran past my memories of him holding the back of my kiddie bike; ran past the ghost of him running down the hill after me, catching me and lifting me off the ground, both of us laughing. It was rare that I got past the bench at the top of the hill without needing to catch my breath but I always stood away from it and looked out at the city in the distance, the glass of the buildings catching the last light of the day. I never let myself look at the bench itself, the memory of the two of us burying my letter to the future there. It was still there for all I knew, in my careful joined-up handwriting: *Dear Person in the Future, I am writing to you from 2005* . . . I couldn't remember the things I'd thought important enough to tell them that spring, months before the bombs had gone off and our lives had started to unravel.

Maybe it was Lex's visit that made me stop a little longer that day. Maybe seeing him look down at Arlo, that wobble in his voice, had made me feel a sort of sadness I thought I'd let go of a long time ago. But I found myself sitting down on the bench, imagining how it had been when I was tiny and he'd brought me there, shown me the skyscrapers on the horizon. *Best garden in the city we've got here*, he'd always told me. He'd always thought of London as his, prided himself on his knowledge of it. All of its secret corners, its shortcuts, at his command. The thought made me shiver even though the evening was warm.

6

When I got back to the flat, Jessie was giving Arlo a bath, and he was showing no signs of being ready for bed. I could hear him singing, huge splashes as he smashed his little hands and feet against the water. I went into the kitchen and downed a pint of water, my breath still coming in hard, listening as she gave up and got him out, folded him into the towel she would have warmed on the radiator ready. We swapped places in the hallway, him bundled in her arms, wet blond hair sticking up in tufts. Jessie rolled her eyes and I tried to smile but something about my run had left me feeling unsettled and strange. It was the thought of Dad, his car crawling down dark, silent streets, but it was more than that; it was that same, persistent sense of being observed, followed. I remembered the figure I'd seen on the Tube, hood pulled up and face turned away from me, and shook my head, annoyed with myself. *All in your mind*, I told myself irritably. Sometimes, back then, I wasn't sure if I was more afraid of Dad actually coming back or that the fear of him would drive me mad.

In the bathroom, I peeled off my sweaty running gear and got into the lukewarm bath as Jessie took Arlo into their room and attempted to get him ready for bed. I dunked my head under the water, listening to her soothing voice, his excited chatter. *The man was nice, Mummy*, he was saying to her. *I know*, she replied.

When the water was cold, I climbed out and dried myself, dressed in the first clothes that came to hand. I tidied up the toys that were strewn over the living room floor, washed the dishes in the sink. Thought of Lex standing there, looking at Arlo's handprints. He'd still been wearing his wedding ring. I wondered if they'd ever given him Liv's back.

It was an hour later when Jessie finally came out of their room, Arlo asleep. She stood in the doorway, rolling her head to crick her neck. Her uniform was stained pale green – mint choc chip or apple, I couldn't decide – and there were purplish shadows under her eyes.

'Just what I needed today,' she said. 'I can't be arsed to cook. Will you go to the chip shop?'

'Okay.' It was the last thing I felt like doing, but I saw the way she sank onto the sofa, her attention drifting to the armchair, where she'd thrown L. K. Cooper's book.

'Thanks.' She tossed her purse to me and fumbled for the remote, her eyes flicking to the book again and then, with effort, at the TV.

*

Out on the street, the night was still and warm again, the air thick. The high street was busy and I walked quickly, sure I felt eyes prickling over my skin, lingering on the back of my neck. I glanced behind me at the pedestrian crossing, got a glimpse of a figure moving towards me through the crowd. Wiry arms; old, faded tattoos. Then the lights changed and everyone around me surged forward, carrying me with them.

As I got closer to the mirrored windows of the super-market, I saw him properly. Standing close behind me, his glasses catching the sinking sun so that they were flashed white, hiding his eyes. A smile spreading slowly across his face.

Dad.

I spun round, disorientated, but the only person staring back at me was a toddler in a buggy, sucking enthusiastically on a dummy.

I turned back to the glass and saw only my own reflection. Lanky and dishevelled, sweat melting away the eyeliner I'd toyed with that morning and making my hair stick to my head. My shoulder thumped into someone else's. 'Watch it,' the woman said sharply and I stepped aside muttering an apology, avoiding her eye as she turned to glare at me. I felt in the pocket of my jeans – I still hated wearing skirts, even in the heat, and my attempts to make cut-offs made me look like a scarecrow – for Jessie's money, pushing damp hair away from my face.

'Addie?'

I spun round, my back bumping someone else.

And there he was. Smiling sadly back at me, hands shoved in his pockets. As casual as if we bumped into each other on the street every day.

Dellar.

'Hi.'

He smiled. 'Hi.'

Another person knocked into me, tutting as they carried on past. I barely noticed them. I couldn't stop staring at Dellar, like he was another vision that couldn't be trusted.

'Got time for a drink?' he asked.

He took me to a place in the market, wobbly enamel stools and a pretty tiled table, a tall, gorgeous waitress bringing us old-fashioned lemonades with striped paper straws. The feeling of sitting opposite him was overwhelming; it choked me.

'I always hoped I'd see you again,' Dellar said, fiddling with the edge of the laminated menu. He still wore the silver ring on his index finger that I remembered, though now there were woven leather bracelets round his wrist which I didn't. He'd let his hair grow out a little, tight curls which made him look younger, but his eyes had started to crinkle at the corners and he'd let his stubble grow out too.

'If there'd been a trial, you would have done,' I said, before I could stop myself.

He looked away, his lips pressed together. 'You're mad at me,' he said.

'No.' I shook my head, reminding myself that it was the truth. 'How could I be? *You* didn't do anything wrong.'

'It's weird.' He went back to studying the menu and then, finally, looked at me again. 'When I mentioned your old man to Ley that time, I was half-kidding. I didn't actually think . . .'

I nodded. 'Well, who would?'

'Just the thought of him there that whole time, with you guys . . . All those years. And now out there somewhere . . .' He shook his head and looked away again. 'Sorry.'

'He'd never hurt us,' I said, and surprised myself. I took a gulp of lemonade and the sourness felt good in my mouth.

Dellar shifted uncomfortably. 'It was really brave, what you did,' he said after a minute. 'Talking to the police like that. You were just a kid. But I wasn't surprised when I heard. I said to Leyton, yep, she was always like that. Always cared about doing the right thing.'

I tried to smile but I didn't recognise the person he was describing. When I looked back at my ten-year-old self I felt ashamed at how easily I'd been led, how easily I'd been silenced. How eager I was to keep everyone happy, always. 'He's been brilliant to us,' I said, truthfully.

'I thought about you a lot, these last couple of years,' Dellar said. 'I always asked Leyton how you were doing. I couldn't even imagine what you were going through.'

I took another sip of my drink. 'We've done okay,' I said. I wondered if he knew about Arlo. He hadn't asked a single thing about Jessie. 'How's Laine?' I tried, uneasy now under the focus of his gaze, the weight of his pity.

He nodded, looking quickly away as if he'd realised he'd made me feel awkward. 'She's good,' he said. 'Still in Norfolk. Frank's five now. He'll be six in March.'

I stared blankly back at him, trying to remember if I'd even known she'd had a baby. We'd become selfish, I realised, Jessie and me. Self-obsessed. As if all that mattered was what was happening within our own four walls.

'That's great,' I said.

Dellar nodded, shifting in his seat again. 'Look,' he said after a second. 'I hope this doesn't sound weird. But I've felt pretty bad, the last few years. Bad that I wasn't there for you. I loved you like you were *my* little sister back then, you know? And then, when you need a friend, I'm gone.' I started to shake my head, to interrupt, but he carried on quickly, as if he was afraid to let me speak. 'I just wondered – is it too late? Or can I be there for you now? I don't know – maybe you need someone to talk to about everything. Or someone to drive you places, whatever. I know it must be tough sometimes, wondering if people are going to stop you in the street. Leyton said you don't get recognised much but still. It must be scary.'

I felt the prickle of tears. Pity I couldn't tolerate, but sympathy was something else. And it was Dellar and I was ten again, asking him to draw me a velociraptor, asking him if he hated Voldemort or Professor Umbridge as much as I did.

'That's nice of you,' I said, drinking more lemonade to push the sadness back. 'Thanks.' I cleared my throat. 'But you shouldn't feel bad. You didn't owe me anything. You and Jessie weren't even together that long.'

He nodded. 'Yeah. Felt like it though, didn't it? It was intense.' He looked down at his hands. 'I really loved her, you know.'

'I know.' I remembered the way he had hugged me, the last day he'd come to the flat, and had to squash down another wave of sadness. 'I remember listening to you arguing,' I said. 'Knowing you were breaking up. I was pretty mad at her.'

He laughed. 'Well, that made two of us then.'

I studied him. 'What did you fight about, that day?' *Lex*, I thought. I wondered again if Leyton had told him Jessie had a son now, whether he had pieced it together.

But he surprised me. 'You, actually,' he said.

'Me? What about me?'

He pressed his lips together, glanced back as if he was going to call the waitress over. 'I don't know if . . . I mean, she was right. It was none of my business.'

'*What* wasn't?'

Something changed in his face then. He wrinkled his nose, shrugged. Sat back in his chair. 'Fuck it,' he said. 'I'm guessing she told you already anyway. We argued about the cards. I told her it was wrong to lie to you like that, no matter how good her intentions were.'

I stared at him. 'What cards?'

He let out a shocked little laugh. 'She *didn't* tell you. Fuckssake. She always swore she was going to but I knew she wouldn't. She would have kept on treating you like a little baby forever if she'd had her way.'

'Dellar. *What* cards?'

'She used to write you birthday cards and pretend they were from your mum. It was so fucking cruel—'

I stared at him blankly. I couldn't think straight.

'Fuck,' he said. 'This is why I *told* her—'

'But the phone calls,' I interrupted, blood pounding in my ears. 'Mum used to call around my birthday. I'd thank her for the cards.'

His defiant act crumbled a little bit then and he looked at me with genuine concern. 'She really never told you. Addie, I'm sorry – those calls weren't from your mum. Jessie used to pay one of the waitresses at that Spanish café near Laine's place to call you. I told her how fucked up it was—'

I pushed back from the table, chair legs squealing against the stone floor. 'You're lying. Why would she do that?'

'She thought it was nice. She wanted you to feel like your mum cared about you. Addie, wait – don't go.'

But I was already standing, my legs shaking. I turned and walked away from him as fast as they'd carry me.

7

When I got back to the flat, the hallway was dark. Jessie had left Arlo's door ajar and through it I could make out a slice of that starlit ceiling, hear the soft fug of his breath. I crept past, the anger still pulsing through me, and let myself into the kitchen.

'Hey.' Jessie had her back to me, was stretching up to take plates down from the cupboard. Another beer was open on the counter beside her. 'Want a beer? I won't tell if you don't. It's been one of those days, hasn't it?'

She found the plates she was looking for and pulled them down, turning to glance at me. 'Oh. Where's the food?'

'We need to talk.'

She laughed. 'Okaaay. Don't tell me – someone else has written a book about us? Or are we getting our own reality show now?'

'I'm serious.' I dug my fingers into my palms. 'I'm sick

of all the lying, Jessie. I want us to talk. I want you to treat me like an adult.'

She folded her arms. 'What are you on about?'

'I just saw Dellar. I *know* you wrote those cards. Pretending to be Mum. I know that was you.'

For the first time in my life, I saw Jessie's face fall. Not just a smile dropped; this was something else, something integral crumbling. It should have scared me. But I had set something rolling which I couldn't stop, and so I turned away.

'You know, most kids get the biggest shock when they find out that their notes from Santa and the Tooth Fairy aren't real. Not their actual mum.'

'Oh right.' I heard her take a shaky sip of her beer. 'You're going to guilt-trip me for wanting you to think you were loved. I'm *so* sorry, Addie, for wanting you to feel that. Big bad me.'

My head snapped back to face her. 'You *lied* to me. You don't get to excuse that by saying it was for my own good. We aren't supposed to lie to each other.' I felt tears rising, hot and unwelcome. 'If we do, what is there left?'

'Oh Addie.' Her voice was thick with tears too and I had to turn away again because I couldn't bear it. 'I never meant to lie to you. I just wanted things to be better for you than they were for me. That's all I've ever wanted.'

'So none of it was real?' I dug my nails in harder, forcing the sadness away. The anger was all I needed, all I could let in. 'Not a single card or phone call? I've never actually spoken to her.'

She was silent until I turned back. '*Answer* me.'

'No,' she said. She wouldn't meet my eye. 'You've never spoken to her.'

'And Spain? Prison? Is that all true? Is that really where she is, or was that just another convenient lie you made up to explain why she never wanted to speak to us?'

She looked at me then, a terrible, desperate expression crossing her face. 'Please. You have no idea what you're talking about. You have no idea what you're trying to undo.'

But I did, I think. I think I always had.

'I just wanted you to know her,' Jessie said softly.

'He killed her, didn't he,' I said, the words so small and so difficult to pull out.

It was the first time I had seen Jessie cry.

'I was just a kid,' she said. 'You were a baby. I didn't know. I didn't understand.'

We were sitting out on the balcony, our shoulders touching, the front door ajar behind us. It didn't feel right to talk about this in the home we had built together, the place where Arlo lived. The place where we were supposed to be safe.

'What do you remember?' I asked.

'They were arguing,' she said. 'They were always arguing. Sometimes I would creep out and pick you up from your cot and take you into my bed. I'd hold the cover round our ears so you wouldn't hear them shouting.'

I tried to imagine it. Tried to imagine their raised voices, things smashing. Tried to imagine a frightened seven-year-old Jessie holding me close under the duvet, pressing fistfuls of fabric against the sides of my face. Waiting them out.

'They'd hit each other before,' she said, and then, as if she'd only just realised she was leaning on me, she straightened up. 'To be honest, I think it was mostly her,' she said, taking a last, long swig of her beer. 'He was smarter than that. He knew how to hurt her, how to say the worst things. If she'd been drinking, she'd slap him. Throw her glass. I used to lie there feeling angry at her. *That's what he wants*, I wanted to tell her. I was seven fucking years old and I could see that.'

I leant my head back against the wall and looked at the clouds drifting across the stars.

'And then, finally, she got smart too,' Jessie said. 'When you'd been born and she wasn't drinking. Then she learned how to use her words too and that made him crazy.'

'That night,' I murmured, something winding tighter in me.

'That night, he lost it,' she said. 'She said something he didn't like and . . . I don't remember the details. I was hiding.'

'You do.' I glanced at her. 'Please. Stop protecting me.'

'Mum was screaming,' she said, rolling the empty beer bottle back and forth against the concrete, clinking it over a loose stone. *Scritch . . . clink. Scritch . . . clink.* 'She was screaming and then she wasn't and you'd fallen asleep curled up against my stomach. I . . . I left you there and I went and stood in the hallway but I was too scared to go any further. It was so *quiet*.' Her voice trembled and she shook her head, the scratching of the bottle speeding up. 'And then, when I finally got brave enough, I went into the kitchen and he was there, standing at the sink washing his hands and the water was so hot I could see the steam coming off it but he just carried on scrubbing, scrubbing. And I said "Dad?" and he jumped, his whole body *jolted*, and he turned round and said, "You should be in bed." In this quiet, dead voice. He came towards me and he crouched down and said, "Jessica, go to bed." And I could see, over his shoulder, behind the table, I could see her *legs*. And one was kind of bent up under her and one of her shoes had come off—'

I heaved, suddenly, surprising both of us. I didn't know if it was a retch or a sob.

'You don't need to hear this,' Jessie said. 'Believe me.'

And because I was afraid, because it was the habit of a lifetime, I didn't argue with her. I breathed in through my nose and looked up at the stars again.

'What happened after?' I asked, when I could trust myself to.

She tipped her head back too. 'He said she'd had to go away and that I needed to be a big girl and look after you.'

'And that was it?'

'No, of course not. I cried. I said he'd hurt her, he'd done something bad, and he got hold of me and he said: "If you ever tell anyone, they'll take Addison away. And they'll take you away. Do you want that?" I believed him. I didn't understand, not really. Not until later.'

A wave of nausea rolled through me as I realised she had used the same reasoning to stop me from telling anyone what I had seen the day of the bombings. When all of this had just begun.

'Jesus. But when you were older, Jessie. When you *did* understand. You could have gone to the police then.'

She stared at me. 'But then you would have known,' she said. 'And I never wanted you to have to live with that.'

I reached out and carefully, very carefully, took her hand in mine. 'Oh Jessie, Liv,' I said. 'You must have known. You knew what he was capable of. You could have gone then.' I'd managed to stop myself from saying *should* just in time.

'I know.' Jessie pulled her hand free, covering her face. 'I was going to, I swear. I thought, this is my chance. But then I met them. Lex. Cara.'

'You loved them,' I said softly. The thing I had always dreaded. That seemed so long ago now.

'I didn't want them to hate me,' she said. 'And I didn't want to cause them any pain. I wanted to help them. I know it was fucked up.'

I looked out at my city, the place where all of those women had walked into the dark and never come back. The place where Cara had lost her mother. The place where Jessie and I had lost ours.

'You should tell him that,' I said. 'I think maybe he'd listen, this time.'

8

I was wrong about Lex, or at least at first. When she went over there the next evening, newly determined, I was sure that he would listen. But she came back an hour later; not puffy-eyed this time but still deflated, smaller somehow. He hadn't even come to the door for her, had asked Lilly – who Jessie learned was Cara's new nanny – to tell her to leave.

But he called a few nights later. He let her try again.

After she left, I went into the lounge and switched on the TV, where a double-decker bus was on fire. 'Reports are coming in that scenes like this one in Tottenham last night are being repeated across the city this evening,' the newsreader said. 'We have confirmation of further unrest in Enfield and Brixton, as protests over the police shooting of Mark Duggan continue.'

I went to the window and looked out at the courtyard and the street beyond. There was the distant wailing of a siren above the thump of music from somewhere out of sight. Fear prickled over me as I stood and looked at the night sky and listened to the newsreader speak to a reporter on the high street, where chants and sirens wound into a chorus behind him. My city disturbed again.

I woke in the night to the thunder of a helicopter, another siren. I sat up in bed, still half-asleep, waiting for the dream to fade away. But the sounds were still there, the siren growing louder. I shrugged on a jacket and shoes and went out into the hallway. The flat was silent, the door to Jessie and Arlo's room closed. I opened the front door and stepped onto the balcony.

Outside there was a smell of burning and the helicopter flew closer and then away again, its blades thwacking the air. There was shouting coming from somewhere; lots of voices, all of them too far away to make out. I closed the door behind me in case the noise woke Arlo – but the thought was distant, hardly even mine. I still wasn't sure if I was dreaming. A breeze whispered against my neck and I pulled my jacket closer around me and went down the stairs and out onto the street.

The helicopter was circling around again as a police van sped past me and up the hill. I walked to the end of our road and stood looking back towards the high street, where smoke was rising steadily. At my feet a Foot Locker box was splayed on the road, tissue paper fluttering in the breeze. A single bright white trainer lay on its side a foot or two away, not yet laced, its tongue hanging out.

Two boys about my age came running up the hill, more shoeboxes in their hands. They laughed as they passed, a rush of cool air following them in the still, smoky night, and I turned and followed them.

Every time I thought I'd gotten rid of it, the image of my mother on our old kitchen floor resurfaced, my father blocking her from Jessie's view. Too late, I was realising the weight of all of the things Jessie had tried to protect me from.

Another police van drove past in the opposite direction, the officers inside in bulletproof vests and visors, their eyes set straight ahead. Up in front the boys were disappearing into a growing crowd and there was the sound of glass breaking and a cheer rose up.

I watched from the pavement as people started spilling out of the broken Currys doors, computers and phones and consoles in their arms, while the alarm blared. The good stuff ran out quickly and soon they were running back down the hill with sheaves of paper, printer cartridges, extension leads. I moved closer and stood in the car park, watching as shelves toppled and people threw things into the boots of cars, scrambled onto bikes.

And while I watched, he watched me.

I didn't notice him at first. But then a girl on a bike, a multi-pack of blank DVDs balanced on the handlebars, sped past me, forcing me to one side. As I stumbled, I looked across the car park and saw a figure there. Standing stock-still, hood up. Even though it cast a dark shadow over his face, I knew somehow that he was there for me.

I wanted to turn and run but I made myself stop. I made myself stare right back.

When he didn't move, I found myself taking a step towards him and then another. He watched me and suddenly I felt like crying again. I felt like running to him, tearing the hood down. *Dad.*

'Move, bitch!' A car swung past me, horn pressed down hard. The backseat full of printers and ringbinders, whole crates of canned drinks from some other looted place. I stepped back onto the kerb, heart pounding. There was the sound of more sirens coming up the hill, the last people suddenly surging away from the store, running.

When the crowd cleared, the figure had gone.

From: ChristinaSouthgate@AMTalent.co.uk
To: laurie@lkcooper.com
Date: November 1st, 2011, 12:33
Subject: Congratulations

Hi Laurie,

Just wanted to say a big congrats on MAGPIE's fifth week at number one. Everyone at Whirlwind is delighted and we're all super proud of you here, too. Drinks needed again soon!

Of course Jane is keen to know what you'll be working on next, and I agree that it would be good to capitalise on our success. Do you have a new proposal almost ready? Send it over when you have and let's get a date booked in for the three of us to discuss.

All best,

Chris x

From: laurie@lkcooper.com
To: ChristinaSouthgate@AMTalent.co.uk
Date: November 1st, 2011, 14:59
Subject: RE: Congratulations

Afternoon Chris,

Thanks so much! Still can't really believe it's happening. It's all thanks to you and Jane, of course, and her brilliant team over there.

Am obviously thrilled to hear they're interested in something new, too. I have a couple of ideas filed away so I'll work on fleshing those out and then maybe you and I could have a drink to discuss which seems strongest before we take it to Whirlwind?

All best,

L x

From: ChristinaSouthgate@AMTalent.co.uk
To: laurie@lkcooper.com
Date: November 1st, 2011, 17:30
Subject: RE: Congratulations

Sounds like a plan. Let me know when you're ready.
C x

From: ChristinaSouthgate@AMTalent.co.uk
To: laurie@lkcooper.com
Date: December 16th, 2011, 09:32
Subject: Hello

Hi Laurie,

Just wondered how you were getting on with that
proposal? Just shout if you need a hand.

C x

From: ChristinaSouthgate@AMTalent.co.uk
To: laurie@lkcooper.com
Date: May 12th 2012, 10:11
Subject: Panorama

Hi Laurie,

How are you doing? I know you've been busy
beavering away on the promo circuit. Hope Jane and
Juliet aren't working you too hard! Look forward to
hearing how it's all been going. Meanwhile, this has
just come in from a friend of mine who works on
Panorama – they're planning a Magpie special to air
in the first week of July and wondered if you'd like
to be interviewed. Obviously I think it'd be a great
opportunity and great to be asked – you're clearly now
the leading expert on Magpie!

Now you're back in London for a couple of weeks it'd be good if we could revisit a proposal for the next – how did you get on with that?

All best,

C x

From: laurie@lkcooper.com
To: ChristinaSouthgate@AMTalent.co.uk
Date: May 12th, 2012, 10:49
Subject: RE: Panorama

Hey Chris,

Oh wow, that's cool – obviously I'd love to. Hard to believe it's been ten years, right? Do you know if Jennifer Howell's family are involved? I don't know if they'd want to be but I'd be very glad to work with them again and I know Emily is always keen to have a platform for her campaign.

I know I've been awful at getting back to you re another book. If I'm totally honest, it's been hard to think of anything but Magpie whilst touring. I'm hoping that after this all dies down, something will come to me – right?!

Love,

L x

From: ChristinaSouthgate@AMTalent.co.uk
To: laurie@lkcooper.com
Date: November 22nd, 2013, 14:31
Subject: The Mail today

Have you seen the story this morning re Addison Knight? Leak from the Met claims Magpie sends *her* the jewellery each July 7th. Apparently has done ever since he disappeared.

> **From:** laurie@lkcooper.com
> **To:** ChristinaSouthgate@AMTalent.co.uk
> **Date:** November 22nd, 2013, 15:01
> **Subject:** RE: The Mail today
>
> I did. Full disclosure, a source did mention this to me a while back, but off the record. Shame as it would have been great to put it in the book. I guess I can talk about it now a different outlet has broken it?
>
> July 7th is her birthday you know. Something extra fucked up about that, right?

From: ChristinaSouthgate@AMTalent.co.uk
To: laurie@lkcooper.com
Date: November 22nd, 2013, 16:31
Subject: RE: The Mail today

Urgh, yes. Poor kid. She's got to be all kinds of messed up.

From: laurie@lkcooper.com
To: ChristinaSouthgate@AMTalent.co.uk
Date: November 22nd, 2013, 16:35
Subject: RE: The Mail today

To be honest, I'm completely fascinated by her. Both of them. I'd love to write something about them. What do you think my chances are of persuading them?

From: ChristinaSouthgate@AMTalent.co.uk
To: laurie@lkcooper.com
Date: November 22nd, 2013, 16:42
Subject: RE: The Mail today

You tried the older one a few times, right? How old is Addison now – 18?

From: laurie@lkcooper.com
To: ChristinaSouthgate@AMTalent.co.uk
Date: November 22nd, 2013, 16:44
Subject: RE: The Mail today

She turned 18 in July, yeah.

There really isn't another story that grabs me the way theirs does.

From: ChristinaSouthgate@AMTalent.co.uk
To: laurie@lkcooper.com
Date: November 22nd, 2013, 17:51
Subject: RE: The Mail today

We could try to reach out. See where it gets us. But I wouldn't hold your breath – I can't imagine the older one's changed her mind about selling her story, not with the kind of offers she was turning down back then. Addison could be different, I guess.

From: ChristinaSouthgate@AMTalent.co.uk
To: laurie@lkcooper.com
Date: May 4th, 2014, 09:01
Subject: Lilly Nordin

Shhh this is top, top secret but we've been approached by the former nanny for Olivia Emerson's daughter. She wants to write something about working in the family after Liv's death – ghost of the mother and all that – but also about the two Magpie girls, because apparently they're back on the scene. The older one is *very* close to Lex Emerson. V weird.

Anyway, I'm not sure whether it's a go-er – not for me anyway, as I think one Magpie expert is enough on my list. James may take her on. BUT, between you and me, I thought it might be a useful bit of information for you to wield if you're still so hellbent on sitting down with Addison.

Unless you've thought of a new proposal in the
meantime . . . (she says, eternally hopeful . . .)

Love,

C x

From The Times, *June 16th, 2014*

Magpie Daughter To Give First Interview

Twelve years after the death of Magpie's first known victim, Jennifer Howell, his youngest daughter Addison Knight will give her first and only interview.

The interview will be conducted by L. K. Cooper, author of bestselling book *Magpie*, and will be published later this month.

The whereabouts of Magpie are still unknown. News broke last year that since his escape from police in 2008 he has sent a piece of his victims' jewellery to his daughter each year on her birthday. Magpie is suspected of abducting at least eight women since 2002, along with the murder of Jennifer Howell.

2014

Watching her is not like watching the others. He keeps his distance, stays in the shadows, doesn't take chances. Watching her fills him with a complex rush of feeling, the thing in the back of his mind silenced somehow. He knows she deserves his hatred just as much as the others – more so, perhaps.

She's dangerous, he knows she is. She always has been.

But he can't help the need he feels to stay close to her.

He can't help the feeling that she should be with him.

1

When I woke that morning, I knew straight away that I had made a mistake. I got up, my stomach churning, and wondered who I had to call to make it all go away.

When I went into the living room, Jessie and Lex were sitting at opposite ends of the sofa, a tray of takeaway coffees and a plate of bagels on the table in front of them.

'We thought you'd probably be feeling nervous,' Lex said, giving me a small smile.

'So we decided to load you up with caffeine,' Jessie laughed but then she got up and gave me a hug. 'Sit down,' she said. 'Have something to eat. Stay calm. It's going to be all right.'

She'd changed her tune, of course. It had taken me weeks to convince her that giving the interview was something I wanted to do.

Wanted is a strong word, I suppose. Needed is stronger, in many ways, but it's probably a better fit.

It had been Lex, in the end, who'd helped me persuade her.

I stared at the bagel on my plate, trying to work up the appetite to take a bite. Jessie picked at hers, the silence in the room growing awkward. We hardly ever had those any more. It wasn't the way it had been when Lex first came back into our lives, when every meeting had been tense, one or both of them always on the edge of snapping, Lex frequently cutting things short or cancelling. But by the end of the first year, we had all settled into each other again. Three years in, I knew he understood why she had done what she had done. I also knew that he would never truly forgive her.

It had been his choice not to tell Arlo who he really was. It would be too confusing for Cara, he said. He wanted to try and build a relationship between them all first. Wait until they were older, when we could explain properly.

I knew Jessie didn't like it even though she was going along with it, grateful for whatever crumbs Lex threw their way. I liked it even less. I didn't want Arlo to grow up with lies the way I had, but neither Lex nor Jessie seemed to care that I had an opinion.

Now, Lex wandered along the bookshelf over our TV, stopping beside my battered old copies of *Harry Potter*.

'Cara should start these,' he said. 'I'm gonna buy her a set.'

'She's seen the films, like, a hundred times,' Jessie said. 'You took her to Harry Potter World last year!'

He shrugged. 'It's not the same. Think of the way you used to get lost in books when you were a kid, Ads. It was like you were on another planet. I kinda wish she had that.' He glanced away. 'A place to escape to, I guess.'

'Cara's going to be a tech geek,' I said, trying to make him feel better. 'She'll probably make millions designing an app or a robot or something.'

Jessie laughed. 'Yeah right. She'll be on stage, that kid. Born celebrity.' We both looked at her, and she shrugged. 'Hey, at least she might be the one of us that gets famous for an actual talent.'

There was a moment's silence and then Lex gave a stiff laugh. 'Well,' he said. 'Here's hoping.'

A fresh wave of fear crashed over me. After years of wanting to disappear, I was stepping out into the light. I was inviting them back into our lives, all because now, suddenly, the price seemed right.

'Hey.' Lex came back over and sat down beside me. 'I know this feels like the exact opposite of everything we've all tried to do. But honestly, I think it'll be good for you. It's your turn to take charge of this story, Addie. You deserve to tell it your way, not his.'

Jessie looked away.

'Thanks,' I said. 'I guess it's too late to back out now, anyway.'

Lex reached out and squeezed my shoulder. 'That's the spirit.' He picked up the last bagel from the plate and took a big bite, wiping cream cheese from his mouth with the back of his hand. 'Anyway, I'd rather you got in there before Lilly. You're not going to tell the world how bad I am at housework or how often I let my kid eat McDonald's.'

I tried to muster a smile. 'Who says?' I said. 'If they pay me enough, I'll tell them anything.'

Lex left before I had to, a hyper Arlo in tow. Getting dropped at the school gates in Lex's Range Rover was the most exciting thing that had happened to him in weeks; he barely noticed the tense atmosphere between Jessie and me.

'Good luck at your appointment,' he said to me, bobbing up and down on the doormat. 'Hey, can we have pizza for tea?'

Jessie shrugged. 'Sure. Why not.'

'Yesssss.' He offered me a high-five and then tugged the front door open. 'Let's go, driver!'

Lex raised an eyebrow. 'Charming. Well, good luck. You'll be great – give him hell.' He gave me a stiff hug. We still weren't really physical with each other; he even treated Arlo like he was vaguely breakable.

'Thanks,' I said. 'And thank you – for coming. And breakfast.'

'Sure.' He gave me a single nod and then followed Arlo out onto the walkway. When they were gone, Jessie and I stood and looked at each other.

'Come on. I'll walk you to the bus,' she said, pulling a coat on.

'You don't have to.'

'I know.' She shrugged. I noticed the hole in the elbow of her denim jacket, the stripe of dark at the roots of her hair. She'd grown out her fringe a couple of years before and it made her face look starker and sharper somehow. Her mascara had smudged under one eye, the jeans she was wearing stretched and sagging around the knees, a splashed stain of bleach across one shin. Lex always made sure that Arlo was well clothed but the days of him giving Jessie new outfits were long gone.

'Okay,' I said. 'Thanks.'

My phone buzzed in my bag and I fished it out and checked the screen. Dellar. Good luck today x I slid the phone back before Jessie could see. I'd reply on the bus, once I was safely alone.

I hadn't meant to keep my friendship with him from her, not at first. But she had been so caught up with trying to build bridges with Lex; so wildly, pitifully hopeful for the first time in years, that I hadn't wanted to confuse things, worry her, with Dellar being back. With the fact that I thought I'd seen a man following me.

And after a while, I'd liked having something that was just for me. A friend who cared about me for the first time since I was ten.

Perhaps, if I'm honest, I liked having a secret.

We were the same in that way, my sister and me.

The paper had reserved a bar on Clapham High Street, paying them to open during the day just for us so that we were guaranteed privacy. I missed the entrance the first time, too busy thinking about the man waiting in there for me. Three years ago, when the book had first been published, the cover had been everywhere. Posters at Tube stations, plastered over display tables in every bookshop I seemed to pass. I didn't know if Jessie had ever read it the whole way through. She had thrown the copy Lex had brought round into a skip, had banned either of us from ever bringing it back into or talking about it in the flat. But I was pretty sure I could recite passages of it back to L. K. Cooper – *Call me Laurie,* he'd said in one of his first emails – if I wanted to.

I had to stop twice on the stairs, breath trapped in my chest, stomach lurching. When I made it to the top, the room was deserted, the shutters down on the bar. The long windows along the side of the room let in murky morning light, the sun hidden behind a bank of thin grey cloud, and the shadows stretched out between tables. He was sitting with his back to me, head bent over pages spread out across the table. I made my way over to him, the door sucking silently shut behind me.

He was broad in the shoulders, a smart black coat still on. But I could see how, underneath the chair, his feet were small in their Converse, one tapping nervously against the carpet. I was only a few steps away when he turned and saw me.

'Oh,' he said, blinking behind his glasses. 'Hi.'

'Hi.' I stood for a second, studying the way his cheeks had gone pink, a cluster of acne scars above one of his eyebrows. He was disappointingly ordinary in the flesh.

'I got coffee,' he said, gesturing to a tray with several mismatched pots and two cups. 'And also tea. I didn't know which you preferred. There's a random chai thing too, if you'd rather. I actually don't know which is which.'

'I'm fine.' I pulled out a chair and sat down.

'Right. Well. Thank you for coming,' he said. He looked at me with something that was halfway between interest and fear. It was a look I'd gotten used to receiving from people over the past six years. I changed my mind and reached out to pour a drink from one of the pots, just to give my hands something to do. Tea. I added milk and sugar, surprised to find that I managed it without shaking.

'I don't want any photos,' I said. 'And no descriptions of me, either.' I had grown my hair out, dyed it darker, anything to feel like a different me. All I had succeeded in was making myself look more like her. Like Mum.

'Understood. That's totally fair. To be honest, I'm never that keen on putting my ugly mug all over the papers either.'

I rolled my eyes. I had seen his face in plenty of papers, on plenty of TV screens. Wheeled out every time it was the 7th July again. Every time another piece of jewellery landed on my doorstep.

'And if I'm not comfortable with a question, I'm just not going to answer it,' I said.

'We're not enemies, Addie. This isn't a battle,' Laurie said quietly. 'I'm on your side.'

'You'll have to excuse me if I find that a bit hard to believe,' I said, taking a mouthful of tea.

He sighed. 'Okay. Well, shall we start?' He took his phone from his pocket and placed it on the table between us.

'Can I ask you a question first?'

A little smile twitched at the corners of his mouth. 'Sure. Go for it.'

'Why did you write the book?' This time, when I lifted the cup, my hand did begin to shake. 'It's kind of weird, don't you think? Getting that obsessed about a murderer?'

He shrugged. 'Not really. Think of Truman Capote.'

'You think you're Truman Capote?'

'I actually think my book is a more objective take—' He stopped himself. 'What I mean is that there's a long literary tradition of books exploring this stuff. It's normal for people to want to understand how a mind like that works.'

'It's gross,' I said. 'Giving him a platform like that. Making him into a celebrity.'

Laurie sighed. 'I think that's the main misunderstanding we have here, Addie,' he said sadly. 'My book was never about your dad. It was about the victims. About who they were, about what was stolen from them.'

I drew back as if he had slapped me. I didn't have an answer for that.

He poured himself a cup from one of the other pots: coffee, the smell making me feel sick as it wafted across the table to me. My nerves jangled with the extra-large Americano Jessie had finally persuaded me to drink at breakfast. I usually preferred it with a lot of milk, three sugars, ideally some kind of flavoured syrup.

'So, tell me,' he said, fiddling with the position of the phone again. 'What have the last six years been like for you? I can't even imagine what you must have been going through.'

He'd given it a good try in several chapters of his book and many interviews, but the fight had gone out of me. 'It's been terrible,' I said, aiming for the truth.

'Did you ever think your dad would be able to stay on the run this long?'

I shook my head. 'No, of course not.'

'And – I hope you don't mind me asking this – are the reports that he sends you jewellery belonging to his victims on your birthday true?'

I drew in a breath. When that story had broken last year it had taken me days to leave the flat. Every time I turned on the TV or the radio, my name was in someone else's mouth. Magpie and his daughter; the gifts he tore from the necks and wrists of other girls. But I had come here to tell my side of the story. I wasn't going to be afraid any more.

'Yes. That's true.'

Laurie closed his eyes just for a second but I saw it written clear across his face: triumph. He had gotten me to say it. It would be the perfect headline.

'How does that make you feel?'

'Sick.' *Curious*. Me sitting there each year, holding each piece up to the light, looking close, so close, to see if there might be the faintest trace of them left there; a single hair knotted in the links of a chain, the slightest smudge of a fingerprint on the band of a ring. 'It makes me feel sick.'

'Do you think it's a message from him?'

I shook my head. 'I think it's a game. I think it always was.'

He leant back in his chair. 'And if you could say something – anything – to the families of the missing girls, what would it be?'

I shook my head. 'I'm not comfortable with that,' I said. 'I don't want to go there.'

He nodded; a single, decisive nod. 'Right you are.' He drummed his fingers against the table. 'Tell you what then. Why don't you tell me about him – tell me about your dad.'

That, at least, was easier.

An hour later, my mouth dry, the tea cold, my words ran out. Laurie was quiet for a moment and then he reached out and poured a glass of water for each of us.

'I'm sorry,' he said. 'That was thoughtless of me before, talking about the girls' families like that. I didn't mean it to come across . . . I didn't mean for it to sound like any of this is your fault, in any way, or that you have anything to apologise for.'

I considered him. 'Is that really why you wrote the book? You wanted to pay tribute to the women? Or is it something your publicist told you to tell people?'

He laughed. 'You're very cynical, has anyone ever told you that? Yes, it's part of the reason. But yes, I'll admit, I was also fascinated by Magpie. One girl, one day, every year – it was interesting, of course it was. And yes, I'll admit that I knew it would sell.' He took off his glasses and polished them on the edge of his jumper. When he put them back on, he looked me straight in the eye. 'So, honestly, what about you? Why are you speaking out, telling your story? It's very clear that you don't want to be associated with your father, with what he's done. You and Jessie have never spoken publicly before. So why now?'

I swallowed, dug my nails deep into my palms. *Say it.* 'It's interesting what you said before about his victims,' I said, my voice coming out shaky. 'About how we should remember who they were, what he stole from them.'

He nodded slowly, a cautious frown forming.

'My father killed a woman nineteen years ago,' I said, 'and I don't want her to go unremembered. I want everyone to know what he stole from her.'

Laurie's eyes had grown wide behind his glasses. 'An earlier victim,' he said. 'Are you sure? Who was she?'

I forced myself to meet his gaze, lifted my chin up high the way Jessie had taught me when I was a kid. 'Her name was Elizabeth Addison. She was my mother,' I said. 'And he murdered her.'

2

We didn't speak about the interview that night at home. We ate pizza and we watched England lose 2–1 to Uruguay in the World Cup, frustrated fans staring morosely out of the screen. When my phone vibrated with a message, I saw Jessie look hopefully at hers, which had stayed silent all evening. I glanced at the screen. Dellar: That's good. Well done mate x

He'd messaged that afternoon, asking how it had gone, and I'd felt like I was telling the truth when I said that it had been okay. Or as good as I could have expected, anyway. Laurie Cooper wasn't the slick, sneaky journalist I'd been prepared for – but then I wondered if that was how he had gotten me to let my guard down. Already I was surprised with myself for how open I had been.

As she was going to bed, Jessie hesitated in the doorway. 'When's it coming out?' she asked. 'Next Sunday?'

I nodded.

'Well,' she said. 'I guess we better start looking at holidays. Now you're rolling in it.'

She was joking, or at least, I think she was. She never let me spend a penny of that money on her. Arlo, yes – I had already booked us tickets to go and stay at Legoland. But Jessie wouldn't touch it. She kept on working at Sundae's; she looked after Cara and Arlo most afternoons after school. The money was mine, it was for me, and I had always known what I was going to do with it.

The open day was that Saturday and I was almost late, too long spent in the mirror trying to figure out how exactly to look like anyone but myself. I leant close to the mirror and painted on a lipgloss I'd bought on a whim that week. I looked like a little kid, candy red streaked round my mouth. I wiped it away with the flat of my hand but the skin stayed stained and angry the whole way there.

All week, the words I had said to Laurie had played on repeat in my head. I still hadn't told Jessie that I had told him about Mum. I hadn't told her that I had as good as told the world. Each time I tried to, I felt defiant – she was my mother, ours, and she deserved to be remembered just the way those other women had been. But when I went to say the words, I couldn't do it. Jessie would be furious, I knew she would.

I knew, deep down, that it hadn't been my story to tell.

The college didn't look too inspiring from the outside; the glass panes of one of the automatic doors cracked and a poster for a sexual health clinic plastered across the other. But it was a start. It was something I'd been looking forward to. And yet, the second I stepped through the doors, the anticipation began to sour. The smell of the cheap floor cleaner, the sound of teenagers jeering at each other somewhere down a corridor – it all made my heart start to pound in my chest. Remembering food pelted at my back, chairs pulled out from under me when I tried to sit down. Fingers knotted in my hair, a foot slammed into my ribs.

'Can I help you?' I had drifted, oblivious, towards a folding table that had been set up to one side, a stern-looking woman with a clipboard perched awkwardly on a stool behind it.

'Hi.' My voice came out in a croak. I cleared my throat and tried again, my lips still sticky with gloss. 'Hi. I signed up for the open day online?'

'Name?'

'Oh, um, Black. Addie Black.'

Hearing the name out loud made my cheeks burn hotter. The deed poll had cost £36 but six months on, it still made me feel guilty in its luxury. Addie Black had no history, no books written about her or her family. Addie Black had not just sold out to put herself through university.

Jessie had refused to change her name.

'Ah, yes, there you are.' The woman crossed me off the

list. 'Information pack there, and there's a welcome talk starting in ten minutes through there.'

I wandered through and chose a chair near the back, hunching down in the same way I always did in public places. Afraid that it was obvious just from looking at me that I was one of the Magpie girls. But when everyone carried on just the way they were, ignoring me, I started to feel more confident. Like maybe I could pull this off.

'Hi.' A girl slid into the seat next to me. 'Did I miss it?'

'I don't think so.' I glanced at her. She was older than me, perhaps even mid-twenties. She wore a tiny sun stud in her nose and I couldn't stop myself from picturing it arriving at my house in an envelope. She smiled at me.

'I'm Chloe,' she said.

'Addie.' Every time I said my name out loud, I flinched inside, waiting for someone to ask. But I hadn't been able to bring myself to change that part of it as well. Because it had been hers. *Elizabeth Addison*. I had never appreciated before that she had given me that.

'You here to do retakes?'

I shook my head. 'I left at sixteen.'

'And now you've changed your mind?'

'Yeah, something like that. I want to go to uni.' It still felt daring to say out loud, gave me a little shiver of pleasure.

'Good for you. I'll be happy just to get an A-Level to be honest, I was terrible at school.'

A woman walked onto stage then, meaning I didn't have to answer.

'Welcome everyone,' she said, a sheet of paper clasped to her impressive chest.

'Oh god,' Chloe said beside me. 'I'm bored already.'

Afterwards, I hovered outside with Chloe, hoping she might ask me to go somewhere with her. I felt light, high, pleased with myself for successfully blending in for an entire day. I felt like this might actually work.

'Do you smoke?' Chloe asked me.

I shook my head although I wasn't sure what the answer would be in a week's time. There was a lot for me to try out now; I still wasn't sure who Addie Black would be. I watched as Chloe lit a cigarette.

'I think a few people are going to the pub if you want to come,' she said. 'There's a couple of girls I went to school with over there.' She shrugged. 'Don't worry if you've got somewhere better to be.'

'I haven't,' I said. 'That sounds great.'

Ten minutes later I was standing awkwardly to one side as the group laughed and joked and shrieked at each other in the nearest pub, topping up their – and my – glasses from the bottle of cheap white wine they'd bought. I didn't drink wine at home. Sometimes I had a beer with Jessie, and Lex had recently attempted to convert me to bourbon although it made me woozy after a couple of sips. But I wanted to fit in, to seem normal – to *be* normal – so I sank each glass in big gulps, trying to enjoy the musky taste of it. When they asked me questions, I tried to answer the way I thought they would, and when they told jokes I laughed along with them. I bought the third bottle of wine and before I'd finished my first glass, I realised I was really, really drunk. My legs felt numb, my face hot. When they told jokes I laughed too late or too loud, and I could feel them starting to look strangely at me.

I excused myself and went to the toilets, stumbling over the step on the way in.

I bent over the sink, my head swimming, and splashed cold water on my face. When I straightened, my skin looked pale and greenish in the mirror, my eyes slow and heavy-lidded. My lips were dry from the wiped-off gloss that morning. I stared at my reflection and I saw my mother. I saw Dad. I saw Jennifer Howell, washed up from the Thames, and Liv Emerson, smiling down at me from her portrait on the wall.

I went home with a boy that night.

I let a boy look at me and touch me and whisper into my ear.

I tried not to imagine his hands around my throat. My bones breaking beneath him.

I let him undress me and climb on top of me and cry out into my hair.

I tried not to imagine my hands around his throat. My father's smile on my face.

I let him fall asleep next to me in his single bed, wedging

me between his thin chest and the pale green wall. I let him make me feel like someone else.

I can't remember that boy's name now. But I loved him for one night, for that.

3

I left before the boy woke up, before I thought Jessie might notice I hadn't come home. As I walked through unfamiliar streets to find the Tube, I tested out the thought of what I had done.

It was funny; it didn't really feel like anything. It was supposed to feel momentous, monumental, or at least that was the impression I'd got from eavesdropping on girls at school. It was supposed to hurt, or have been awkward, or been embarrassing or romantic, or at least that was how it was in novels. When it was happening, it felt like I was taking something back. Putting something between myself and the girl that L. K. Cooper had written about in his book, the girl that people had felt sorry for and written about in comments sections and police reports. But now it was done. And I was still that girl. I always would be.

Crossing a deserted road not far from the last place Katherine West had been seen on CCTV, I thought I heard a set of footsteps matching mine. But when I turned to look behind me, there was nothing. Just the shadows shrinking back as the watery dawn light grew stronger.

By the time I got back to the flat, the last traces of my happiness were fading. I felt empty. Wrong.

I got in the shower and let the water run over me, tepid but fast, drumming against my scalp. I tried to remember what his hands had felt like on me but the memories had evaporated, just patchy flashes left between shots at the bar and the awkward fumbling off of my clothes. I looked down at my body, hoping for bruises or some kind of visible sign, but it was just the same as it had been the morning before – pale skin, slight pudge of belly, the gravel-shaped scars on my side from falling off my bike aged seven. I closed my eyes and stuck my head back under the flow, trying to let the water wash away the memory of my drunken reflection in the mirror. Of my dad's face smiling back.

I went back to the college on Monday to hand in my registration forms. I dreaded seeing the boy, whose name I would never find out, or Chloe, whose number I had found in my phone even though I couldn't remember us having exchanged them. I handed the forms in and scurried away as quickly as I could.

'Addie!'

The sound of my name shouted across an open space still frightened me. It made me think of journalists outside our house or the police station. Drunk people standing outside bars on Brixton High Street as Jessie and I tried to creep past. It had been years since it had actually happened but the fear still felt brand new.

I forced myself to glance back. A boy had stopped five or six feet down the path, half-turned towards me. As if he'd seen me and only a minute later made the connection. The fear tightened round my heart. *Recognised.*

But he was smiling. Coming towards me, a hand raised in an awkward sort of *hi*. And as he got closer, the fear melted away.

'Henry?'

He'd put on weight since I'd last seen him (although he could probably have said the same about me). His hair was still thick and stuck out at the crown but he'd let it grow down over his ears and it curled and spiked around the arms of his glasses – thicker than the ones he'd had as a kid, hipster frames which were straight-edged at the top of the lenses but round underneath, like those a reporter or scientist from some old black and white movie might wear.

'Well this is weird,' he said.

'What are you doing here?' I laughed. 'How *are* you?'

He grinned. 'I'm all right. Resitting A-Level Physics, unfortunately for me. The parents are *not* happy, as you can imagine. How are you?'

'I'm . . .' I faltered. The excitement of seeing him again was slowly being replaced by dread. 'Well, it's been a weird few years.'

He looked away. 'Yeah. I would've got in touch but . . . I thought you probably wouldn't appreciate hearing from some kid you used to know when you had all . . . *that* going on.' He managed to meet my eye again. 'I'm really sorry, Addie. If that's even the right thing to say.'

I nodded but the feeling of dread kept growing. 'The thing is, I don't want . . . I've changed my name and stuff . . .'

'Oh,' he interrupted, a hand out to stop me. 'I would never say anything. To anyone. I totally understand.'

'Thank you.' I tried to feel relieved, or at least ignore the dread. 'I really appreciate it.'

'So what's the new name?'

'Black.'

'After Sirius?'

I laughed. 'You know, you're the only person who's figured that out.'

'To be fair, I'm probably the only person who last saw you as a Harry-Potter-obsessed ten-year-old.'

'To be fair, I'm now a Harry-Potter-obsessed nearly-nineteen-year-old.'

He smiled. 'Well, it's nice to know some things never change.'

'And you?' The strangeness of seeing him overwhelmed me suddenly and I laughed again. 'What have you been doing for the last . . . nine years?'

He laughed too. 'You know, that sounds like the kind of conversation that should be had in a pub.'

That night when I got home, Jessie was already in her pyjamas, she and Arlo cuddled up on the sofa watching one of my old Harry Potter DVDs.

'Hello, Miss Stop-Out,' she called as I let myself in. 'Two nights in a row! You've got a busier social life than Cara these days.'

'We're watching *Harry Potter*,' Arlo said, flopping the duvet down so he could see me properly. 'The CGI is *rubbish*.'

'Oi,' I said. 'How dare you.' I sank down on the arm of the chair. 'I've got a friend who used to think it was the best thing ever.' I glanced at Jessie. 'I bumped into Henry today.'

She frowned. 'Henry . . . *That* Henry? Oh my god!'

'I know.'

'What's he like now?'

I laughed. 'Pretty much exactly the same.'

I saw the sadness that flickered across her face and I knew she was remembering us both when we were ten. I wondered how much I had changed.

'Right, LB,' she said, ruffling Arlo's hair. 'Bedtime. Maybe Addie might read to you tonight?'

'I'd love to.'

'Awesome!' Arlo jumped up and ran ahead of me.

'He's keen,' I said, and Jessie gave me a weak sort of smile, that sadness still lingering. I got up and followed Arlo into his room.

Arlo thumped onto his bed and produced my battered old copy of *Charlotte's Web* from under his pillow. 'Mum's been reading me a chapter of this every night,' he said. 'She says it was your favourite when you were little.'

269

My throat burned. 'Yep, that's true,' I said, swallowing hard. 'Let's have a look where you're up to.'

I read two chapters to him and had almost started the third before I realised his eyes were closing. I shut the book and slid it under his pillow, then clicked on the stars nightlight he sometimes pretended he was too old for. 'Night, little bear,' I said, leaning over to kiss him on the forehead. He mumbled in response, eyes closed properly now, and turned onto his side.

In the living room, Jessie had turned the DVD off and was watching an old rerun of *Friends*, an episode I was sure we could both recite by heart. TV was the only thing that had kept us sane sometimes, especially in the first weeks after Dad went on the run, when we were holed up, trying to avoid the press or the police standing guard outside. I didn't think I'd ever be able to sit through *Family Guy* or *How I Met Your Mother* again.

'You okay?' I asked, sinking down into my corner of the sofa and pulling the duvet over my knees.

She shrugged. 'So Henry, eh? How come you saw him?'

'He's retaking one of his A-Levels at the same college I'm enrolled at. So I guess at least I have a friend there now.' I thought of Chloe, her eyes narrowing as she looked at me over her glass of wine. I tried not to think of the boy, the eager way he'd pulled his T-shirt over his head. The cautious way he'd touched me.

'Must have been a pretty weird catch-up chat,' Jessie said, changing the channel as the *Friends* episode ended.

'Sort of.' Actually, it had felt like the easiest conversation I'd had in weeks. We'd talked about politics and Ebola and *Sharknado* and A-Levels. We'd talked about Michael and Jessie and Arlo and the word 'magpie' hadn't been mentioned at all. 'But actually, it was nice.'

She smiled at me. 'Well, that's good. I'm glad.'

'Yeah.' I snuggled deeper under the duvet. 'Me too.'

She reached out and pulled my feet into her lap. 'What do you want to watch? You choose, seeing as you're honouring me with your presence this evening.'

I laughed. 'One night out in nineteen years and suddenly I'm Kim Kardashian.'

'Hardly.' She tossed the remote at me. 'I'll put the kettle on, shall I?'

'Yes please.'

But she stayed sitting there, watching me. 'I'm really proud of you, you know,' she said.

'I know,' I said, and felt sick.

4

The article was published that Sunday as planned. When Arlo woke that morning, I made him breakfast and kept the kitchen door closed. 'Let Mummy sleep,' I told him, and we ate jam on toast together and talked about Charlotte and Wilbur and the other residents of Zuckerman's farm.

'It's really late,' Arlo announced, studying the digital clock on the oven. 'Eight-three-zero! We normally get up at seven-zero-zero! Can I go wake Mum up now?'

'Yeah, you can wake her now,' I said, and when he ran in to her, I slipped out of the front door.

I bought a copy from a newsagent at the other end of the high street to us, afraid somehow that someone would see me, know what I was doing. I rolled it up tight and kept it clutched in my fist as I walked back up the hill towards the park. It was busy, the sun already climbing and dog walkers and joggers starting to fill the paths. I cut across the grass, sweat trickling down my neck as the slope got steeper. I stopped when I got to the top, a sudden nausea swelling up. I had walked on autopilot to my bench, to *our* bench. I shook my head, tried to push the feeling away. Tried to tell myself that it was fitting. That it wasn't our bench any more.

I sat down and unfolded the paper, my eyes scanning over the articles without understanding or caring about them. For one, frantic moment, in a rush of panic and relief, I thought it wasn't in there. I thought that they had changed their minds.

Then the plastic sleeve of magazines slid out of the middle and it was right there on the front page: *Daddy Dearest: How it feels to grow up as the daughter of a serial killer.* I wondered how the daytime TV presenter who was on the cover felt about having that headline slapped across her chest, her own relegated to a corner: *Kayleigh: The Reinvention.* I dropped the rest of the paper onto the bench beside me and tore the sleeve open, accidentally sending a load of leaflets fluttering to the floor. I flicked the magazine open with shaking hands.

They had used an old photo of my dad, one I'd never seen before of him in a pub somewhere, grinning as he leant against the bar. A pull quote filled one corner: 'He killed a woman nineteen years ago and I want her to be remembered . . . She was my mother.' There it was. The truth out and free. Impossible to take back.

I read the article once and then twice, my eyes catching on different sentences each time. *Addison Knight is,*

perhaps understandably, guarded when I meet her . . .
Addison admits that it's true her father sends her a single
piece of jewellery belonging to his victims on her birthday
each year – the flourish which originally earned him his
moniker . . . Addie's eyes fill with tears as she tells me the
dreadful truth: 'She was my mother. And he murdered her.'

My phone bleeped, making me jump. I pulled it out of
my backpack and glanced at it. Dellar. You ok? I can meet if
you need to talk. D x

So he had seen it. I tried not to picture the article posted
on the paper's website, the link being shared across social
media, the comments starting to appear below the line.

I tried not to picture Jessie logging on to the laptop to
look at it.

Reading the article through a second time, I tried to tell
myself that it wasn't bad. That it had been what I wanted.
I wanted people to know what he had done. I wanted
justice for her. It had felt powerful, when I'd decided to do
it. But seeing it in print, in a bold 24-point pull quote, it
just felt cheap.

I knew Jessie would be appalled. I couldn't bring myself
to go home and face her.

I sat on our bench and watched the city carry on as if
none of it mattered at all.

5

I spent the day walking. The bar where Katherine West had bought her last drink had closed down long before, had been a noodle bar and now a steakhouse. The tiny shop under the arches which had been Laine's had been turned into a delicatessen, the counter which Jessie had stood behind replaced by a glass display of cheese and meat. I stood there and pictured her, pictured my ten-year-old self on my little stool in the store room. Nine years ago – I felt a sudden pang of sadness, of something like being homesick. I turned away, left the memories there.

I walked through the market, watching people eating breakfast and then lunch, papers open on the tables in front of them. I saw my father's face staring back from the magazine as a woman turned the page, took a bite from a pastry. He was there again, abandoned on a table in the dark pub where I nursed a cider for most of the afternoon, the wet ring from a glass spreading slowly across him, wrinkling the page.

Each time I stayed in a place too long, I started to feel people's glances lingering on me, started to hear whispers begin. *You asked for this*, I told myself. I paid for drinks I didn't want and food I couldn't eat with the money I'd been given for selling us all out and I dreaded checking my phone and seeing a message from Jessie.

But none came. The dread got worse.

I hadn't had a panic attack for months but as I tried to make my way up the high street towards the flat that evening, I found myself trapped in a crowd. A fight had broken out outside the Underground, people gathering round to watch, station staff trying to herd everyone back. My chest started to feel tight, the cider I'd drunk making my head spin. I took a step back and connected with some-one's chest. 'Sorry,' I mumbled, but when I tried to move away, someone in front was knocked back, bumping into me. I squeezed my eyes closed, tried to keep control. I could hear my breath coming in short, tried to draw in a longer gulp.

'Fucking *bitch*,' someone yelled, and I opened my eyes, scanning wildly for a way through the crowd. I had to get out of there.

I pushed past the person next to me, felt them shove back. I struggled through a gap at the edge of the pave-ment, not caring about the oncoming traffic, and moved as quickly as I could up the road. It wasn't until I was almost home that I felt the tightness in my chest start to loosen, felt like I could breathe.

And then I was climbing the steps to the flat and the

panic started to rise again at the thought of facing Jessie. Those words danced in front of my eyes: *She was my mother. And he murdered her.* I thought of Jessie crying in the kitchen the night the truth had finally come out, the secret that she had carried alone for sixteen years. That was now public property, just like us.

The lights were off in the flat and, when I unlocked the door, I saw that her keys were missing from their hook on the wall, hers and Arlo's shoes gone from the mat too.

I went into the kitchen and put my backpack on the table, working up the courage to call her. But when I unzipped the pocket and slid my hand in to find my phone, my fingers touched paper instead. I frowned as I pulled it out. A folded scrap of lined notepaper, nothing I remembered stuffing in there. When I opened it and saw the writing, my stomach lurched.

The address was printed in a careless, familiar scrawl. Beneath it, he'd written:

Please come. She hasn't told you everything.

Dad.

I remembered the crowd outside the station, people pressing in from all sides. Tried to picture him slipping his way through, thin fingers unzipping my bag. Sliding the note inside.

I closed my eyes and took in one breath after the other, willing my heart to slow down. When I felt like the world wasn't closing in on me, I put out a shaky hand and dragged my bag towards me again. I fished around in it until I found my phone and, when I managed to unlock it, I found Jessie's number in my contact list and pressed call. The robotic tone of her voicemail clicked in straight away.

'It's me,' I managed. 'Please call me back. I need . . . I need to talk to you. Please.' My eyes fell on the note on the table again and I hung up and dropped the phone, ran back to the front door and put the security chain on.

I waited. I waited and waited for her to come back, for her to tell me what I should do. That's how I like to remember it anyway, although the truth is that perhaps I wouldn't have told her at all, not once I'd calmed down. Read it over and over. *She hasn't told you everything.*

I guess he knew me better than I'd realised.

When I was sure that Jessie and Arlo weren't going to come home that night at all, I made up my mind.

6

The address was a dark mews of garages and outbuildings somewhere in Streatham, all with heavy corrugated metal shutters or graffitied barn doors. The uneven road outside was lined with rusting cars, some on blocks. The single street light near the middle was broken. I made my way along it, every nerve in my body screaming at me to turn back. But I carried on until I saw the spraypainted 77 on one metal panel, faint in the moonlight. The padlock which held the makeshift door closed hung open, a chink of dark visible. I stepped forward, trying to peer inside, but the black was thick, dancing, and I reached out a hand and pushed the door open, forced myself to take a step inside.

The space smelled of petrol and dirt, a steady drip coming from somewhere in a corner. I fumbled my phone out of my pocket and used its weak light to illuminate an old pair of work boots, a rusty wrench. A length of piping. I thought I heard something scuttling along the back wall and I spun, trying to get the light to reach it.

'Dad?'

He moved quickly but it was the quiet that I'd remember later. I still think about it now. How he moved without a sound, how I didn't know he was behind me until he was pulling the bag down over my head. Over the top of it a hand clamped down hard over my mouth but I was too stunned to scream. Frozen, barely noticing as he tugged the phone from my hand. As he pulled my wrists together, icy metal digging into the skin as he clicked the cuffs closed.

He dragged me through the dark and I was dimly aware of the outside air against my skin, cool seeping through the weave of the fabric covering my face. I heard the clunk of a car door opening, felt the pressure of a hand on the back of my head. Not hard – tender, even. But then a shove, pushing me down onto the seat, the car door slamming shut behind me.

He didn't speak. I listened to the sound of my own frantic breath inside the bag, tried desperately to stay calm. I was terrified that the panic would start to take hold, and so I tried to stay numb instead, to keep track of time as we drove, the roads beneath us changing from busy city to motorway to something rougher. Then, finally, the car was slowing, stones crunching beneath the wheels. I heard the driver's door open and then slam and I tensed, waiting to see what he would do.

The door beside my head opened, hands reaching in and hooking under my arms, pulling me out. My legs had fallen asleep at some point in the journey and I struggled to stand on them, leaning my weight against him.

He lowered me onto something scratchy that smelled of grass. When the hood was tugged off, it took a moment for my eyes to adjust. But I felt the straw under my hands, smelled the bales of it stacked around me. I was in a barn, hay loft above me and empty milking stalls at the opposite end.

And him, standing beside me, looking down.

'Hey, kiddo,' he said.

'Dad,' I said and then, shocking both of us, I started to cry.

'Now, come on.' He turned away. He had never liked it when we cried. 'No good crying now, is it?' He sighed and sank down onto a hay bale in front of me, rested his elbows on his knees. 'I didn't much like the things you had to say about me in the paper today.'

'I didn't much like having to say them,' I spat.

He shook his head. Disappointed in me. 'You've got it wrong, Addie,' he said.

Another sob shivered up inside me but this time I swallowed it back. 'You killed my mum,' I hissed.

'Addie.' His voice low, slippery. 'This is not about her. You need to listen to me—'

'You *killed* her,' I interrupted. 'You *murdered* her, Dad.'

'You don't understand. Yes, I did a terrible thing. To her and to you. But I've spent my life trying to make it up to you and that's not—'

'You've spent your life *murdering* other women.'

In the silence that followed, he studied me, face unreadable again. And it was me, then, who was afraid.

'You really believe that, don't you?' he growled. He ran a hand over his thinning hair and I knew that his temper was stretched almost to breaking; recognised the warning signs even though it had been so long since I had seen him last.

But I didn't care, the words still spilling out. 'Tell me where they are,' I said. 'Do the right thing.'

He laughed, a horrible, cracked sound, a smile spreading slowly across his narrow face. 'You can't stop digging, can you? Okay, Addie, if you're so sure that's what you want, let me tell you a secret.' He leant forward, put his face close to mine. His breath smelled rotten and I hated myself for flinching. 'Our place,' he whispered, and then he drew back. 'Go there. Then you'll see how guilty I really am.'

'What do you mean?' A sick feeling started rising. 'Why are you saying this? Why are you here, Dad? Why have you been following me?'

He leant in again then, a frown deepening. 'You need to be very careful,' he said. 'I haven't—' But then the first thwack-thwack of a helicopter echoed through the rafters and he froze, his eyes still level with mine. 'What did you do?' he whispered.

I forced myself to move closer, our noses almost touching. 'What did you?' I whispered back.

His whole body sagged, a sudden fear crossing his face. 'I did this for you,' he said.

'For me.' I let out a sudden, terrible laugh. 'All of this is for me. That's all either of you ever say. You did it for me. How can you possibly say you did any of this for *me*?'

Understanding dawned then; I watched it light up his narrow, bloodshot eyes and then fade away again. 'She didn't tell you why,' he said. 'She didn't tell you what me and Lizzie fought about that night.'

'She doesn't remember,' I tried to say, but a wave of fear – of knowing – swept over me and the words were carried out as a whisper. 'Tell me,' I said. Outside one siren after another screamed its way closer, blue lights streaking across the rafters above us. There was the slam of doors, the thud of feet.

Dad's face twisted into a sneer. 'She said the baby wasn't mine,' he said, as if the baby wasn't me, wasn't sitting there in front of him. The barn door flew open, police streaming in dressed in body armour, guns held up.

'Get your hands up!' one bellowed. 'Get your hands in the fucking air.'

Dad stepped back from me, his hands raised slowly though his eyes didn't leave mine.

'Addie,' he said, and there was panic in his voice again now, his hands forced behind his back as he was pushed down to his knees. 'Addie, listen, you're in danger.'

'Shut your mouth,' the same officer commanded. He cuffed Dad's wrists, then pressed a boot into his kidneys so that he cried out, his forehead bowed down to the barn floor.

'Addie.' DS Jones came surging up from the line of officers, the helmet and goggles ripped off his head. 'Are you okay?' He dropped to his knees in front of me. 'You did so good, Addie. I was with you the whole time.' He fumbled his phone out from a pocket on his vest, showed me the screen where he had been tracking me, just like he'd promised.

'Addie, please.' My father rising up from the floor again, swaying like a snake. 'It wasn't me. I didn't send them—'

'Shut your fucking mouth, scumbag!' There was a crack and then a chattering ticking sound, Dad dropping to the ground, his body rigid. The officer holding the Taser watched him calmly, didn't stop even though he lay still.

'Come on.' DS Jones helped me up, draped a jacket round my shoulders. I hadn't realised I was shivering, my teeth clattering against each other. 'Let's get you out of here.'

7

Jessie and I sat side by side in the waiting room, a clock ticking loudly behind us. The sound of the Taser echoed in my ears and I couldn't stop picturing the faces of the officers looking on. They hated him. They wanted him to get what he deserved.

I didn't know what I wanted any more.

Jessie got up and started pacing. 'This is crazy. They can't keep us here.'

I ran a finger round the bruises on my wrists, the marks from the handcuffs he'd put on me. 'They said it's for our own good. The press are going mad outside.'

DS Jones was trying to find somewhere to send us, somewhere to wait it out. But a night in a hotel or, worse, some kind of safe house, wasn't going to be enough. People wouldn't give up that easy. They would want to hear how we were feeling, what we knew. I didn't know why I'd ever thought I could sell my story once and not have people coming back for more.

Jessie looked at the clock. 'I hate the idea of Arlo waking up without me.'

I didn't think Arlo would care all that much, waking up in the spare bed at Lex's house where there would be chocolate cereal for breakfast and Cara's PlayStation to entertain him. 'What do you think's happening to him? Dad, I mean.'

She shook her head. 'I'm not sure.' She scratched at a patch of eczema on her wrist. I hadn't noticed she'd had another flare-up. 'I guess there'll be a trial.'

'But will they . . . Where will he go before that?'

'Will they let him out, you mean?' She paced over to the door, glanced out at the corridor. 'No. I highly doubt that.'

I nodded. Tried not to think about his face level with mine. *I did this for you.*

Jessie glanced at me, a thumb rubbing at the patch on her wrist again. 'Do you want to talk about it? About what he said?'

I shook my head, avoiding her gaze. 'What is there to say? He killed her because of me.'

'*Don't* say that. There would've been something. He would've snapped eventually. That's who he *is*. He can't control himself.' She came over and sat back down, put a hand over mine. Her voice was gentler when she spoke again. 'None of this is your fault. It never has been.'

I turned to her and the words came out in a whisper. 'You did remember, didn't you? You knew all along what they argued about that night. You knew she'd said I wasn't his.'

She looked away and then, after a second, nodded. 'I'm sorry.'

Suddenly I found I didn't care so much about the press after all.

Dellar lived in a flat near Clapham North station, on the sixth floor in a new development with a gym in the basement and mirrored walls in the lift. I stared at the floor, ignoring my own reflection. When the doors slid open, he was standing at the end of the hallway, propping open the door to his flat with his foot. He stood aside to let me in.

'Nice place,' I said. It was all sleek and new – shiny white counter and breakfast bar in the open-plan kitchen, black leather L-shaped sofa in the living area and a wide-screen TV mounted on the wall.

'Thanks.' If I'd woken him up by calling him at 4 a.m., he didn't show it. 'What do you need? Tea? Coffee? Wine?'

'Wine.' There was no question there. I wanted to drink until I stopped thinking. Drink until it all seemed far away, like it was happening to someone else.

Dellar poured me a glass from the bottle on the counter, put the kettle on to make himself tea. 'It's all over the internet,' he said. 'Magpie finally caught.' He handed me my drink as I sank onto the edge of the sofa and watched as I knocked back half of it in a couple of gulps. 'Take it easy,' he said. 'You're probably in shock.'

'I was there,' I said, staring into the glass. 'I tricked him, actually. Led them right to him.'

He raised an eyebrow. 'Jesus. You okay?'

I drank the rest of my wine instead of answering, handed him the empty glass. He went back and refilled it without comment but when the kettle boiled he made two mugs of tea instead of just his own.

'So, I hate to ask the obvious,' he said, putting both my drinks down on the glass coffee table and then taking a seat in the armchair across from me, 'but how come you're here and not with Jessie?'

I took a big gulp of wine but the woody taste was starting to make me feel sick. 'She lied to me,' I said, and then, because I hadn't said the words out loud yet, 'Apparently he's not even my real dad.'

Dellar leant back in his chair, let out a low whistle. After a few minutes, he asked, 'Isn't that a good thing?'

I looked away. 'I guess so. And I had a right to know.'

'Yep.' Dellar took a sip of his tea, then rested the mug against his leg. He was wearing soft grey jogging bottoms, his feet bare. I definitely had woken him up when I called.

'I just don't know how to feel.' I gulped down some more wine, my cheeks warm. 'It's like everything I knew about myself – about who I was – is gone, just like that.'

'Okay, first of all, do you even know it's true?'

I shook my head. Maybe it was just something Mum had said to hurt him, something in the heat of the moment. *She learnt how to use her words too*, Jessie had said.

'Second of all,' Dellar continued, 'this doesn't change anything about who you are. It doesn't matter where you come from, Addie. That doesn't define you.'

I looked at him doubtfully.

'I'm serious. Look at Laine – she knew Frank's dad was bad news so she decided she was going to have him in Norfolk, just like that. Fresh start from day one for both of them. DNA isn't some unbreakable sentence the way people think it is, Addie. It's just cells. You're your own person, you always have been.'

'Yeah, well, unless Frank's dad happened to be a serial abductor of women I don't think it's the same, legacy-wise.'

He winced. 'Yeah, sorry. I wasn't trying to say . . . You're right, I guess being a bit of a lowlife dealer isn't exactly in the same league. I just meant . . . I don't know what I meant, really. I just don't want you to feel like this is the thing that's most important about you.'

'It's okay.' I smiled. 'Honestly. I know what you meant. Thank you.' I lifted my wine to my mouth again and noticed my hand was trembling.

'And look, if what he told you tonight *is* true . . . I dunno. Maybe he thought it would free you, or something.' He shifted in his seat, coughed uncomfortably. 'Sorry. I'm not saying any of this right. Try and drink some of your tea. I put extra sugar in it, for the shock. *Tea* I can get right.'

But I'd stopped listening. Something was wrong, the beginnings of a realisation scratching its way to the surface. 'He wouldn't come back just for that,' I said slowly, more to myself than to Dellar.

'You what?'

'Just to tell me he's not my dad.' I put my glass down, trying to remember the way he'd looked, the things he'd said. 'He said I had it wrong.' I remembered the way his face had changed when I'd asked him about the women he'd taken, about where they were. *You really believe that, don't you?*

'I think he came to tell me that it wasn't him,' I blurted, a sudden, sick certainty dawning. What was it he'd said? *I didn't much like the things you had to say about me in the paper today.* 'It wasn't him,' I said again slowly, testing the words out. 'Those women. It wasn't him.'

Dellar frowned. 'Addie, I know you're upset but think about what you're saying. Of course it was him. He's been on the run for six years. What more proof that he's guilty do you need?'

I shook my head. 'I don't know. I just . . .' My head was spinning. 'What proof do we even really *have*? The purse.'

'The blood,' he said quietly. 'They found Olivia Emerson's blood in his car.'

'A tiny trace,' I said hotly, surprising myself. 'That doesn't prove anything. It doesn't mean she was in the car.' I stopped suddenly, a thought turning my blood to ice. 'It could mean that the killer was, though.'

Dellar leant forward and carefully put his mug down on the table. 'Look, tonight's been crazy for you. But don't . . . . I just don't think this is helping.'

I picked up my wine glass again and then changed my mind and went for the tea. 'Someone could have framed him, even. Put the blood in the car, hidden the purse.'

He stared at me, silence unfolding between us. 'I really think it's a bad idea to go down this road, Addie.'

'It makes sense though.' I drank more of my tea, no longer shaking, my brain working overtime.

'It really doesn't. You *saw* him come home with blood on his clothes. And when you told the police, he ran. Come on. Don't let him get into your head, not after all this time. He killed her. He killed all of them.'

The words stung but they stopped me in my tracks, the hopeful energy I'd felt a second ago evaporating. In a small voice, I found myself repeating the question Dad had asked me in that dark barn. 'You really believe that?'

Dellar sighed. He sank back, tapped his fist idly against the arm of the chair for a second, as if he was trying to make up his mind about something. Finally, he looked at me. 'I don't know how to say this but . . . Well, it's something that's been playing on my mind a lot. It's kind of the reason I wanted to get in contact with you, actually. Because I think you deserve to know.'

The icy feeling spread. 'What?'

'I've always wondered . . . I think . . . I think Jessie knew. What your dad was doing. I think she knew.' He glanced at me. 'She used to ask me stuff. About Leyton. The investigation. This was back when it wasn't all public knowledge, when they were keen to keep it under the radar. She was, I don't know. Too interested, I guess.'

I swallowed. 'So she suspected, you mean. She was worried it was him.'

He shook his head. 'No. Well, I don't know. But the more I think about it, the more I think that she *knew*. The reason she was so interested was that she was trying to figure out if the police knew. If they were going to catch him.'

'I don't believe that.' Except that I could believe it. I no longer had any doubt that Jessie would do anything to protect us. Me. No matter who else got hurt along the way.

But then I was remembering Dad in that dark barn. *You can't stop digging, can you?* And the way he'd leant close, almost smiled. *Our place. Go there.*

Then you'll see how guilty I really am.

'I have to go,' I said.

8

I walked up Tulse Hill, all of the houses quiet and dark, the first streaks of dawn just beginning to paint the sky. A black cab pulled up outside a house in front of me, a girl stumbling out with her shoes in her hand, her dress riding up. I looked at the hoop earrings she wore, the chunky gold bracelet around one wrist, and imagined them slipped inside an envelope, landing on Leyton Jones's desk.

The gates to the park were locked, no sign of anyone inside. I waited for a bus to pass and then, when the road remained empty, I slung my backpack on and climbed over the railings. It had been nine years since I'd last climbed a tree with Henry, and I'd lost most of the boldness I'd had back then. I wobbled on my way over, my foot catching under the top bar, and I landed awkwardly, rolling my ankle. I forced myself to get up, hoping no one had seen me from the street.

I limped down the path, turning as soon as I could so that I was out of sight of the road. The park was dark, trees whispering in the breeze. Pools of cool shadow between them where anyone could hide. Jessie had complained about the lack of CCTV in the park earlier in the year after someone had been attacked and I thought about the headlines if that happened to me, Magpie's daughter. I wondered if Laurie Cooper would write about it.

I wound my way round the greenhouses and headed up the hill, remembering how much harder the climb had seemed when I was little, my hand in his. The way sometimes he'd taken pity on me, hitching me onto his back. The way we had run back down the hill together when it was time to go, my belly tumbling and my arms held out, ready to take flight.

When I got to the bench I stood for a second, looking out across the dark to the red and white lights of the city. My favourite view and yet now it looked hard, cold. Hostile. I thought I heard footsteps behind me but when I turned there was nothing, just the trees looking back. Red seeping into the sky behind them, the stars disappearing.

I sank onto my haunches and rested my back against the bench, trying to remember it clearly, Dad standing over me and me choosing the place I wanted, jumping up and down with excitement. Him digging carefully with a trowel borrowed from Mrs Klusak.

I didn't have that luxury. I started pulling lumps of dirt free with my hands, still listening for the sound of someone climbing the hill behind me. The soil was dry and grainy, shifting easily as I found my rhythm, as if it had been recently disturbed. But I started to panic as I got deeper.

Maybe I had imagined it, maybe I had read him wrong. *Our place*. He could have meant the flat, though that had been combed over so intensively by forensics it seemed impossible that he could have hidden anything there.

But then a clod came free and I saw a corner of plastic sticking out from the hole it had left behind. I clawed away more soil, tearing a nail and making the skin bleed, but I managed to tug it free.

I brushed the clots of mud away, staring at the bag. I knew immediately that the phone that was sealed inside was my father's. I could see the familiar cracks spiderwebbing the corner of the screen, the way the case, which had also cracked when he'd dropped it once, didn't quite fit. He'd wrapped an elastic band round it to hold the back on and the battery in. It looked oddly pathetic in there and I felt unexpectedly sad.

I unzipped the bag and slid the phone out. The battery would surely be dead; I'd already started wondering if any of the stalls on the market would sell the right charger for it as I pressed the power button. But the screen lit up, the phone giving a feeble buzz in my hand. The buttons were stiff and it took me a minute to work out how to use the track pad but soon I was moving through the icons on the screen, searching for whatever it was he had left for me there. The messages were empty. He'd never set up an email address on it. No photos, no contacts – all of it deleted.

All of it except for a single file, tucked in the final folder on the screen. A recording. No name on it, just the date it had been made: 18th September, 2008. The day he had run.

I wiped the blood from my thumb and hit play. I had to bring the phone close to my ear to hear it properly.

The sound was crackly – he had hidden the phone inside a pocket; a coat or jacket by the sound of it. I was impressed by his cunning. It was a Jessie sort of thing to have done; I supposed she had to have gotten it from somewhere.

'What was the big rush?' I heard him say. 'Your message didn't make any sense.'

Whoever he was talking to was too far away to make out and the crackling sounds got louder as he moved towards them.

'—saw her with that detective. I think . . . I think she'll tell him.'

I sank back against the bench. The other voice belonged to Jessie. Whatever it was my father had hidden for me here, he had hidden it from her.

'Fuck.' The sound scrambled and then cleared; I pictured him rubbing a hand slowly over the back of his head, the way he did when something had surprised him. 'What now?'

'Now,' Jessie said calmly. 'You run. Run and keep running.'

He laughed, a cold, humourless bark. 'And you? What happens to you in this scenario?'

'We'll be okay. As long as they don't find you.'

'You want me to take the blame for this.' The words coming out in a growl.

'Yes. About time too, don't you think?' She took in a deep breath. 'If you don't, I'll tell the truth about what happened to Mum. About what you did. I'll tell Addie everything.'

There was a long pause. Through the crackling of fabric, I could hear my father breathing. 'You wouldn't,' he said.

'I would.'

He scoffed. 'I don't believe you. You love her too much.'

'So do you.' When he didn't reply, she added, 'She'd forgive *me*.'

His breathing got louder. 'I helped you,' he said, eventually. 'When you needed me, I was there. You called *me*. And I took care of it.'

Then it was Jessie's turn to laugh. 'What,' she said, 'you want me to say thanks?'

'You're doing all of this for her. I'm your *family*.'

'She's my friend. You've got friends too. I'm sure they'll help you.' In the background, I could hear baby Arlo crying. 'There's something else you should know,' she said, that slyness I hated most creeping back into her voice. 'I sent her wedding ring to the police. They think Magpie got her.'

There was a silence as he took that in, and then a shaky laugh. 'You are a fucked-up girl, you know that?'

'You practically murdered my mother in front of me. Why are you surprised about that?' When he didn't reply, her voice got louder. She was coming closer, the way she did when she knew she was winning. 'I think you better go. They might already be on their way.'

I realised, with a sinking sense of horror, that he was crying. 'And if I go?' he asked. 'What happens then?'

'You stay gone,' she said. 'If you stay gone, we'll all be all right.' I thought I heard something like pity in her voice. 'It won't be so bad, Dad. I'm sure you'll figure it out. You're a very resourceful man.' I heard the softness turn sour and realised I had been wrong. There was no pity there. 'Just stay gone. I'm going to look after them now.'

The recording ended and I sat in the dirt and stared at the screen.

9

I ran. I stumbled on my way back down the hill and lost my footing, managed to get my hands out in front of me just in time to stop my face hitting the path. I bit my tongue, my mouth filling with hot, bitter blood, but I pushed myself up, the two phones rattling around the bottom of my backpack.

'You okay?' a woman jogging past asked me. The park gates had opened, the place coming back to life as dawn turned to proper day as if the whole world hadn't just changed. I nodded and carried on walking, swallowing hard.

When I reached the entrance, I realised I had nowhere to go. I couldn't go back and face Jessie, not with her lies laid out in front of me. *I helped you*, Dad had said, and she hadn't argued. *What, you want me to say thanks?*

What had she done?

They think Magpie got her. She'd sounded so pleased with herself. And I couldn't stop seeing that picture of Liv that hung in the hallway of Lex's house, the picture which had watched me and my sister walk past, year after year, while her purse was stashed behind a mattress in our flat. Jessie had seen that picture every day and she had sent that woman's wedding ring to the police in an attempt to hide whatever had really happened to her.

You are a fucked-up girl, my father had said. Except he wasn't my father, was he?

And who was she?

She's my friend. I couldn't stop turning over the way Jessie's voice had changed as she'd said that. More like the Jessie I knew: defensive, protective. There was only one person in the world Jessie would have called her friend.

I found my phone at the bottom of my bag and dialled.

Henry picked me up an hour later in a florist's van he'd borrowed from Michael's girlfriend, Kate. As I climbed in, he shifted a tray of pansies off the front seat and onto the dashboard and looked at me over the top of his glasses.

'Best I could do,' he said.

'Thanks for this,' I said. 'I . . . I didn't know who else to call.'

Henry fumbled the van into gear and pulled away from the kerb jerkily. 'You want to tell me what's going on?'

'I found something out,' I said. 'Something . . . I don't even know. I just have to find out what it means.'

He nodded as if any of that had made sense and indicated to take us back onto the main road. 'I saw about your dad. Is it true you were there?'

I nodded. I saw his face in front of me. *What did you do?*

'Wow.' Henry tried to change gear and failed, the engine roaring in protest. 'Sorry,' he said. 'I'm actually quite a good driver. Just not used to this, that's all.'

I didn't answer, turning my face to the window. For the first time since I'd heard the recording, I felt tears rising. Henry had learned to drive, had probably had girlfriends and jobs. The first time I had made money of my own was by telling a journalist how my father killed my mother. Would I ever do something as simple as borrow a friend's car, pick up another friend?

'Addie,' Henry said. 'I'm good at looking at stuff. Figuring things out. If you wanted to tell me what you're worried about.'

I was quiet for a long time. Wondering if I could trust him. Wondering if it mattered. We left London behind and drove on through an endless stretch of anonymous motorway, the pansies on the dashboard shaking their heads at every turn.

'I don't think he killed them,' I said, eventually.

'Oh,' Henry said. 'Fuck.'

The house was small, with greyish pebble-dashed walls. It stood at the end of a terrace, yellowing net curtains at its windows. It didn't look anything like anywhere I imagined Laine living. But it had been a long time since I'd last seen her, and I guessed we'd both changed.

'You sure this is it?' Henry frowned. 'Doesn't look like anyone's home.'

But I had seen the net curtains in one of the downstairs windows twitch. Rain started to patter on the windscreen of the van, fat drops which blurred the view of the fields and the road in front of us. I hesitated. In the corner of the narrow front garden, I saw a child's bike, abandoned on its side.

'We can go, if you want,' Henry said.

'No, it's okay.' But I still couldn't make myself get out of the car.

'You don't think . . . I mean, is she dangerous?' Henry looked nervously at the house.

'No.' The thought was so ridiculous it spurred me on. 'No, not at all. But she knows something and I'm not leaving until she tells me what it is.'

He nodded. 'That was actually pretty persuasive.'

'Thanks,' I said grimly. 'You okay to wait?'

'Sure.' He pulled a *National Geographic* out of the side pocket of his door and flicked it open. He glanced back at me with a grin and a shrug. 'Some things never change, right?' His face paled, his mouth pressed tightly shut. 'Sorry,' he said. 'That was—'

I shook my head. 'It's fine.' I shut the car door behind me and walked up the front path, the smell of rain and field clinging to me. I saw the curtains twitch again in the window, the small hand which clung to the corner of them, a little eye glaring out from behind. I raised a hand and knocked on the glass panel of the door, rain soaking the back of my T-shirt as the wind picked up. A shadow came down the hallway, hesitating there. Then there was the sound of a chain being pulled back and the door opened.

Laine stared back at me, her face set hard. Her hair had been scraped into a short, tufty ponytail, none of the long, glossy extensions I remembered. She wore a long, baggy beige cardigan over leggings and a faded T-shirt. Her nails, pressed white against the edge of the door, were short and bitten.

'Addie,' she said. 'What are you doing here?'

But I could see that she already knew.

'Can I come in?' I asked.

We sat in the living room; me perched on the edge of the sticky leather sofa, Laine in an old patterned armchair. Frank lingered in the kitchen but I could see him out of the corner of my eye, peering round the doorframe. He was small for eight, but stocky, too; thick-necked and barrel-bodied, his eyes narrowed. He hadn't spoken as I came in. On the living room wall was a magnetic chart: *Good behaviour*, columns for the days of the week spaced out across it. There was a lone star in Wednesday's column. It was Monday and the rest of the stars were huddled together in the bottom corner. Below them was a dent in the plaster, a small fist shape.

'How did you find me?' Laine asked. She pulled the sleeves of the cardigan down over her hands. The house was cold even though it was June; a wet, thin sort of cold that crawled across your skin.

303

I shrugged. 'I asked Dellar. He obviously didn't get the memo that you didn't want to be found.'

She chewed her lip. 'And why *did* you want to find me?'

I glanced back over my shoulder at Frank, who shrank back out of sight. 'I . . .' I met her eye. 'Why did you move here? Why did you leave London?'

'I was pregnant,' she said quietly. We watched each other.

'When?' I asked. 'When did you move?'

'I . . . Summer. 2005, I guess. After the shop closed.'

'July,' I said. 'You left in July, then.'

She swallowed and didn't answer.

'What happened?' I asked, my voice as quiet as hers. 'That day. What happened to Liv?'

Her mouth opened and then closed. And then she got up and shut the door.

'Jessie told you,' she said, and I shook my head.

She closed her eyes. 'When I saw he'd been caught . . .'

The words fizzed on my tongue and so I said them aloud, tried them out for size. 'You killed her.'

'*No.*' Laine shook her head and then stopped. She glanced at the door and then at me. 'It was an accident,' she said, and I felt something inside me fall in, break.

'What was? What happened?'

She scratched at her face and then pulled her sleeve down again where it had ridden up, though not before I saw the faint bruises around her wrist. 'We'd done it before,' she said. 'It never went wrong until then.' She glanced at me, her expression hardening. 'You were just a kid. You have no idea how hard it was for Jessie back then.'

'I *do*,' I said hotly. 'Of course I do.'

She ignored me. 'I tried, obviously I did. But then I lost the shop and I felt like I'd let *her* down as well as myself. So when she asked me to help her sometimes, I did. I'm not proud of it.' She shivered. 'Elliott would've killed her if he'd known. But she always picked the rich bitches, you know? The ones who could afford it, who it didn't matter to. She wouldn't have done it otherwise. She's not a bad person.' Suddenly, without warning, she started to cry. 'Neither of us were.'

I pictured Liv, stepping out that morning from her beautiful big house. Dressed in some of the expensive clothes that would hang undisturbed in the wardrobe, gathering dust, until Lex finally gave them to charity. Until he gave them to Jessie.

'What did you do to her?' I asked.

She took in a deep, shuddering breath. 'It was so small-time. So amateur. I'd park my car somewhere, some quiet street in whatever place Jessie had picked – Chelsea, Hampstead, wherever.'

'Pimlico,' I said, and she shivered again.

'I'd pretend I'd broken down or got lost and ask someone on their own to help me. She preferred women. Easier to dip into a handbag without anyone noticing.'

'She pickpocketed them,' I said, disgusted.

'She was good at it. Little, quick. None of them ever

noticed.' She sighed. 'But *she* – she was on to us straight-away—'

'Her *name* was Olivia.'

She flinched. 'Olivia, she turned at the wrong time and saw Jessie with her hand in her bag. Obviously she tried to get hold of it, tried to pull it free. Starts making a fuss, starts struggling. She had hold of Jessie's hair. And Jessie freaked – she . . . she punched her. Square in the face. And then she grabbed the straps of the bag and pulled the whole thing right off her shoulder and ran.' She closed her eyes. 'I thought Olivia would chase after her but instead she turned on *me*. She was losing it, shouting, breathing all funny. I panicked. I just wanted to get away, I didn't *think*—'

Her voice had grown louder, the panic surfacing after all those years, and she stopped herself. 'I jumped in the car,' she said. 'But she got in the backseat, started yelling at me to take her to Jessie, to get her bag.' She opened her eyes, stared up at the ceiling. 'I thought she was crazy, I didn't realise she just wanted to get it back, that she couldn't . . .'

She swallowed. 'I drove, I just kept driving, and all I could think was that she'd seen my face, she'd seen my face and she was in the car and we were in big fucking trouble and I was going to end up having my baby in jail, all because Jessie wanted to take you for fucking pizza on your fucking birthday—'

I reeled back like she'd hit me.

'And I realised that she couldn't breathe, that she was trying to tell me to get the bag, to get the bag because—'

'Because her inhaler was inside.'

She nodded, the tears bubbling up again. 'I didn't know what to do, Addie, I swear. I just . . . didn't know and I kept driving and then . . . then it was too late.' She looked at me, eyes swollen. 'I wasn't that much older than you are now, that's what you have to remember. Jessie was seventeen. We were just babies. We never could have known—'

'So you called my dad,' I interrupted.

'Jessie said she'd take care of things,' she said. 'I was a wreck. I wanted to drive straight to the police, as soon as I realised. As soon as I snapped out of it and saw what we'd done. But she wouldn't let me. She kept telling me to think of my baby. To think of you.'

Me. So many things they had all spent so long excusing because of me. Blaming on me.

'She was with you,' I said. 'She didn't come home that whole day. She said she was looking for Dellar. But she was with you, wasn't she?'

She closed her eyes for a second. 'You can't even imagine the state I was in. She stayed with me. She helped me think of a plan.'

'And it was her idea to move away?'

'I couldn't stay,' she said. 'I couldn't stay there, knowing. Waiting for the police to show up at the door any day.'

'They wouldn't have,' I said. 'The two of them made sure of that.'

'I swear,' she said. 'I didn't know about the Magpie thing, not till later. Sending the ring. I don't know why she did that.'

But I thought that I did. I remembered how the inquest had returned an open verdict on whether Liv had been on the Tube that day. That last tiny hope for Lex, and my sister had found a way to smother it. To make everyone stop looking.

'Leyton's your cousin,' I said. 'He's spent his whole career on this. Don't you care about that, at least?'

'What am I supposed to do, Addie? After all this time? And she's dead. That's how the story ends either way.'

10

That's how the story ends either way. I thought about that as Henry drove us away, leaving Laine watching us from the window. Waiting there to see what I'd do, who I'd tell. Waiting to see if it was all about to come crashing down on her.

And did it really matter, in the end, who had done it or why? Would it help anyone for the truth to be out, for Lex and Cara to know how much Jessie had truly betrayed them? I couldn't stop thinking of Arlo, of Frank. I thought about Dellar and how he'd feel – but then I remembered how easily he'd handed over Laine's address when I'd called him, without even asking why, and I wondered if he'd had his suspicions all along. She wasn't as practised as Jessie at hiding her feelings, that was obvious even nine years on. No wonder Jessie had told her to leave London.

But none of it mattered, I realised. Because Dad had been caught and now he would surely tell the police what had really happened. Jessie had broken her half of the bargain after all, when she'd told me what he'd done to our mother. And then he had risked getting caught, all because I had told his darkest secret, the only thing she truly held over him. He had come to tell me that Jessie was just as guilty as he was. He had come to tell me something that was worth leaving his hiding place for.

'He said I was in danger,' I said, with a sudden bolt of fear.

'What?' Henry, surprised by the first sound from me in sixty miles, jerked the wheel to the left and had to hurry to correct it to stop us leaving the road. But I didn't care, or didn't notice. Because all I could think of was the way he'd yelled before the Taser had hit him. *I didn't send them.*

'The jewellery,' I whispered, every hair on my body standing on end. 'He didn't send the jewellery on my birthdays.'

My dad wasn't Magpie. But Magpie had still found me.

'Where shall I take you?' Henry asked, shooting a worried look at me as we left the motorway and began winding our way back into London. 'You could come back to ours with me?'

It was tempting. The idea of stepping into a normal family, even for a moment. Sitting to watch TV, listening to Michael and Henry bicker. Laughing at their dad's clumsy jokes, helping their mum set the table. The image felt so real I wanted to reach out and touch it.

'I think I need to go to the police station,' I said.

Henry nodded. 'Okay. I'll stay with you. If . . . if you want.'

For a moment, I almost said yes. I still wasn't ready – I wouldn't be ready for a long time after that – to do anything on my own. But then I looked at Henry, his face so kind, so concerned. I thought about the man out there somewhere who had taken those women and sent me their jewellery. I didn't want to drag Henry into that. Not if I was in danger.

But I had thought of someone else who might be able to help me. I reached for my phone and found his number.

11

Laurie Cooper's house was at the end of a long terrace in Canonbury. When he answered the door, he was flustered, his glasses steamed up. 'Come in,' he said. 'I was just having a tidy-up. The house is . . . not looking its best.'

I followed him into the kitchen. The oven hung open, some kind of lethal-smelling foam bubbling around its sides, and the cupboard doors were all open too, plates and mugs and glasses stacked on the counter, various spray bottles and cloths abandoned along the way. But it was a beautiful, big room – light and airy, windows looking onto the narrow garden. A set of framed film posters were artfully arranged on one wall; a set of shelves with cigarette cases and hip flasks lined up on another. On another shelf, high up above the door, were old editions of books whose titles I couldn't make out, arranged in descending order of spine. The huge oak dining table had been stacked with pans and dishes, another spray bottle and cloth beside them.

'Sorry,' he said. 'I tend to clean when something big happens. Helps me focus. I have to admit, I really didn't expect this day to come. Is it true you were there? When they caught him, I mean?'

'No comment,' I said, turning away and pulling out a chair.

'Sure, of course.' He picked up a frying pan from the table and stood uncertainly with it for a second. 'Do you want a drink?' he asked, putting it back down.

'No,' I said. 'Thanks.'

He nodded, but fumbled around getting a glass down anyway before realising what I'd said. 'Sorry,' he said again. 'I'm a bit out of sorts today. My phone's been ringing off the hook.' He picked the glass back up and filled it from the tap, taking a sip. 'Worse for you, I'm sure. Anyway. You were pretty vague on the phone – what do you need?'

'I have an exclusive for you,' I said, and he tipped his head to one side, intrigued.

'Now that was not what I was expecting you to say. Go on.'

I took a deep breath. 'My dad is not Magpie. Magpie's still out there. And for some reason, he's taken an interest in me.'

Laurie put the glass down shakily, almost missing the edge of the counter. 'I'm not sure I understand.'

'My dad didn't kill Olivia Emerson although he was involved in covering up her death. And he didn't kill any of the other women, either.'

'And you . . . you have confirmed evidence of this?'

Laine's stricken face flashed into my mind and I forced myself to push the image away. 'Yes. Which means that there's a murderer out there who likes to send his victims' jewellery to me once a year and I think you'll probably understand when I say I find that quite upsetting.'

He blinked, swallowing hard. 'Gosh.'

'It also means that your entire career has been built on a lie, so, you know, sorry.' Fear had made me brittle. I felt a rush of understanding for Jessie.

'Well.' He blew out a breath. 'I don't know what to say.'

'You're supposed to be the country's leading expert on Magpie,' I said. 'You know all there is to know about those women, about the nights they were taken. There has to be something the police have missed. Something that will tell us who he is.'

He gave a shocked little laugh. 'Addie, what makes you think I can solve this when the entire Met has got it so wrong, according to you?'

'Because you have to. We have to.' I felt light-headed, overwhelmed. 'It's the only way to put all this right.' All of those families were out there, thinking that the man who'd taken their daughters, their wives, their sisters from them was now in custody, that justice would be done. I wondered if Dad was already talking. What if Jessie had already been arrested? Arlo – Arlo was still at Lex's. I'd need to go and get him. The room swam, a sudden wave of nausea hitting me. I gripped the table, took another breath. 'I need to use your bathroom.'

'Sure.' He looked at me with genuine concern. 'Here, let me show you. Are you sure I can't get you a drink? You don't look so great.'

I shook my head, not trusting myself to speak, and he directed me to the room at the top of the stairs, tiled all over in brilliant, blinding white. I closed the door behind me and then crouched in front of the toilet, waiting for the sick feeling to pass. I couldn't remember the last time I'd eaten or slept. When I was sure I wasn't going to throw up I sank back against the wall, the tiles cool through my T-shirt. I wanted to stay there forever, locked in that little bathroom. Let Dad say whatever he was going to say, let Jessie and Laine look out for themselves.

But I couldn't. Not because the real Magpie had for some reason taken a shine to me. Not even because I knew Leyton Jones and the families of those women needed to be told that he was still out there.

I had to tell the truth for Lex. For Cara. Because she was nine years old and she deserved to grow up knowing exactly what had happened to her mum. I wouldn't take that away from someone the way it had been taken away from me.

I stood up, splashing cold water on my face and trying not to picture Liv leaving her home on the morning of July 7th, not knowing that, only a few streets away, my sister and Laine were waiting for someone just like her.

I stopped, the tap still running. I stared at my hands over the basin.

Liv had never made it to Pimlico station. She'd jumped

into Laine's backseat and she'd never gotten out again, not until my dad showed up and dragged her body into his own car.

But Laurie had written in his book that he'd knocked her over outside King's Cross.

I reached out to turn the tap off with a shaking hand, thinking it over again. Artistic licence – that was a thing. But why? Why insert himself into Liv's story and none of the others?

I unlocked the bathroom door as quietly as I could and stood at the top of the stairs, trying to stop my whirling thoughts. Downstairs I could hear the clatter of plates being replaced in a cupboard, the scratching of a scouring pad on the counter. I lingered there in the dimness, my pulse pounding in my ears.

A door stood ajar at the other end of the landing, the edge of a desk visible. I went closer, pushed the door open wider.

The study was small, a skylight in the eaves showing a stretch of rooftops and a greyish square of sky. His desk was neat, just a laptop and another pair of glasses, a notepad and pen. I moved closer and flicked through the top pages but they were all blank. I turned and looked at the framed pictures hanging on the wall behind me. There was the cover of *Magpie* – the hardback one I remembered so well, and another; the paperback, maybe. A few foreign editions too, each of them printed out in black and white and carefully arranged around the original. And then, beneath those, a row of portraits, also in black and white.

I recognised Jennifer, Katherine, Anita. Maria, Anna, Mae. The women whose stories he had told, along with mine. Liv's photo wasn't there.

A chill ran over me, my mouth turning dry.

I crept as carefully as I could across the landing and moved quickly down the stairs, keeping close to the wall. The front door loomed ahead of me but I stopped when I reached the bottom, listening to the sounds from the kitchen. More dishes being stacked somewhere, the gush of a tap.

Now. I skidded down the hall, got my hand on the latch. I didn't look back as I turned it.

The door wouldn't open.

'It's locked.'

I spun round. He was only a couple of feet away, the key held up in front of him. He gave a sad little sigh, smiled sympathetically. 'You really didn't have to come here,' he said.

12

I took a step slowly back, pressing into the door. 'I need to go,' I said.

'That was quick.' He came closer, the key shoved into his pocket. 'I thought you wanted my help?'

I stared back at him. 'You wrote a book about them,' I whispered.

'A tribute,' he said.

'You lied about Liv.'

He held his hands up, a *You got me* gesture. 'I couldn't help myself. Anyway, I'm sure she *would* have helped me if she'd been there when I got hit by the van. She sounds like that kind of person.'

I glanced past him, trying to see into the kitchen. Had there been patio doors back there?

'You're not going to try and run, are you?' He was close now, so close. 'We don't have to do this, you know.'

'You sent me their jewellery,' I spat, edging to my left, the kitchen tantalisingly in sight.

'A tribute,' he said, and this time he smiled. He took a step closer, placed a hand on my shoulder, his head on one side as if he was admiring me. 'You have to understand, Addie, that I was very interested in you. The girl who mistakenly accused her own father of being Magpie.' He squeezed the top of my arm in a chummy way, but when I looked down I saw the handle of a knife sticking out of the waistband of his jeans. 'I had a lot to thank you for,' he said. 'You and your family made life so much easier for me.'

I lunged forward and drove the heel of my hand up into his nose, heard the bone crack. 'You're fucking welcome,' I said, and as he moaned and staggered back, blood pattering onto the pretty tiled floor, I ran for the kitchen.

He grabbed me from behind just as I made it to the doorway, swung me round so that I staggered against the wall. Before I had a chance to right myself he was lifting me, slamming me against the wall again, my head smacked back so hard that the world blurred. Blood streamed down his chin, his nose already swelling. He turned his face and wiped it against his shoulder, vivid red against his white shirt.

He slammed me again, hands gripping both my shoulders now. 'You're full of surprises,' he hissed, his voice ragged and his breath thick with iron. 'I really did like you.'

'You killed them,' I managed to splutter. 'Why?'

I saw a new light come into his eyes and I knew I had

said the wrong thing. 'Because they deserved it,' he spat. '*She* deserved it.'

His hands were round my throat so suddenly, so tightly, that the world dimmed, my heels kicking helplessly against the wall.

'You know,' he said, almost conversationally, his blood-streaked face only inches from mine. 'I never thought I'd do this to you.'

A terrible, faint rasping sound was coming from my mouth as I tried to draw in breath, spots dancing across my vision. He leant even closer, our foreheads touching, his whole body trembling with excitement.

'But it's probably for the best,' he whispered. 'Those girls were trouble. And you would be too.'

I was still struggling but I could feel myself drifting, the drumming of my kicks against the wall and against his legs getting slower. Even the pain seemed to fade as everything got dark and I realised that it was really happening. I was dying.

'Let go,' he whispered. 'It's all over now.'

I let myself go limp, let my eyes roll back, and I heard his breath coming in fast. He pressed against me, took the weight of my body on his as if I was a sleeping child he was about to carry to bed. He rested the side of his head against mine for a moment with a deep, delighted sigh, and the grip of his fingers slowly loosened from my throat.

With the last of my strength, I sank my teeth into his neck and slid the knife from his waistband.

13

He screamed, dropping me as he tried to pull away, my mouth filling with hot, shocking blood. I drove the knife as hard as I could into his side and he shrieked again, collapsing against me. I pushed him back and he staggered against the stairs, hand pressed to the wound. My lungs were burning as air flowed back into them, as I drove the knife hard into his stomach again. I did it again and again and I realised suddenly that now it was me who was making awful, hoarse screams, not him.

He slumped towards the floor but I dragged him up, shoved my hand into his pocket. The key was slippery in my fingers but I tugged it free. I ran, skidding on the bloody floor, my shoulder slamming into a mirror and sending it shattering to the ground. I fumbled the key at the door, dropped it. Behind me I heard him groaning, the thump of his hand against the wall as he tried to push himself upright. I got the key in on the second try, turned it with numb fingers. My hands leaving red streaks against the paint, blood already turning tacky on my face.

As I pulled the door open, I heard the sound of him falling; a heavy, meaty smack, a reedy gasp of breath. And I ran.

I spilled out onto the street, half-stumbled down the steps.

'Help,' I shouted, my voice rough and frightening. 'Help me.'

I heard footsteps thundering towards me and turned, the world dipping and whirling beneath me. Henry, his eyes widening at the blood around my mouth, down my front, on my hands.

'Addie, what—'

A car stopped in the road in front of us. People were stepping out of their front doors and staring from their windows, and I heard the first cry of a siren, somewhere in the distance.

I sat on the edge of the ambulance doors, listening to the thunder of the news helicopter overhead. Watching as the second ambulance, its doors closed, drove away, lights flashing frantically.

'Why did you come back?' I asked. My mouth tasted sour and of metal; the paramedic had not been allowed to swab away the evidence.

Henry shook his head. 'I don't know. Just a bad feeling, I guess.'

We watched in silence as police and forensics filed in and out of the house, the yellow tape blocking the road ahead fluttering in the breeze. Front doors all along the street still gaped open, people watching with hands pressed to mouths. Their phones capturing every moment.

'They'll find them now. The girls,' Henry said, quietly. 'They have to.'

I watched as an officer lifted the tape, let the sleek black car drive under. Watched as it swung to a stop in front of us, as DS Jones climbed out of the driver's side, left his door hanging open too.

As he came towards me, I saw myself as he must have. Black-mouthed and wild-eyed, so different from the girl he had met in the courtyard of our estate six years earlier. He stopped a few steps short of where we sat, his breath coming in heavy bursts.

Then he came the rest of the way forward and hugged me.

HM Prison Belmarsh
1st July 2017

Dear Addie,

*I never really know if you want me writing to you. I
don't even know if you get the letters – they say they
have to send them on but it's hard to trust some of
what people tell us in here, and I guess this is just the
kind of thing which might end up for sale on some
freaky auction site somewhere.*

*I've been thinking about your mother recently. I hope
you aren't offended by me saying that. Sometimes I like
to replay the moment you first told me about what
happened to her. Because that's the first time you really
surprised me, Addie, and I liked it. I guess I'd thought
I had you all figured out but I had no idea that your
life had started that way. And I suppose I always find
it interesting, hearing about the men who kill women.
My father didn't kill my mother but he came close
plenty of times before he left, or that's what she always
told me, anyway. I grew up thinking about that a lot.
Some girls are just trouble, my mother used to say*

*when I got old enough to start looking at them, and
I think that's kind of funny, now, because she was
pretty troublesome herself. I learnt pretty young that
I couldn't trust the things she said to me but that's one
that always stuck. I've been wondering if your mother
was trouble too.*

*It was special that you trusted me with that story that
day, in our interview. And in return I have decided it's
time to tell you one of my own.*

*There was a girl who lived on the same street as me
for almost the whole time we were growing up. Her
name was Audra and she had hair that came right the
way down her back even when we were teenagers.
Sometimes we'd walk to school together or I'd catch
up with her on the way home. I used to live to make
her laugh – have you had that with someone? Where
you spend the whole time scoring yourself on how
often they've smiled, how often they've touched you
or, best of all, laughed at your jokes? I had that with
Audra and the longer we spent together, the higher my
scores got. I understood her in a way no one else did,
I know I did. I could make her laugh, this little nervous
laugh she had, like she was afraid to show how happy
she really was.*

*I spent a lot of time on Audra. I really did. I did a lot
to make her happy. I know that you're like that too –*

a natural-born pleaser, right? – so I guess you probably understand how it felt once I finally got up the courage to ask her to be my girlfriend when we were nineteen. For weeks I'd watched her looking through the window of the jeweller's in our little town square as we walked home, always staring at this bracelet. It had her birthstone – amethyst – I knew that because that's the kind of person I am. Details are important to me. Anyway, I bought it for her and gave it to her with a note in the box, because I was shy back then. Actually, I would say that I'm shy even now. I like to express myself in words on the page, I'm not so good when it comes to the face-to-face. I don't like things when they're unpolished, unedited. And I guess Audra wasn't so good with the face-to-face either because she posted the bracelet back through my door that night, a note of her own inside: I'm sorry. I don't see you that way.

But I know that wasn't true. So I was patient. I waited and I kept finding ways to talk to her, to let her know that it was okay, that I would be there until she was ready for us to properly be together. And you know what she did? Nothing. She let five years pass and then on July 7th 2001, she turns up at my house and tells me that she's getting married. Addie, I know that you've been betrayed by people you love so I'm guessing you can imagine how that felt. So I'm hoping that maybe you'll understand why the things that happened next, happened.

I can still feel the way it felt to squeeze the fucking breath out of her. Sometimes I lie awake at night and think of those blood vessels in her eyes popping, the white flooded red. True beauty is so rare but in that moment, as I took her life, as I finally made her mine, I experienced it.

The thing is, that first time, with Audra, I was so angry. Too angry to really appreciate it, to enjoy it. One minute she was standing there talking, the next she was dead, my hands still round her neck. And the interesting thing to me is that I didn't stop being angry. The anger just changed. It felt like something more powerful. It's an addictive feeling but it's dangerous and after that I knew I had to set limits. I wanted my killings to mean something, I wanted them to be special. Details are important to me.

I guess many people will – if you share this letter – choose to think that Audra was the reason I did what I did. And I do like to think of those girls as a tribute to her, as a celebration of women like her (trouble!) finally getting what they deserve. But I do also believe that killing would always have been in me. I've tried at various points in my life to outrun it and it's always found me, a voice I've tried and failed to shut out. On that day each year it just spoke loudest. It still does. There are many reasons we do the things we do and sometimes that reason is just that it feels good.

It felt good to kill them. It felt good to toy with the police, with their families, with you.

But I meant what I said to you that day in my house when I almost killed you (and, I guess, when you almost killed me ☺). It felt good, the way it always did, but at the same time I really didn't want to do that to you. I like you. I see something of myself in you. I think we have a connection and I think maybe that's another reason why I liked to send their necklaces and things to you. Like maybe you deserved nice things more than they did. I watched you then and I will watch over you as best I can now – until, I hope, we meet again.

Yours,

Laurence K. Cooper

2017

'Come on, mate, get a move on.' I pace, impatient.

'I don't know what to wear,' comes the familiar whinge.

'What you have on is fine.' The same thing I have to say every time we go out. 'I'm leaving in five . . . four . . .'

Arlo appears at the top of the stairs. 'I'm too old to fall for that,' he says, but he comes down anyway.

'You've got taller again,' I say, my heart swelling a little at how carefully he's matched his socks to his T-shirt, worn his clean new Converse, his prized possessions. This obsession with the way he looks, with wanting to impress, is new. I'm not sure if I'm supposed to quell it or address it or just let it be. I never know. We have to muddle along and hope for the best.

And I understand. I'm nervous too.

'Come on, buddy,' I say. 'Time to go.'

On the Tube, I watch him reading, see the way he doesn't turn the page, no words going in. I try and remember everything that was going through my head when I was nine, try and remember how much worse things are for him. Sometimes, the pressure of being all he has overwhelms me, makes it hard to breathe.

On those days, I understand how hard it must have been for Jessie.

I try and hold onto some of that sympathy now. It makes it easier. We are where we are. They're both doing their time. And Arlo has me. I'll never let that change.

The letter from Laurie went straight to DS Jones, the same way all the other things he used to send me did. But the words stay with me. *There are many reasons we do the things we do and sometimes that reason is just that it feels good.* It's the closest thing to honesty I think I've had from him. When he was first on trial a family friend sold their story and claimed that he was psychologically abused for years by his mother. Perhaps that's true; perhaps what he says about Audra, his original victim, is too. But Laurie is a man who likes to tell stories, who likes to have control of them. I looked him in the eyes that day and I could see that, deep down, he hated women because it felt good.

The thought makes me long, briefly, for the taste of his blood in my mouth again.

As we get off at our stop, Arlo looks up at me, uncertain. This is new, too, the fear. In the last couple of months, he has watched as TV screens flood with stories of a concert in Manchester bombed; of Borough Market, where he and I like to walk some weekends, under attack. Of a tower block across the river burning uncontrollably. I try to remember how I felt when Jessie tried to change channels or hide headlines, and try and talk to him instead. Explain. Because the world is a scary place and we, more than anyone, can't be shielded from that.

But it's hard. I want to protect him. He's already had to grow up so much.

'You remember the way, right?' I ask him, giving him his Oyster card so he can swipe himself out of the barriers. He nods, skipping a couple of steps ahead, and I'm glad. He's excited to see her.

It's busy, the same as it was last time we came. We queue to get in the door, the family ahead of us flustered and irritable, sniping at each other as they juggle bags and a buggy. The woman letting them in is equally unhappy, scowling at them as they negotiate their way to a table.

'Do you have a reservation?' she asks me, daring me to say no.

'I—'

'Addie, over here!'

Cara stands by a table in the corner, hands on her hips. I shoot an apologetic look at the hostess as Arlo hares past and make my own way over to the table, where Lex has risen out of his seat and turned.

'Hey, dude!' He high-fives Arlo then straightens up, his eyes meeting mine. We stand, uncertain, and then he steps forward, offers me a hug.

'Hi,' he says.

Cara pulls out her seat, its legs screeching against the floor, and flops into it. 'I'm so glad you guys are here,' she says. 'Dad wouldn't let me order and I am *starving.*'

'Me too.' Arlo hops into the chair beside her, not quite daring to look at her. She terrifies and fascinates him in equal measure, the same way she did when he was a baby.

'Dad,' Cara says, shoving the menu away. 'Can I get a freakshake?'

She's twelve now and she fascinates and terrifies me, too. Her hair sandy blonde like her father's but her face a perfect replica of her mother's, the likeness chiselled deeper every time I see her.

'Sure,' he says. 'Just don't complain when you eat half of it and feel sick.' He notices I'm still standing and pulls out the seat beside him. 'Please,' he says. 'Sit.'

I do. I do my best to smile when Cara tells me she likes my top, when Lex jokes with Arlo about the bruise on his elbow he got from trying to breakdance in our back garden. I order coffee and I drink it, gulp it back black and bitter the way I like it now.

'Why don't you guys go check out the cakes on the counter,' Lex suggests to the two of them, holding out a twenty-pound note. 'Pick a couple of things for us all to share.'

Arlo rushes off and Cara slopes after him. 'Sorry,' he says. 'She just loves this place. I think it reminds her of this ice-cream parlour my mom used to take her to in the States.'

'That's okay. It must be tough for her. Settling back in.' They left soon after Dad was caught. Just after Jessie and Laine were arrested too. The three years between have seemed like forever to me but perhaps for them, there, it was different. I hope so.

He shrugs. 'This is her home. I think I always knew that. It's where her mom is.'

Liv. Finally laid to rest, once my father confessed the places where he had hidden her. The overgrown copse where a branch had scratched his cheek, his arm. The abandoned length of sewer his friend Leonard had once told him about. The reservoir behind a half-finished luxury development of flats and the landfill site far from the centre of the city where she had died. Because though he hadn't been guilty, he *had* been good at what he did – he had thought carefully about how not to get caught; how to make sure she was never discovered, never identified. In the end, though, it was simple to find her – I asked him, before the trial, to tell us. And he did.

The women Laurie murdered were easier to find; in that, at least, he proved less inventive than my father. In that Canonbury house his study was lined with their portraits, the basement with their bones.

'And it's where Arlo is,' Lex says softly, interrupting my thoughts. 'And that's important too. I'm sorry it's taken me a while to figure that out.'

I turn my head, watch Arlo weighing up the benefits of a giant treble-tiered chocolate cake over some kind of elaborate, sweet-stacked cheesecake.

'No one could blame you,' I say.

'It'll take time.' He fiddles with the edge of his napkin. 'But I'm trying.'

When the kids return, we eat cake. We talk about Arlo's school and Cara's, about the shows we all like on television. We talk about the weather and the summer ahead.

We don't talk about my father or my sister. We don't

talk about Laurie Cooper or any of the other women who lost their lives on a day in July.

When it's time to leave, Cara hugs me tight. 'Can we do this again soon?' she asks, with a momentary earnestness that punches me in the chest, reminds me of her as a little girl.

'Sure,' I say. 'We'd like that, right, Arlo?'

'Yeah,' he says, attempting and failing to feign cool. 'Hey, maybe next time we can go to Laser Quest!'

Lex laughs. 'Yeah, maybe. See you later, bud.' He offers him another high-five, a fist-bump, and then turns to me.

'I'm glad we did this,' he says, and this time when he hugs me, it feels warmer. Safe.

On the way home, Arlo is more relaxed, loses himself in his book. I sit and fiddle with the bracelet that was returned to me by DS Jones two years ago. The one piece of jewellery that didn't belong in an evidence bag, that hadn't been taken from one of those women. Instead my father bought it from Leonard on the night before my tenth birthday, one bracelet from a box which Leonard and his brother had stolen from a warehouse somewhere.

I don't know if what my mother said was true, whether the man who raised me is my real father. It doesn't matter to me; he's still the man who murdered her. But I like to wear the bracelet sometimes. I like to think of myself on that last night, like to think of Liv alive somewhere in the city.

It's easy to forgive, Dellar told me once. *It's trying to understand that's the important part.* He and his mum share custody of Frank, who is starting to adjust to life here. He'll have to – the judge was far harsher on Laine when it came to sentencing, despite her guilty plea. Frank will be in his twenties before she's released.

'What are you thinking about?' Arlo asks me. He's finished his book, is leaning against me as we shuttle in and out of stations.

'I'm thinking,' I say, putting my arm round him, 'what a nice day I've had.'

The phone's ringing as I open the front door and I run to answer it, Arlo already heading for the fridge. The boy has a never-ending appetite and I'm already wondering what I'll make for dinner. My skills have had to improve rapidly, both of us learning together. He's had to put up with beans on toast more times than I can count when a recipe I've tried out for the first time has gone wrong.

'Hello?' I hear the sound of the fridge door closing, a cupboard opening. He's going for the crisps, taking full advantage of the fact I'm occupied.

'It's me.'

Suddenly I'm not listening to the sounds of the flat around me. I'm listening to the distant hum of voices on the other end of the line, someone yelling something incomprehensible.

'Hi,' I say, and the two of us are silent for a second. And then:

'It's good to hear your voice,' Jessie says. 'You okay?'

I swallow, lean back against the wall. 'I'm okay,' I say, surprised to find my voice steady. 'Are you?'

'Well, you know. Not exactly kicking back in five-star luxury but yeah, I'm all right.'

I always feel a longing to joke back with her but I'm not quite ready, not yet. I want to be.

'How's the boy?' she asks.

'He's good.' I think of the morning we've just spent with Lex and Cara and bite my lip, wondering what Jessie would say if she knew. There's time to figure that out, at least. 'I'll get him for you, hold on.' I know she doesn't have long; can hear other inmates getting impatient behind her.

'Okay, thanks.' She draws in a breath like she's about to say something but seems to change her mind. We are both quiet, waiting.

'Well, take care of yourself,' I say. This is normally the part where she says she will. Where she thanks me for looking after her son.

But today is different.

'Happy birthday, Addie,' she says.

Acknowledgements

Thanks first and foremost to Cathryn Summerhayes, for all her wisdom and support – I feel very fortunate to have you on this journey with me. I'm also really grateful to Irene Magrelli, Melissa Pimentel, Callum Mollison, Martha Cooke and all at Curtis Brown.

Ella Gordon has been a wonderful editor – endlessly patient and incredibly insightful. You really have helped me bring this story to life and I can't thank you enough. Huge thanks too to Kate Stephenson for all of her help during the tricky 'Which book am I actually going to write?!' initial stages, and for reading it when it finally emerged despite having a far more important project on her hands. And to Alex Clarke, captain of the good ship Wildfire, for all his support.

Thank you so much to Jenni Leech for doing such an amazing job getting me and *The Tall Man* out there in the world, and for all her enthusiasm about this book. I also owe a vat of wine and huge gratitude to Becky Hunter and

Acknowledgements

Georgina Moore who have adopted me at various points. Thanks to Jenny Harlow and Phoebe Swinburn for taking such good care of me along the way, and a special shout-out to Vicky Abbott and Joe Yule too. Frankly, everyone at Headline is unfailingly brilliant and I wish I could list all of them here.

I'm especially grateful to all the bloggers who read and reviewed *The Tall Man* – I can't tell you how much it meant to me.

Love and champagne to the Ladykillers who have done an excellent job of keeping me sane during the writing of this book – an extra-special giant thank you to Karen Hamilton for being the kindest of listeners and the loveliest of train companions.

And to all of my friends and family who've offered an ear, an opinion or a stiff drink along the way – I love you. But especially, as always, to Margaret, Richard and Dan Cloke: I'm so lucky to have you. Thank you for all of it.